Shane Jensen is the nom de plume of a Sydney-based author,
artist and hermit.
MA studies in writing have failed to socialise her.
The Literature Board of the Australia Council has paid various
professionals to mentor her, but none have succeeded as yet.
While they were seeking to steer her efforts, this feral novel
slipped through the net.

I0524595

Shane Jensen

Hum

New Generation Publishing

For
Annie
&
Antonio

Published in 2009 by New Generation Publishing

First Edition

Published by New Generation Publishing

Cover art by Shane Jensen
shanehjensen@hotmail.com

Eternal thanks to Peter B and Faye for their insights into *Hum* at different stages; and to Heather, Julie, Kirsty, Derek, George and the Friday Night Writers' Group for their eternal patience. Above all, thanks to Michael for emotional and technical support.

Contents

·I·

The Temple

ONE

Where There's a Will There's a Whale

*Call it low self-esteem, co-dependency, lack of personal bound-
aries, whatever — I've read all the books, done all the courses,
self-helped myself to the end of my tether — but letting Teresa
set the agenda seemed better than being alone.*

*Before we met, I'd aspired only to fame as an artist. She was
the yoga devotee. Then her obsession with enlightenment cast its
shadow on me. We were different enough that I should have
known — I was destined for endarkenment.*

This is not what we came here for. Maybe it's a bad sign.

'Push!' Teresa yells again, like some battleaxe of a midwife.

But nothing will be born of our struggle — the baby's about
to die. The three beachcombers who helped for a while have
vanished around the headland, and with them our last hope of
liberating this ton of washed-up blubber. My jeans are soaked to
the tops of my thighs and more salt water's rolling down from
my eyes, but I can't bear to tear myself away from the whale.
The suffering of wildlife touches me more than that of humans.
As a child I felt closer to birds and animals than I did to my
family. It's still true, now I'm twenty-two. Wild things seem so
defenceless.

That's not why I feel close to Teresa, though her gelled,
bleached crop looks wild. My best friend likes to take care of
herself, and others besides.

'Push harder!' she bellows. 'Let's give it one last try!'

We strain with all our might but still the whale's bulk won't
shift. We've tried scooping sand from under it but the tide's
begun to slip out; and the sight of the gouges riddling its hide

3

only deepens my doubts. Silently, so Teresa won't notice, I pray as I search its clouded eye.

'We've done our best,' she says, 'but it doesn't want to budge. There's no point wiping ourselves out for nothing.'

Just as I concluded after ten minutes on the loo this morning; but that's my pitiful little secret. When I confessed, once, that I was bunged up, Teresa showed me some yoga poses. She's never known a day of constipation in her life. Her colon works as forcefully as her mind does. If she'd been practising yoga for longer she'd know how to make the whale levitate. We turn our backs on it for the first time in hours, wade through the wavelets, and walk up the beach to retrieve our gear from the foot of the dunes.

'Your lips look blue,' she says, shaking sand off her boots.

'As long as the shade suits my skin tone,' I say.

'You must have inadequate circulation.'

I imagine her tone says, *and that's not all.* She might be right. Her lips look much warmer than she sounds, despite their thinness. I keep mine clamped together as we climb a path that threads through scrub. We didn't come up the coast for a dip on this late autumn day. Our purpose was the *invocation* — Teresa's word — of a soul mate.

'Maybe it's a sign,' I say, when we pause on the crest of the headland. The stiff walk's stilled my shivers and dried my clammy jeans. 'How often do you see a whale that's gone astray?'

Teresa sits down on the flattest rock she can find. Her wraparound shades hide her piercing green gaze and mirror me back doubly, two moon faces framed by short copper hair on fire in the afternoon sun. Though she went under the shears first, I'd planned to anyway.

'Don't take it so personally, Skye.' She rummages through her leather bag. 'There's nothing more we could've done. Whales beach themselves for a reason. You can't save something — or someone — that doesn't want to be saved.'

Why would it have a death wish, I wonder as I sit beside her, when it was so young?

Teresa takes out her pen and journal. It's back to business as usual. 'Let's start by making lists.' She'd rather not keep her soul mate waiting.

I open my gilt-trimmed blue diary, the one friend with whom I share all my secrets, and we fall silent to contemplate what traits our ideal mates will need. The decisive scratching of her pen leaves my guesswork for dead. Trust her to know exactly what she wants. I'd sooner die than be left behind, except that I wonder if treating Spirit like Santa Claus isn't a touch presumptuous. Not that I'd question her faith to her face. She can't stand fears and doubts.

'Do you want to go first' — she caps her fountain pen — 'or shall I?'

'You can,' I say — she looks like she can't wait — then fear that she'll think I'm too subservient.

'Creative, innovative, self-assured,' she reads out. 'Intuitive, visionary, versatile, imaginative, well-informed, devoted to social transformation . . .'

I hope we don't fall for the same man. But that's unlikely. Our sculpture tutor hasn't impressed her at all.

Now it's my turn to place a male order.

'Alcohol-free, nature-loving, environmentally aware, a healer of others and the planet, a creative genius dedicated to self-transformation . . .' Neither of us specified height, colouration or style — we trust Spirit to surprise us with the packaging.

Teresa nods approval and upgrades her list.

'Do you think these profiles sound more like gurus than equals?' I say. A man fitting our descriptions might want a woman who can change the world. We couldn't even save one baby whale.

'I expect nothing less of myself.' She pulls on her leather bomber jacket. 'We need to ask for what we deserve or men will keep disappointing us. If we think of them as inferior they'll fulfil our expectations.'

So the problem isn't the men I meet, but my attitude towards men in general? '*You* fit my list.' It's true if I overlook her binge drinking and leather. 'My ideal can't be too unrealistic.'

'And you're my equal in every way,' she says, 'except that we're not gay. So we'll need to find male lovers.'

'I've been looking,' I remind her.

'I'm not proposing a total lack of judgement!'

Will she ever forget my art-school indiscretions? 'Okay, so I made a mistake or two.' I can tell from the way her brows lift that she's rolling her eyes behind her shades. A cloud drifts across the sun and the wind's bite smacks of oncoming winter. One of my legs has gone numb against the rock.

'Not all men are useless,' she says. 'The best ones can be fun. That's why matriarchies died out. Women got bored with each other.'

Is she trying to tell me something? 'We have fun together,' I say.

'Up to a point,' she says. 'But I have sexual needs. Men exist to add spice to life. To inject excitement.'

'Up to a point,' I agree. Her last injection, before I met her, happened at gunpoint. We never discuss *that*.

'You're full of shit,' she says.

If only she knew. 'Maybe,' I say, out of sheer perversity, 'all things come to those who wait. Maybe, if we can just be our-selves, the right man will find us.'

'Like Prince Charming found Sleeping Beauty?' She laughs. 'That's a patriarchal myth. Passivity won't transmute nuclear waste or save whales from extinction.'

And doing downward dog pose or breathing through alternate nostrils will? But then I remember she said she was sleeping when that psycho found her. That would make anyone want to change the world.

'So why write lists?' I close my diary and bury it deep in my bag. 'Let's scout for talent at art events or target men on the street.'

'If you go shopping without a list there's more danger of impulse buying.' She puts her pen and journal away. 'If you don't align your will with Divine Will the warped wills of others will sway you.'

'How can you tell "Divine Will" from yours?' I'm guessing her hash smoking might distort things.

'They should be one and the same,' she says. 'Aimed at the highest good.'

Our sculpture tutor's face floats into my mind, dreamy and kind-eyed. I've been thinking he's too good for me. 'You think I should aim higher?'

As she eyes me steadily I see my two selves reflected again. 'Skye,' she says, 'we can't aim high enough. If you shoot at the sun you're more likely to hit the moon than if you aim at a tree.'

'Is that an old Sanskrit proverb?'

'No, old English,' she says. 'I've adapted it.'

'I can never remember those right,' I say. 'You've inspired me.'

With a smile so subtle it might disguise boredom, Teresa shifts her gaze towards the horizon. The sight of the distant white lines of breakers mirrored in her wraparound shades makes me yearn for a love I can lose myself in, the love of a soul mate.

TWO

Hero Today, God Tomorrow

The world doesn't need a saviour. That's taken me half a life-time to see. All I've managed to save, in the twenty-two years since I first met Zane, is me. Still, looking back now, I can see how far I've come. That's the beauty of inner achievement. You can't undo the past, but you're free to stop repeating it.

Banners and robes emblazoned with symbols that might well be alchemical adorn Zane's neatly ordered room. The student who referred me to him said he's an alchemist. It can't be worse than that old psychic who twirled a crystal over a dial and asked if my father had molested me. He must lay that on all his female patients. But he guessed wrong in my case. Since I was small, my father has avoided so much as eye contact.

Zane kneels at my side and gazes straight into my eyes. His gold-flecked irises remind me of amber, and echo his long, tawny hair. 'What can I do for you?'

I reel off my symptoms and a brief history. 'Doctors are use-less,' I conclude. 'They just prescribe laxatives. I want to bring my body back into balance.'

'Mainstream medicine treats the parts instead of the whole,' he says. 'But doctors believe in restoring harmony too.'

'Now I'm confused.'

'So are they, with all the holes in their knowledge. Can you take off your jeans and lie on your back?' He politely averts his gaze till I'm ready.

Then he begins to knead my belly low on the right near my appendix, working up, across, and down the left side. His firm, subtle touch assures me that he knows his way around, but as he massages my middle the pressure makes me gasp.

'Just focus on your breath,' he says.

When I close my eyes to concentrate, rainbows shimmer inside my lids. Zane's hands feel so divine as they follow the flow of my chi that I lose track of time. Yet I find myself counting the months since I last had sex. Zane's in his thirties and so magnetic; he must have had plenty. I wonder if Teresa's presence in my life has deterred men.

'What did you find?' I say when Zane withdraws his hands.

'Our bodies tend to exaggerate our state of mind —'

'So it's no secret that I'm feeling stuck?'

'Maybe you worry too much.'

'So I need to unwind?'

'You can treat it from either end. Banishing the physical symptoms would ease your worries so I've started there. But I'd like to see you again.'

I'm relieved that he feels the same. 'What did you have in mind?' Dinner and a movie cross mine, but I'd settle for coffee initially.

'A follow-up in a few days — I do discounts if you can't afford it.'

As I realise he hasn't asked me out, my smile collapses. What if he has a girlfriend? There I go, worrying again.

'How about Tuesday,' he says, 'at eleven?'

'Cool. How much do I owe you?' Twenty, the student said. I slide two tens from my wallet.

'Ten's fine.' He writes down the details in a graceful, even script. Unlike that of the doctors I've been to, it's legible. But why the new address?

'Moving already?' I say.

'Something better came up.' His gaze lingers on mine.

As he lets me out of his flat I feel hopeful that he'll propose a date next time.

Since we rented the second floor of a derelict seven-storey warehouse — to save money and Teresa's nostrils; her last flat-mate dealt coke — she says we live in its navel chakra. Its throat chakra's blocked, she jokes, because of the fifth-floor junkies.

10

She wasn't laughing when one left in a body bag the Tuesday after Easter. We passed the men hefting his corpse downstairs as we lugged our groceries up. From the smell we guessed he'd died on Good Friday, which the coroner later confirmed. His mates had gone away for the long weekend.

I'd rather die surrounded by friends. More feasible now I live with one, but that didn't help our neighbour. I must take care, I think as I wash up, not to die on a public holiday.

Still, I chose the isolated back studio 'for the view', hoping the nearby bathroom might inspire regularity. It hasn't. But Teresa makes regular visits and I have to listen.

I'm peeling an onion when she emerges from her private front space, and leans her latest paintings against one wall of the middle ground by the kitchen.

'Is veg curry the only recipe you know?' she says. 'I'm bored shitless with Indian.'

'You always cook Italian,' I remind her as I chop.

'Only because you say you like it so much.'

My eyes begin to water. 'I do, but pasta turns to lead in my gut.'

'That means your navel chakra's blocked. Impure thoughts make the body sluggish.'

'Maybe I, too, could think pure thoughts if I smoked as much hash as you?'

'You already do. I've shared my stash with you for the last six months. And not once have you deigned to contribute. It's high time we stopped sharing everything and going everywhere together —'

'We don't.' My heart's hammering. 'I took the psych strand knowing you'd do philosophy, and —'

'People have asked me if we're lovers. Or *twins*.'

'How superficial.' We're both short with short hair, but she's pear-shaped. My boyish hips aren't made for breeding.

'We're as good as married. That's what others notice.'

'If you're hung up on what others think you'll never get enlightened.' I make a mental note to look for new recipes in the cookbook that a Hare Krishna gave me on George Street.

'It's not just others. I feel you're too dependent.'

'Then why spit the dummy whenever I go to bed with some guy?' I yell. 'You act like you're at least as needy as I am.'

'There's a big difference, Skye — you're desperate.' She mounts the ladder in the common space and starts swinging my hammer.

'Didn't we agree to exhibit jointly in here?' I say.

She twists around. 'That's right. That's why the wall's empty on your side. Why should I hide my light under a bushel just because you're not ready to shine?'

Seven small paintings of chakras, like flowers, are propped against the partition on her side; their colours, Sanskrit symbols and numbers of petals traditional. Derivative, and so twee, I think, but I look up at her and say, 'You'd make a killing if you sold those to some meditation centre.'

'Your work would sell too if you'd pull out your finger. Felix thinks I should take on commissions.'

'Who the fuck's Felix?'

'Our downstairs neighbour.' She beams down at me. 'Who'd have guessed the man of my dreams was right under our noses?'

'Not the actor?' That shifty-eyed fatso who always wears black? 'You don't fancy him?'

'He doesn't just act, he writes and directs. And he happens to fancy me, too,' she says.

'I hope it works out for you.' No I don't. Felix seems self-indulgent to me.

'It might take time. He already has five lovers, and he's bi-sexual.'

There you go. 'Sounds complex.'

'He fits all the requirements on my list.'

'Sex addict? Still, you did specify "versatile".'

'He might settle for one woman, if she's *the* one.'

'I met a candidate today,' I say impulsively.

'Someone you'll be seeing again?'

'Definitely. It was mutual.'

'Where did you meet?'

'He gave me a treatment.'

'You can't fall for a healer!'

'Why not?' He has to be safer than a neighbour who might be using or dealing.

'If you don't know shit about him or his lifestyle it's too easy to idealise him. Can you hand me up the base chakra?'

'That's red, right, with a tiny white elephant at its centre? His bedroom's incredibly tidy for a guy's, and he's —'

'You went into his *bed*room?'

'That's where he treats his patients.'

'That's so unprofessional, Skye.' She hangs the base chakra lopsidedly.

'It means he can keep his fees down for those who couldn't afford help otherwise. You need to drive that nail in more.'

She lifts the canvas off with her left hand and taps with the right, but the nail just bends. 'Did he try anything?' she says as she prises it out of the plywood. It's not like her to make a mistake and she looks suitably mortified.

'No.' I pass another nail up to her.

She hits it squarely. 'He *could* be legit.'

'Don't forget to return my hammer.' I walk off before I can attack her with it.

Come Tuesday at eleven, I reach Zane's new front gate, wearing new hipsters under my best jeans. Since his healing touch moved me in more than one way, I can't help feeling he just might be my soul mate.

On the first-floor balcony, a mass of bobbing shapes resolves, while I squint, into nine or ten strangers and Zane. As I walk up the path they all wheel in formation, outspread arms floating like wings. Though I feel as forgotten as a flightless dodo, I ring the bell on principle.

Zane looks spun out when he opens the door. 'Did we have an appointment?' He taps his forehead when I nod. 'Sorry. But we've done our tai chi, so I can still see you.'

From the sofa I watch males and females of assorted ages file out. Unlike art students, they smile at me. Maybe I should explore tai chi, I think, as I follow on Zane's bare heels.

'This space feels colder than the other,' I say in his room. 'Your toes must be freezing.'

He shakes his head. 'Kerosene's expensive. I save it for when it's most needed.'

The expense didn't rate a mention last week. I stare at my feet and wait.

He relents and lights the heater. I peel off my jeans, feeling hotter already.

'You might as well take everything off if you're not too cold now,' he says.

I've undone my bra before I wonder if I heard right. I feel too confronted to ask. He's not looking as he drags the heater across, so I strip then stretch out on the mat. If he's indifferent now, I've got nothing up my sleeve.

He kneels next to me and his hands trace my colon the way they did four days ago. As if he's immune to distractions. He must be accustomed to naked patients. Or taken. I squeeze my eyes shut. His hands seem to know my gut better than I do; or they're just intimate with guts in general. Even as I want to resist, my muscles let go and my breathing deepens. How many patients have lain on this same mat, dying for special treatment? No-one's ever touched me with such awareness — but do others feel likewise? I open my eyes.

Zane completes the healing with a silent prayer. I feel incomplete.

He bends over me and blows a stream of air between my breasts. Then the wind of his breath travels all the way down to my pubes, where he plants a kiss. My back arches involuntarily, which he takes for consent. He's right; and his harem pants drop to his knees and he's got nothing on underneath.

Now the outer world falls away, as I've imagined for four days, and the rainbows I saw with my eyes closed before coalesce into kaleidoscopic patterns that run rings round Teresa's chakra paintings, while Zane and I fit in to each other like yang and yin forming a wheel of light and dark, motion and stillness, tension and release, until I feel at one with the source of all creative inspiration. And then I remember: I promised Teresa that I'd do the shopping. Though she'll disapprove of what I'm

14

doing, if Felix had time she'd be doing the same. I concentrate on synchronising my hip thrusts with Zane's until her image fades into a star-shot dome spun from exploding nerve endings, a vision that dissolves in turn when someone bangs on the door.

Zane groans. 'I forgot all about my band rehearsal.' At least his forgetting our appointment wasn't personal. 'This has never happened to me before,' he says with a euphoric smile.

'Me neither.' It can't be the first time he's kept his band members waiting; he must mean that he's never ended a treatment that way.

As he crosses the room, still bottomless, a scar on his left buttock catches my eye, but I scramble for my clothes so I'm presentable when he opens the door. Two men stand outside, one chubby-cheeked with red-gold ringlets, the other black-bearded.

'Sorry,' Zane mumbles and turns to me. 'Meet my bass player and flautist. And this is —'

'Skye.' Is it such a forgettable name?

'Luke.' The cherub-faced man winks at me.

The flautist just nods, then they retreat discreetly.

'You're welcome to stay while we rehearse,' Zane says. 'It won't take long.'

'I've got things to do.'

'Then why don't you come back later?' His eyes widen. 'Please?'

'How'd you get that scar?' I ask. He looks blank so I step around him to touch the purplish dent in the flesh of his butt cheek.

'It's a bite mark,' he says matter-of-factly.

'Human?'

'Yes and no — she'd over-identified with her animal totem.'

'Lucky she came at you from behind. She must've been out of her mind.'

'Her kundalini went haywire because she raised it too fast,' he says. 'Poor lady.'

Teresa knows all about kundalini, the sacred serpent fire sleeping at the base of the spine that burns away dross once it's stirred up until nothing's left but enlightenment. As Zane walks me to the door I'm touched by his compassion for a woman who scarred him for life.

Maybe the groceries could have waited, but I need a breather. On the bus I rehearse what to tell Teresa. Zane fits all the specs on my list. We're soul mates. It's predestined.

I just hope she doesn't get jealous.

·THREE·

United When Stoned

Hordes of people use drugs without going over the edge. Teresa still smokes dope, a habit she passes off as 'partying'. So it makes sense to investigate other causes. Tantric sex has been known to derange the mind. Zane indulged in plenty with me. Could those factors have had such potency, though, without the magic *ingredient? The practice of obscure rituals can be a sign of insanity. Yet which came first in my case — or did they intertwine?*

As I wake to Zane's warm embrace in my space for the first time, I feel content. Though I first woke in his bed just three days ago, he'd have seen me each night since if I'd let him. Instead, I've been taking his book to bed. A step-by-step guide to ritual self-initiation, it's blowing my mind no less than our sex is.

'This space would make a perfect dance studio.' Zane's gaze sweeps the worn wooden boards and high ceiling in the mid-morning light.

'True,' I say, 'if it wasn't already a perfect painting studio.'

'Are these yours?' He nods towards the abstract canvases facing my bed.

I thought he'd never notice. 'Yes.' I wait with bated breath.

'What wild talismans!' he says. 'They're *elemental*.'

A cloud of vapour escapes my lips as I sigh with relief. 'We can't afford heating' — I laugh, high on praise — 'in such a big place.'

'How many artists live here?'

'Just me and Teresa.' We missed her last night, coming in late, and with luck she'll have left early. 'So you're a dancer?' That could explain his sexual stamina.

17

'I'm in training.'

'I'd love to be a dancer.'

'Then why don't you take classes?'

'I'm too old.'

'That's no excuse. I started when I was your age.'

To ask him how old he is now seems rude. 'Should I make us breakfast?' I say.

'I might wait till I've done my yoga. It's better on an empty stomach.'

'How disciplined.' No wonder he's supple; but why is he tubby round the middle? 'Coffee then?' Clangs in the kitchen announce that Teresa's just risen.

'Do you have herbal tea?'

'I'll go and see,' I say.

'I'll come with you.'

We pull on our woollens and Zane wanders out ahead of me. To justify my lust, I've told Teresa what a wizard he is — writer, artist, guitarist, teacher, healer, high priest and more — and she was gratifyingly awed. Now I wish I'd played it down, or sown seeds of doubt, mentioned his callgirl flatmate.

'Hello,' I hear her say. 'So you're Zane? I've heard so much about you.'

Though I've taken care that he can't claim the same, he says 'Ditto' anyway, and they're smiling broadly if awkwardly when I enter the common space.

'I'm brewing real coffee,' she tells him.

'That sounds great,' he says.

'Sure does,' I say.

He sits down at the table and takes a gladbag from his pocket. Dope on an empty stomach; that should stimulate the munchies. Too bad I left *nonsmoker* off my list. At least he disapproves of tobacco.

'You'll be late for yoga,' I tell Teresa, and sit thigh to thigh with Zane.

She pulls up a chair opposite us. 'I'll go this evening instead.'

Zane crumbles some leaf onto a rolling paper. 'What sort of yoga?'

18

As they bond via the intricacies of asanas, bandhas and pranayama, I don't know whether to feel pleased for them or left out.

'Who painted the seven chakras?' Zane asks, as he lights up his number.

Teresa smiles at me like the cat that swallowed the cream. 'I did.'

'Your paintings possess real power.' He passes her the joint.

'Thanks.' She takes a toke. 'Skye told me you paint too.'

'Not lately — but I had some success in my teens.'

'If your work sold, why did you stop?' She holds out the joint. I pass. Zane reclaims it.

'I didn't,' he says. 'My art just changed form. I diversified. Specialisation divides a society and limits self-sufficiency.'

'I guess I'm a specialist,' I say. 'All I've done since leaving school is paint and nothing's sold.'

The old don't-get-me-started look ignites in Teresa's eyes. But she regains control and fetches the coffee pot.

'Milk?' she asks Zane.

'No thanks. I'm vegan. Art can inspire change in the group mind' — he hands her the joint — 'and the fate of the Earth depends on what we all visualise.'

I'm grateful that he's back on my side. But what's the 'group mind'?

Teresa nods. 'That's why I dropped out of college.'

My jaw drops. 'Since when?'

'Since yesterday. There's more inspiration in this ware-house.' She blows smoke and yawns. 'That place is a refuge for losers and poseurs and head cases.'

'There's a gifted woman painter in post-grad,' I protest, 'and Chris is different —'

'That ideologue? He called these *derivative*.' She indicates her chakras and sniffs.

'You're lucky,' I say. 'He rarely gives feedback.' Though he has critiqued my work too, since I attracted his interest.

'And do you have much to do with Chris?' Zane asks me obliquely.

'Not a lot,' I say, 'but he's more spiritual than most tutors.'

19

'Skye says you're an expert on temples and sacred circles,' Teresa cuts in, 'and you've led thousands of spiritual seekers in initiatory rites —'

'Hundreds, maybe.' He stares at his bare feet. 'I'm hoping to start a new magic group.'

'I'd like to join it,' Teresa says.

'Me too.' At least, I'd hate to be left out.

'My flautist has volunteered,' Zane says, 'but we'll need five to work circles. Do either of you know anyone else who'd be interested?'

'A friend of mine from yoga might.' Teresa tops up her coffee.

Just what I need — a whole group of yoga freaks so I can feel more excluded.

'Why five?' I ask, at the risk of sounding useless.

'One for each of the four directions,' Zane says, 'plus a moderator.'

Teresa straightens her shoulders as if she can't wait. 'We could set up a temple here in the exhibition space.'

Safe in her shell, Pearl can let the conceptual crap swirl by. Students who hang on long enough get a key to their own studio, and her cramped, stark white cell is heaven compared to the space I have to share, a labyrinth with ghetto-blasters and dope fumes. I don't fit in. The others shared first year. I've been granted advanced standing. You lack a personal style, they said, when I showed my slides. At one school you painted figuratively, at another you tried on expressionism, then, at the next, abstract expressionism. You adopted the style of each school, they accused.

Now I'm trying on concepts, like they are, but I still don't fit in. Pearl doesn't either. We both have technique. That's why she's invited me to visit.

Dozens of pairs of eyes peer out of the paintings on her studio walls. Always the same eyes, despite varied settings, wary and vigilant. Awed by her skill, I ask if she began with a concept. More of an interest in shamanism, she says. That's why her figures fly over the canvas, and transform into eagles or seagulls.

As we lounge on the stained seagrass matting that hides her concrete floor, I tell her I've met my soul mate.

'For a while I thought Chris was my soul mate,' she says. 'But I'm starting to think it could be a woman.' She gazes at me, her pale face and hair luminous under the overhead skylight.

To avoid any ambiguity, I sing Zane's praises ad nauseam.

'He's crammed so much in to his life,' she says. 'How old did you say he was?'

'Thirty-three or thirty-four — he's not sure.'

She giggles. 'He told you that?'

I nod. 'He ran away from home at fifteen.'

'Or could he have been sixteen?' she says. 'Was he sure?'

'He lost track of calendar time when he tuned in to lunar and stellar cycles.'

'Shamans tread lightly in this world because they're focused elsewhere,' she says.

I picture tribesmen suspended from hooks by their nipples, with quills through their cheeks. 'How would you become a shaman?' It wasn't an option when I chose a TAFE course to sidestep the HSC.

'It's a calling. Some sort of crisis marks you and once you're chosen there's no going back. Refusal of the initiation means death.'

'In ancient societies?'

'In any society.' Her wide eyes narrow till they resemble the painted ones above. 'You know, I feel sure that we've known each other before.'

'The eyes in your images look familiar,' I say. 'Which tech did you go to?'

'I meant in a past life.' Her gaze intensifies. 'It's like I've always known you.'

As I gather that what she means is she'd like to know me now, I look up and see an om symbol in one of her paintings. 'Do you meditate?'

'Most mornings.'

'What about yoga?'

'No,' she says. 'Why?'

'No reason,' I say. 'By the way, Zane and I want to start a ritual magic group. There's four of us and we just need one more. Are you interested?'

Her stare wavers. 'I'm honoured to be asked.'

'Does that mean you'll consider it?'

'When would we start?'

My mother looks askance at Zane's bare legs when she opens the door.

'Sorry we're late,' I say, 'but we've come straight from our dance class.' I almost warned him to change out of his shorts, but that would have delayed us more.

'Come on in — *Zane*? That's different,' she says. 'Is it short for something?'

'No, it's the name my mum gave me,' he says with great solemnity, reminding me that he must have one, though he's never mentioned her.

My father stands to shake Zane's hand. 'Can I get you a beer, mate?' he says.

'No thanks — I don't like alcohol,' Zane says in his most fastidious tone.

'You haven't been smoking mari-joo-*ah*-na?' my mother hisses in my ear on our way to the kitchen.

I shouldn't have kissed her. 'What if I have?'

Thankfully, a more serious matter distracts her. 'Zane, let me get you something to sit on!' she calls, and marches off down the hall.

'I'm fine,' he yells after her as I join him on the lounge.

But she returns with an old towel. 'You'll be all sweaty after your dance class.' She motions him up then lays it out.

With a shrug, he plants his bare thighs on the towel — and bare feet on the marble coffee table. My father shrinks into his chair, eyes round. I swallow. He's done it now.

'Zane,' my mother shrills, 'we don't put our feet on the furniture here.'

Jolted upright, he removes them, wide-eyed with surprise.

22

I quietly despair of his ever redeeming himself in her eyes — or of her ever redeeming herself in his. Yet Zane and my father appear to bond via talk of martial arts, and before long we're sitting down to dinner. My mother starts to unwind as Zane shares his knowledge of herbs, and we all get on famously until dessert.

'Would you like ice cream with your rice pudding?' she asks Zane.

'That sounds yummy,' he says, and blows his nose on his paper napkin.

When my mother and I have done the dishes, we step into her sewing room. Drawn blinds emphasise the smallness of the space where I slept as a child. I unwrap my bolt of deep violet velvet.

Magical tools are as good, says Zane, as the heart and art with which they're made. First, we need a purple cloak for ritual wear. Teresa owns a sewing machine, so she's got hers all ready. And Pearl sews as well; but despite or because of her keenness to help me, I've asked my mother instead.

Soon we've cut out the pattern and pieces of fabric and pinned them together, and my mother's running up the seams on her Singer.

'What did you say it was for?' She loads a bobbin with violet thread.

'I didn't,' I say from the doorway, 'in case you made light of it.'

'Oh, Skye.' She forces a light-hearted laugh. 'You're always imagining things.'

I force an indulgent smile. 'To protect our auras while we do pagan rituals to heal the Earth.' Zane never said to keep it secret, just to use our discretion.

'That sounds very interesting.' She licks the loose end of the cotton and threads the poised needle. 'Where will you do that?'

'I'm not sure. Indoors, I guess — or outdoors, in nice weather.'

'Just be careful you don't drag the hem through the mud. Velvet isn't the sort of thing you can just wash after each wearing.'

'So you know what an aura is?' A few hours in this house and already my jaw feels tense. I'm talking about a whole planet and my mother's stuck on a few damp square metres.

'Let's see — that's the field surrounding our bodies, that clairvoyants can read?' Her foot depresses the pedal and her hands guide the velvet unerringly. The cloak will be near perfect. Might Zane think I'm cheating by letting her help?

'Yes,' I say when the clatter dies, 'we're going to learn to see auras.'

'That sounds very interesting.' Her smile makes me wonder, for once, if her green eyes see more than I've realised. But in a blink they mist over, and I doubt it. 'Did you want that silver trim on the edge of the hood too?' she asks.

By the time the cloak's done it's late, but Zane lets my mother lay on tea and cake.

'Since when have you eaten dairy products?' I ask him on our way home.

'It isn't healthy to be too rigid about anything,' he says. 'Besides, your mum's pudding had stronger shakti than her pie did.'

I'm not sure what 'shakti' is, but she always steams the life out of the greens. That would explain why Zane left his. 'My mother *bought* the ice cream,' I say.

'What we eat harms us less than our beliefs about it,' he says gently. 'If you tell yourself ice cream is bad for you, your body will manifest proof.'

I'm not the one who can't squeeze into jeans, but that seems too petty to say. Zane's perfectly healthy — just a smidgin overweight.

The first ritual won't take place in the communal warehouse space. Zane feels it's too cold, and his callgirl flatmate told us to use their front room; she would have loved to join in if she'd had a free afternoon. She's an initiate magician, Zane said, or I'd never have guessed. What will I be after I initiate?

'My head aches,' I tell Zane, while we wait for the others, 'ever since I put on my seal.' Pearl and I made our silver discs with jewellers' tools at college. Zane says they'll protect us — and others — while we learn to flex psychic muscles, if they're worn at our throats throughout the 'neophyte' phase.

'The right side of your brain's adjusting.' He knows without even looking, as he sits in a lotus pose like the porcelain Buddha on top of the TV he's watching.

'Then why does the other side hurt?'

'It's not your brain that's hurting,' he says, 'it's your head, on the lunar side. Pain is only energy distorted by suppression. The talisman tells the universe you're ready for more power. You're opening up what's been shut down.' He turns back to the TV and rolls a joint, just in time for the arrival of Teresa and the flautist.

As we wait for Pearl, I'm the only one not partaking. 'Your book says neophytes shouldn't use drugs or alcohol,' I say.

'When you want to undo societal conditioning, addictions can cloud the issues,' Zane says, 'but abstinence isn't as crucial for our group as it was for the first few.'

The other two nod like they understand.

'Why not?' I say.

'The work done by those before us has energised the new thought forms.' The flautist trades looks with Teresa and offers the joint to me.

As I waver, the bell rings and Zane opens the door. Pearl sidles in, swathed in a shawl, and shyly says 'Hi' with lowered lashes.

'Skye tells me you're a gifted artist.' Zane sounds so stiff, I could swear he feels challenged. 'Now we're all here, let's get started,' he says. And he and the flautist begin to undress.

Teresa beats me to the bathroom — it's a miracle I found a man first — so I slip into Zane's room to change, and Pearl follows. As she sheds layer after layer, I focus on my bootlaces, terrified that she'll seek my approval. Yet when her flat chest and birdlike legs stand revealed, she looks oddly cute.

'I've stopped using soap and shampoo,' I confess, to lessen the tension.

'You don't have to go without,' Pearl says. 'I'll lend you the money.'

'I can afford them. But they bleach the nerve ends and blunt auric sensitivity. Zane says a clean *aura* matters more and, without interference, our skin makes its own soaps.'

Pearl shakes out her cape — of the same shade as mine, we shopped together — then puts it on. 'Why not?' she says. 'Mine exudes enough oils.'

Soon five of us, naked beneath our new cloaks, sit cross-legged on the rug. Pearl keeps glancing at me. Embarrassed, I glance at the others. The flautist — in lilac, like Teresa; a purple of sorts — has closed his eyes. She keeps hers trained on Zane, who appears to be meditating.

Then he takes my hand and I guess he wants us all to join hands. He starts to speak in a low, even voice. Electrified, I stop noticing the meaning of his words, as energy flows into my left hand and out through my right in an unbroken circuit. My sense of myself ebbs until I'm aware of just pure light. Linked to four other luminous points suspended outside time, I dissolve into an ocean of light. For a moment, the circle drops away. Then we're all chanting a repeated, drawn-out om. Teresa strikes the highest, clearest note. Pearl's tone sounds as deep as the men's. Mine wavers between. Our voices rise and crest and fall in overlapping waves.

After, we sit around comparing notes. To my relief, the others felt similar sensations. Zane makes cups of tea. Pearl hugs her knees, her cloak wound tightly about her. The flautist strums Zane's guitar, and I realise he's not just a flautist. Teresa glows, as if she's taking it all in her stride. Maybe yoga has primed her. Yet I wonder how she feels about making my lover her personal spiritual guide?

Teresa doesn't give her trust lightly.

·FOUR·

Let Big Guns be Big Guns

Sex on a first date is always a mistake, Teresa would say. And I learned the hard way. Sex clouded my appraisal of Zane, a virtual stranger. Our premature intimacy put a spin on my already fragile state, leaving me more vulnerable to other dangers.

But it took me another decade to come around to Teresa's point of view. At twenty-two I confused sex with love and wanted love badly. As for sex before a first date, I forget Teresa's policy. And maybe she did too.

High heels aside, the astrologer's still tall for a woman. Big-boned, nails alternate pink and orange, lips bright red, she looks like a trannie; not that Pearl said. But she told Pearl her moon's conjunct a black hole; sucked her right in.

'Did your father ever hit you?' the giantess asks, well into side B of the tape. That's Jupiter on the poster behind her. I recognise the red splotch on its face.

'He spanked me once while my mother watched.' Shouldn't I be asking the questions?

'And you may find you're attracted to women.'

'My mother would slap me when she lost her temper.'

'Moon sextile Uranus can indicate bisexuality. Don't be afraid of those feelings.'

'I'm not. But I met my soul mate two months ago and he's male.'

'Yes, I was getting to that. The big guns have triggered your Venus.'

'Who are they?'

'Jupiter, Saturn and Uranus — is he a popular, older man, and offbeat, even zany?'

27

'You could say that.' She's hooked me now.

'Pluto's hit your moon, too. Have women been difficult lately?'

'How do you mean?'

'Power struggles . . . envy or jealousy . . . undermining behaviour . . .'

Teresa's gone into orbit round Felix. 'Nothing out of the ordinary.'

'Just keep an eye on it. By the way, you're a healer. Sun conjunct Chiron.'

'Actually, I'm an art student. My soul mate's the healer.'

'That's why you've met him,' she says. 'It's time to awaken to your inner healer.'

'But I don't know the first thing about healing.'

'You don't have to. The aspect's exact. It's an energy you give off without doing anything. Just by being. Soon Saturn will leave the house of group ideals, and enter the house of self-undoing.' With a clunk the tape runs out. 'Don't worry,' she says. 'We retain what we need to.'

'What did you mean,' I say, 'by self-undoing?'

'Friends and groups will let you down. You'll have to seek wisdom within.'

There's something to it, I think on my way out. Interpretation's the key. By the time I get home, I can't wait to study astrology.

'That's spot-on,' Teresa says as we play back my reading on her ghetto-blaster, and I choke on the sickly sweet smoke, from an incense cone, thick in her studio.

I pause the tape. 'What?'

'Envy and jealousy.'

'I can't identify.'

'That's great — because, last night, when you went down to the phone booth, Zane offered me the main part in his play. He said he needed a shit-hot singer.'

It's no secret that I can't sing — we chant during rituals — so why not ask her in front of me?

'That's great,' I say, swallowing. 'He needs others, with all his ambitions.'

28

Last night he did say he's lucky to have such a pretty girl-friend. And now Teresa can feel she's been chosen — she's not the star of Felix's show. If Pluto hadn't hit my moon, I wouldn't be jealous at all.

I've begun to shut my eyes during sex so I can't see Zane's rolling back in their sockets, and inside my closed lids I see visions. They feature Zane as we make love tonight, but his skin's red and nubs of horns jut from his head. When at last we lie spent and entwined on my futon, I share my impressions.

'That was Pan. He's a playful nature god. You're a seer,' Zane says.

'Is that like an astrologer?'

'Yes, but it's more straightforward. Why?'

'Just curious. I saw Pearl's astrologer today.'

His eyes narrow to slits. 'So what did she say?'

'Have you ever heard of a planet called Chiron?'

'It was sighted seven years ago — after our ritual to heal Lucifer.'

I picture a circle of Satanists. 'As in *fallen angel*?'

'Planets were angels to the ancients. Since Lucifer fell from its orbit and split into asteroids, it's been disowned. Our work helped make Lucifer whole.'

'Metaphorically speaking?'

'No, we initiated real change.'

While I want to believe him, that sounds grandiose to me. 'The astrologer said my sun conjunct Chiron makes me a healer. Is that how you see it?'

He nods. 'Your art is a channel for healing.'

'She said that I could heal just by being.'

'She did, did she?' He smiles to himself. 'Let's go visit your gay friend,' he says.

Pearl's house feels like the heart of a forest, painted emerald green inside. The dense perfume of Indian incense reminds me of Teresa's space. Dark as Pearl is pale, her gorgeous girl guru adorns all the walls, contracting or expanding to fit the frame.

At Zane's request Pearl lies face up on a yoga mat. She's asked me to be present while he treats her congestion. I assured her that he's harmless, but she freezes up when she's alone with men.

Zane kneels at her feet. I sit by her head, set to watch. But instead of starting, he stares at me.

'Go on then. Heal her. If you think you're already a healer.'

Pearl's still, a bridge between us. My eyes fill. He's perfected techniques over years, more years than he'll admit to.

'I don't know how,' I say, feeling foolish.

He proceeds to explain.

Abstraction gave me somewhere to hide; it's taken me this long to see. Yet Chris said I'm on the right track when he critiqued my tentative figure sketches. I've spent half the day at home painting two nudes that don't look half like Zane and me, so I feel naked too when I hear determined footsteps coming closer.

'Skye, I need to talk to you,' Teresa says from the doorway.

My neck tenses. It's not her style to hang back politely. 'Come in.'

She does, but stops short. 'Zane and I had sex in my studio yesterday.'

I stoop to dunk my brush in turps, but I miss and it daubs the floor. 'You *what*?'

'Yesterday afternoon.' She shifts her weight from one leg to the other. 'Zane fucked me.'

I retrieve the fallen brush and ram it into the jar near my feet. 'Why?'

She shrugs. 'He was treating me. It took us by surprise, but I told him to stop soon after he started because it didn't feel right.'

'Treating you for what — frigidity?' I repress an urge to lash out at the canvas she still hasn't noticed. 'How *did* it feel?'

'Dubious but healing — I think that's all he intended.'

'Did you think to use a condom?'

'Zane practised semen retention.'

'So much for hygiene — did *I* rate a mention?' My throat's become a black hole, muffling sound. When we make love Zane

30

controls his breath and contracts certain muscles, and energy shoots up my spine. Did his technique blow her mind?

'I'm sorry. I haven't had sex since the rape. Nothing else entered my head.'

Maybe I'm selfish to begrudge her affection — but why Zane's? I stare at the random splatters of paint on the floorboards till she walks away.

The darkness that stuck in my throat now swallows me whole. Rain lashes the windowpanes as I sprawl facedown on my mattress and bawl. Between the floorboards lie broken needles. They evoke scenes of rows of sewing machines, the rag trade of former days. Why haven't I seen any signs before? I wish I could slip through the gaps in the splintery floor and not have to come back. The pit of my stomach feels bottomless.

When Zane turns up after nightfall, I know he knows I know. From my swollen, mottled face. Or did he know Teresa would say?

'I'm sorry to have to tell you,' he says, in the hush of my space. He looks more attractive than usual, if only because I feel disgusting. 'Teresa and I made love yesterday.'

'Sorry you made love — or sorry you're telling me?' But I see the lines scoring his face; hear his voice crack. 'Thanks for your honesty.' Still, would he have owned up if she hadn't?

His eyes search mine like he'll find forgiveness if he looks deep enough, and I try to put myself in his place to understand how he could do what he's done.

'It didn't feel right,' he says, 'so I stopped straightaway.'

'But you would've kept going if it had felt right?'

'You're the best lover I've ever had, Skye,' he says. 'It won't happen again.'

·FIVE·

Wounds Will Never Cease

I must have been mad at them. But if so, where did my anger go? I didn't express it openly, as anyone in her right mind might have. Did my pain come out sideways — as travel plans, scrawled in a diary from those days? Only a torn page remains, and not a word of Teresa or Zane. Looking back, I don't think a trip to India could have saved me from the fate that astrologer said she saw in the patterns the planets would trace — the undoing of the self I'd known.

The magic group can go to hell. I'm creating my own private temple. One with a door I can lock. The other second-years never accepted me, so I'm not afraid of their jealousy. My sculpture tutor took a close look at my work after I mentioned magic. When Chris saw strings stuck on one painting he urged me to make the leap into 3D — *installation* in artspeak — and gave me his office key, no strings attached.

Though I've tacked abstractions to all four walls and painted a spiral on the floor, I'm not yet sure how to shift from two dimensions to three. Still, at least I can forget about a love triangle.

Last night Teresa started asking questions in Zane's absence; he's teaching tai chi up north for two weeks. Before their fuck she followed him blindly, but now she disputes his sense of direction. Fire's south, but south of here's Antarctica, not equatorial heat. And air's east, but east of Sydney is ocean. Why is west water if it's dry? When I said the attributions are symbolic, not literal, she scoffed that the same could be said of Zane's ideals. Lucky we'd just worked a healing circle, or I'd have wished her harm.

33

She'd be appalled to see I've devoted the eastern wall to air. Strings tipped with white feathers evoking flight — or writing quills — hang from the canvas. At the hub of the spiral stands my crude gesture to the fifth element, a hollow plaster egg so large a dinosaur could have laid it. My temple feels ripe with potential.

With Teresa gunning for me, and Zane away, I'm not inspired to rush home today. Instead I open a library book a third-year called Damian recommended, on representations of kundalini, the sacred serpent power, in art. An erotic print's caught my eye when I hear a knock.

'Can you hang on?' I call.

'Okay.' The deep, resonant voice sounds like Damian's.

Flustered, I slam the tantra book shut. Where to hide it? I slide the book through the hole in the eggshell, and dust off my jeans. 'Door's open.'

'Wow,' Damian says as he steps across the threshold. 'You've got your own sanctum. What god do you worship in here?'

Before I can think of a suitably smart-arsed retort, he spies my cracked egg.

'You worship a giant serpent?' He peers in. 'How about that. It's begun to hatch.' Swift as a flash, he plucks out the book, holds it up and whacks it, like a doctor delivering a child. Then he sees the title and his sharp, blue eyes narrow. 'You're not going to believe this, but I've just read that.'

'No way?' He's forgotten our chat. And no wonder — on our campus, males are outnumbered. With his high forehead, angular cheekbones and definite chin, he's handsome enough to distract passing women. And he's younger and thinner than Zane. My eyes focus on the scar between his: a depression as wide as my silver seal, right over his third eye.

'It's only skin-deep.' He grins. 'Don't worry — they didn't remove my brain.'

Yet I noticed he took the book for an omen. He's less rational than he pretends to be. Soon he's sitting inside the spiral on the floor with me, and I've told him all about Zane, our circles and

34

the Tree of Life. Damian listens intently until I grow self-conscious.

'The Garden's hidden within us,' he says. 'God didn't punish us for knowledge, we've banished ourselves out of ignorance. The Tree of Life's a metaphor.'

'No,' I explain, 'it's an actual filter we program into our auras.'

He smiles at me patiently. 'And what's the point of that?'

'Enlightenment without a guru, the Tree's like a map.'

'Isn't Zane a guru of sorts?'

'No, he's just someone who knows the way.'

'But how can he guide others to somewhere he's never been before?'

'You haven't even met him,' I say.

'I can't wait to meet Zane.'

We smile at each other, and I'm confused as to why I didn't meet Damian sooner.

'In twenty words or less,' he says, 'what do you want from your quest?'

I'm afraid he's teasing me. 'Ideally?'

'No holds barred.'

'Repair of the ozone layer, world peace, harmony between races and species . . . Gender equality. Reforestation. Global disarmament. Renewable energy —'

'What about for you personally?'

'Living a holistic lifestyle with Zane in a like-minded creative community —'

He raises an eyebrow. 'Paradise, eh? We all need our fantasies.'

'You jaded old cynic.' But since we've been talking, I feel free from pain for the first time in days. Already I'm looking forward to seeing Damian again.

Alone in the sun with my breakfast on the external fire escape, I'm rattled; not by the wind vibrating the rickety stairs, but at hearing my name.

'Skye,' Teresa repeats from inside the exit. 'I need to talk to you.'

Here we go again, I think as she steps outside. The landing creaks.

'I've booked a flight to Bombay,' she announces evenly. 'One way.'

I hug my knees and squint at clouds hugging the horizon, beyond the reach of countless red roofs. It's not a total shock — we used to talk of going to India — but we've barely talked at all for weeks, so I'm shaken. And yet I feel weak with relief.

'That should cure your aversion to curry.' Not that I've made any lately. Since Zane's return we've been eating out.

'I'm sorry it's short notice.' She sounds almost sincere.

'I'll advertise your space and Zane can find another singer.' I could sing for joy at the inconvenience.

'I'm angry at Zane for coming between us and turning you against me,' she says. 'Divide and rule. And you fell for it. But he won't be satisfied until he owns you.'

'You turned against me first. It wasn't like he raped you.'

She stiffens. 'I said I was sorry.'

'You thought the sun shone out of his arse too.'

'His knowledge seduced me briefly, but it's no substitute for truth.'

'You think you'll find your precious truth in India? Wasn't that what we wanted from magic — to look for enlightenment here?'

'Then look at yourself, you silly bitch, instead of listening to Zane!'

'He's only human, as you found out firsthand. But that's not enough for you.'

'I'm concerned for your sake, Skye. You've made him the centre of your life.'

'He's the *love* of my life. You're just jealous — or why try to take him off me?'

Hurt gleams in her green eyes. She puts on her shades then hurtles away.

36

'What'll you do now?' Pearl says, in my temple, when I've told her the latest.

'The water wall's next. Ear-shaped curves? Rhythmic lines rippling out like soundwaves . . .'

'No,' she says, 'about the rent. Would Zane want to move in?'

I wince. 'He's been dropping hints, but it's difficult. He's always horny. If I'd been meeting his needs Teresa mightn't have tempted him. He says transmutative work stirs up powerful sexual energy so maybe we should all go into a dark room and fuck at random just so no-one takes it personally, says it's an old sacred rite.'

To my amazement, Pearl giggles. 'How tribal. What'd you say?'

'That the others mightn't want to. He never asked whether I would.'

Pearl doesn't either. 'My flatmate's moving out too,' she says, then hesitates. 'Hey, I don't suppose you and I could share?'

It pains me that we share a dance class. She wears more layers than a mummy, and flat-footedly copies me, not the teacher. Like Zane, she's advancing as Teresa's retreating. Too skint to live alone, I'm caught between the devil and the deep blue sea.

'That's a thought,' I say at last. 'Why's your flatmate leaving?'

'She's saved enough for a trip to her guru's ashram in India.'

Teresa's just finished packing her cookware when I arrive home. Three overflowing boxes and the bare shelves underline how little I own.

'In case you don't know,' she says, 'Zane won't be replacing me.'

I try to out-smirk her. 'That's not your choice to make.'

'It's not yours either. We've been given notice. All seven storeys,' she says. 'The warehouse is scheduled for development.'

·II·

The House of Self-undoing

SIX

Out of the Prying Hand Into the Fire

*The other day I searched through a rusted tin filled with snaps
spanning more than four decades. The earliest shows my father
cradling me.* ARNOTT'S FAMOUS BISCUITS, *the tin's label
used to say, but it's rotted away; only* NOT FAMOUS *remains.
And under some slides, at the bottom, I found a print I'd all but
forgotten.*

*An elfin-faced man sits outside a spiral painted on a floor.
Behind him hangs an abstract canvas. In front juts a gut fore-
shadowing midlife. At arm's length from him, a young woman
sits inside the spiral. A silver disk dots her throat. Summer's
turned their limbs golden. White gauze strips like stretched-out
prayer flags fall from above, dividing the picture plane and the
lovers — my only photo of Zane.*

*His body faces mine, but he's staring into space and his
crossed arms guard his heart. My down-turned gaze contradicts
my open posture. What* weren't *we saying?*

College is out for summer. More time to spend with Zane. At
least I'll know what he's up to — and vice versa. Each morning
we drive to the dance studio where Pearl and I did classes. As
when Chris gave me his office key, it's an honour, to train with
the company, though the dancers only endure me because of
Zane.

After ninety minutes of yoga, Zane leads the tai chi. Everyone wants his knowledge, so I melt into the background. Then
we do an advanced dance class. I stand out like an ugly duck-
ling. The swans eye me askance when I can't get out of their
way fast enough. Technically they all leave me for dead.
Between routines, a few males watch me in the wall-to-wall

mirrors, and not, I don't think, just because I'm with Zane. The females look through me.

All except for mad Margot. No-one calls her that to her face. But with her demented attempts at ballet, it's ironic she shares Fonteyn's name.

'Fie, fie, fond love! Thou art so full of fear,' she declaims today, sinking into a plié — while the rest of us strain to perfect downward dog pose — then shrieks, 'EEYAIR-EEYAIR-EE-YAIR-EEYAIR!' as a fire engine roars by outside.

Some dancers titter, some roll their eyes. Others ignore her completely. As usual, I'm grateful that she's deflecting negative attention from me. She scowls at me as if she can sense how I feel, then makes eyes at the man leading the class. Everyone admires his loose, wild grace. But the wildness in Margot's eyes makes me think of a beast caught in a trap.

When Zane and I get home — as we now call the small cottage Pearl vacated — he turns on the TV and rolls a joint. The emerald walls, so charming while Pearl's guru beamed down from them, press in on me biliously, lately. Green, the colour of Venus — and of weeds, pond slime and mould, the colour of a decaying, low-rent hole.

For once, I decline a toke when Zane offers. Marijuana seems to aggravate my constipation, making me even heavier on my feet. Zane's pressure-point massages always give me relief, but in my present state I'd feel more trapped if I got stoned. Now we share a bed, I have no room to call my own. Incensed that he'd rather watch a cartoon than communicate, I spring up and head for the kitchen.

Since the end of semester I've missed college staff and students. I've even begun to miss Teresa. Though I no longer know who she is, and I'm questioning who I am, I miss our conversations. We didn't need TV to entertain us.

'If you're making ginseng tea can you brew enough for two?' Zane calls, as if unaware of my rising angst.

I stifle an impulse to scream at him to turn down the fucking TV.

'Why don't you just ask?' he says when I bring in the teapot and mugs.

42

'What?' My throat tightens as I kneel beside him on the rug. Even if I'd thought aloud, Astro Boy would have drowned me out.

'If you want it turned down all you have to do is ask.' He looks at me as if he can't understand why I'm so hard on myself.

My thoughts begin to swarm and bounce off one another like bees. Can Zane read my mind all the time? I flinch from that thought as if I've been stung. How can he love someone so naive?

Never taking his eyes from the screen, Zane edges closer and slides a hand inside the waistband of my dance tights. My thoughts can't agree. Don't rebuff him, hums one, you're lucky to have him all to yourself. I want to smash the TV, buzzes another.

After a struggle I manage to voice a third thought. 'If you don't want to turn me off, can we turn off the TV?'

He jerks his hand free as if it's been bitten by something inside my tights. Maybe he feels betrayed. I've never complained when he's watched it during a fuck. But I've seen these cartoons more than once. More than twice. I used to switch on the box when I came home from school and watch until bedtime.

In a huff now, I say, 'TV sucks.'

'It sucks, alright' — I gape at his statement — 'because most viewers are passive,' he says. 'But I'm reprogramming the group mind via the set.' My confusion, as usual, hasn't fazed him. 'Because it's tuned in to the television networks, I can make more of an impact using the power that's raised during sex.'

'Sorry.' I'd assumed the cartoon reruns amused him — after all, we have sex so often — but of course any adult would find them boring. Once again, I feel ashamed that I've underestimated him. His focusing on the TV instead of me grates less now I know what it's for.

The photos of my installation look better than the real thing. Like a proud parent, Zane praised my 'talisman', so a friend offered to document it, shooting a whole roll of film including a snap of Zane and me. Not my best angle or his, but at least it's a record of us I can keep.

I thought he must have borrowed the prints when I noticed they weren't where I'd left them, on top of my wooden chest by the bed. It never occurred to me that he'd search through my things; still, until we moved in together, I can't say I ever left him alone with them.

'You're paranoid,' I say again. 'Damian's just a friend.'

Zane glares at me across the futon. 'He wants to be more.'

'If you can read Damian's mind why can't you read mine?'

'You're harder to read.' His eyes narrow, as if he's in pain.

'So you read my diary instead.' My face burns with shame. Records of Chris's and Damian's comments and a hug from the head of sculpture — reminders that others like me and take my work seriously — sound petty compared to Zane's behind-the-scenes global healing. 'Why bother if you already knew what you'd find?'

'I wondered why you needed to hide it.' His folded arms declare that he's closed his heart so I can't wound it again.

'Don't you own anything personal that you never let anyone see?'

'Magical tools.' He sighs as if despairing of a wayward child or pet. 'That's the danger with your diary. What you write about is what you'll manifest.'

How can I disagree? I wrote Zane into my life. 'Friends are all I'm writing about,' I sob, feeling misunderstood. Maybe he can't mind-read after all.

Zane turns on his heel with a shrug and heads out to a house call. As the front door slams behind him, I recall his suspicion of male friends, magicians, who covet his lovers to whom they assume he's taught every trick he knows. Is that why he never teaches me any tantric techniques?

When the sound of his engine has faded I take out my diary. More than anyone named on its pages, it's been a trusted friend. It knows more about me than anyone does; except Zane, now.

Our house features a real fireplace. With luck, the owners won't return before winter and we'll be here to enjoy it. Pearl says they're due back sometime this year.

44

I lay my little blue book on the grate like a newborn in a basket of rushes. Nothing can ever be truly destroyed; it just changes form. Those weren't Zane's exact words, he's more eloquent than I am, but I'll try to make my words count from now on.

I strike a light on a matchbox from the bar where Zane plays with his blues band. Then, like that goddess who held a baby in a fire to make him immortal, I pass the flame underneath mine. As the white leaves catch and flare up, the cover flies open. Heat flicks through pages tattooed with ink and furry tear stains. A sky-blue flame licks their edges, like the etheric field, I imagine. Zane said the densest part of our aura looks blue to sensitive eyes. As flames eat the words I never uttered, sound crackles out of them. Tears drop onto my bare thighs. Maybe Demeter cried when she passed that child through the fire, missing her own, immortal, stolen daughter.

For a heartbeat, I want to snatch the diary back from its pyre, if only to read it one last time. Details of all the praise staff and students heaped on my installation. Chris understood that I just needed privacy.

On the sideboard I find a giant acupuncture needle of Zane's, and stir the charred fragments until every last word disintegrates. The cover hasn't quite been consumed, but that doesn't matter. I'm free to turn over a new leaf — as soon as I stop shaking like one.

·SEVEN·

More Spaced, Less Heed

My biscuit tin holds a little black book inscribed front and back like the silver seal, a record of all the rituals I performed in a group and alone. Though I wrote up just those actions and impressions that Zane sanctioned, it's indirectly revealing — for, over the months, the entries lose focus.

If only I hadn't burned my diary. If only I'd kept writing in it; a lifeline of words, like Ariadne's golden thread, to lead me out of the labyrinth. Once my unravelling had begun, was there some way I could have reversed it? And if not, was there a way I could have assisted it? The answer to that might depend upon why and when I came undone in the first place.

By the time the thread began to unravel again, two decades later, I'd retrieved enough memories to realise that I was the maze.

Passing fields give way to thighs as Zane guides my head down, while driving north up the highway for his midsummer tai chi workshop. I nearly choke with surprise. When did he undo his fly? And can I anticipate more stunts like this now we've left civilisation behind? As I strain to hold my cheekbone clear of the steering wheel without losing contact, he swerves off the sealed road and speeds down a rutted dirt track. Jolted, I withdraw my head from his lap, the better to grit my teeth, and when the traffic fades to a distant drone he grinds to a standstill. Yet he doesn't seem like himself as he humps me in the passenger seat, and instead of the visions I've come to expect, I see only winged things splattering the windscreen. Please let that be a detour, not a sign of what's to come, I pray, once Zane's come inside me and we're back on the highway.

47

He looks so blissed out that I hate to voice doubts, but I'm too afraid not to. I didn't survive chronic constipation to have my belly bloat with a pregnancy.

'If I'd known you were going to come,' I say, 'I'd have taken precautions.'

'That's okay,' he says calmly. 'I knew it was safe.'

'How can you be so sure if I can't?'

'Your smell's a giveaway.'

My missed orgasm seems trivial in the light of how lucky I am to have found a man who knows the female body so intimately.

'I've dreamt about you for a long time, Skye.' A faraway look enters his eyes. 'Maybe one day we can move up north and have a child together?'

'Maybe.' I'm sure he'd make a great father. Children adore him. He even delivered his own baby once, though he's vague on how long ago. It's sad that the mother denies him visiting rights. I'd love to give him a child when I've worked through my hang-ups. Children make me feel self-conscious, but that might change if I had my own.

In my dreams of rural seclusion, I have Zane all to myself. In fact, there'd be an unending flow of friends through our home. *His* — I know no-one up north yet — but I'll make new friends, he said this morning, as we passed through his home town without stopping. It's true; I made a few at art school, and all sorts of artists must live on the land. I'm about to find out.

We drive straight through to Seraphine's. Her handmade wooden house is hidden amid emerald hills. As we near the front door, it swings open and she emerges, pale and slender. In the dusk I can just see a riot of flowering vines; and some dope plants that tower over me. Illogically, I sense them watching me through their serrated leaves, and tell myself I'm imagining things as Zane embraces Seraphine, but the down on the back of my neck stands up.

As tall and stately as her plants, Seraphine beckons us in. We sit at her kitchen-cum-dining table and share a joint after our long drive. 'Heads,' she says as I suck smoke into my lungs, like we're playing a game of chance. But heads are more potent than leaves. Two tokes does me. I've sucked on enough for one day.

Now night's fallen I can't see the crowns of those plants at the window behind Seraphine, and I start to unwind as she and Zane reminisce. Close to his age yet built like a dancer, with heavy, dark tresses and light blue eyes, she must be the most striking woman I've ever seen.

Just as I'm wishing *I* looked like a gypsy queen, Zane shoots up off his chair into the air, and crashes down backwards onto the floor. When he rises, unhurt, a flower of broken blood vessels blooms on his forehead. How can that be when he fell face up? Could it be symptomatic of brain damage wreaked by the home-grown heads he's smoked? Zane's often said he'd love to be able to levitate. Was that an attempt? His rapt smile and Seraphine's hysterics mystify me more.

My impression that everyone in this dimension wields special powers but me persists until Seraphine turns her attention to mundane matters like crushing garlic.

'Skye's a gifted artist,' Zane tells her over ratatouille. 'She made a temple at art school dedicated to the four elements.'

I bask in feeling special until Seraphine clears the table and lays out her vibrant paintings of the Tree of Life. A serpent twines around the glowing fruits.

'It's high time we shed old skins,' she says obscurely.

Zane smirks. 'Speak for yourself — I already have.'

'You can't fool me.' She laughs. 'I'm a rat too.'

Before he can answer, in walks a tall, thin man with long, thick hair — the gypsy king. He greets us warmly and the banter moves on to new subjects of which I know next to nothing.

Soon Zane starts to yawn, so Seraphine shows us to our bed. Zane drifts straight off, but I lie awake trying not to moon over Seraphine's man, and freaking out at a dragging, scraping sound. As dawn breaks I vow to myself to refuse all future offers of heads; I can barely cope with the usual voices in my own.

When we surface around midmorning, Seraphine's brewing coffee. 'Did you hear the diamond python in the roof?' she says.

To my surprise Zane nods. 'It must play havoc with the rats.'

So that's what they were talking about before we went to bed? I don't admit that I spent the night squirming in a paranoid sweat.

The tai chi workshop's first day, held on private land not far away, passes as fluidly as a dream. We shape-shift into cranes, tigers, monkeys and dragons; floating, crouching, springing and lashing our tails. The others always include me, smilingly passing me joints in the breaks, but after my all-night guilt trip I'm not tempted to partake. While I envy their laid-back lifestyle, they also have problems — physical ones. After the day's tai chi they seek treatments from Zane. As I wait for him to finish laying his hands on them, I feel a profound identification with Mary Magdalene.

Between patients, I show Zane some itchy red welts on my arms. He says they follow my colon meridians. Insects aren't the enemy, they just target blocked chi, he says. Maybe they do. I'm constipated again. As soon as he's seen his last patient, he shows me a colon meditation. To my relief it works next morning when I try alone. I'd begun to fear I could only ever shit if I stayed home.

Later in the week, a gaunt older woman approaches me. 'I'm so happy that Zane's found someone who loves him for himself,' she says.

What's he been loved for in the past? I want to ask, but just smile.

'Zane's a rare man. I know you understand. Without him I wouldn't be here now. He cured my cervical cancer.' Before I can answer, she holds out a small, sealed jam jar.

I take it, hoping the dark globs inside aren't tiger turds or monkey glands. 'Thanks.'

'Don't look so stunned, they're a gift from the land.' She laughs at me. 'Magic mushrooms sweetened with honey. For you and Zane to eat — and enjoy.'

Chickens peck and scratch near my head as I lie, face up, on Seraphine's floor, legs spread, barely daring to breathe. Zane's begged to shave me for months and I gave in, at last, because

50

dark pubes look unnatural with copper-dyed hair. He finishes without one nick and rocks back on his heels to admire the view.

'Your vagina's the prettiest I've ever seen,' he croons.

And he's seen plenty. I've met some of their owners this week, and compared, while we skinny-dipped in the river. Yet the confirmation of his praise, his hard-on, intimidates me. In-explicably, I think — smoothness should reduce friction. Then I remember.

This morning we woke up on the spare mattress of a couple we'd visited late, when their three year old charged in and threw herself at Zane. He tickled her and she squealed as they rolled around amongst the covers. The uneasiness I felt while they giggled together still hasn't gone. I have to keep reminding my-self that he always wakes up with a hard-on.

One sun-drenched morning after the workshop's finished, Zane suggests we eat the magic mushrooms; so we scoff them for breakfast, washed down with coffee, and go for a swim in the river. He urges me to use his snorkel to look at some fish under-water, but as the trip comes on I'm absorbed by some insects above the surface. Undeterred, he forces the mouthpiece be-tween my lips and pushes me under. As my mind expands into the riverbed I lose touch with where I begin and end, swallowing and breathing water during our slow-motion struggle. Fear of drowning engulfs me in the space between each heartbeat and for an ever-expanding moment I panic that Zane will snuff me out. Not until I've gotten about as light-headed as I can bear do I gather that he just wants his snorkel back. I surrender it, grateful to come up for air.

We wander back to the house and discover a fruit-salad land-scape indoors, as a goddess, sheathed in a sarong like a skin ripe for peeling, beams and pours fresh cream over delectable golden ridges until smooth, pale rivers flood shimmering valleys strewn with walnut boulders. After Zane and I eat in rapture, the god-dess glides away. Insides glowing, we slither to the floor. I con-template an exotic pink fruit dotted with tiny red bumps for what seems like an eternity, mesmerised by its beauty, yet unable to identify it. When the scenery shifts to a furrowed, dark hole with a tangy smell, I realise I've been staring at Zane's scrotum. Sublimely juicy sex follows, as we pour through each other like cream.

Down by the river again, I hear myriad sounds interwoven — birdsong, trickling water, rustling wind — into an exquisitely orchestrated symphony of dazzling complexity. Not a single note is random, contrary to what I might have assumed before listening through the ears of the fungi.

As I gaze at Zane, and a halo of rainbow rays of light fans out from him, reaching into me and beyond, touching heaven and earth, it seems that a brooding, hawknosed pagan god stands before me — my ultimate soul mate who gives my life meaning and answers all my questions.

I feel as if the gold tops have opened my eyes, not just to the truth of the web embracing us, but to Zane's true nature. While I've glimpsed it before when stoned, the insight faded with the high. But this revelation of Zane's enlightenment won't be denied. My desire for him has merged with the rhythms of sap singing through the trees, water warbling over stones, and the sacred kingfishers' wing-beats.

I'm watching thunderclouds mass when Seraphine's gypsy man enters his studio. Synthesised music soon fuses with rolling thunder and the swelling hum of the land, and reverberates through the hills, while Zane swells beneath my hand until the whole valley ripples orgasmically in harmony with my hills and valley.

By the time raindrops kiss my bare skin, the trip is beginning to ebb.

EIGHT

Bad Things Come in Trees

It's true that I used to dwell too much on the past. Zane would be appalled if he knew that I'm still doing it. Yet he never dwelt on it enough, or he'd have seen patterns repeating. And sometimes things change superficially, making the pattern harder to see. I learned that lesson not long ago in therapy with Josh, who asked about my family tree at one of our first sessions.

The next healer to make much of an impression on me, Josh seemed far removed from Zane, and not just by the passage of time. Josh, I've no doubt, would say that Zane's past defined him because he denied it; that all his behaviours were defences against it. Hard to tell, when Zane seldom mentioned his family. Though perhaps that's telling in itself. Anyway, Josh's approach intrigued me partly because of its contrast to Zane's. He guided me to focus exclusively on the past.

My magical work lapsed during our holiday. But, as we drive out to the coast to see an initiate friend of his, Zane says all work and no play won't hasten initiation.

Handsome in a weathered way, Miles looks older than Zane and seems to rival him for healing knowledge. An expert iridologist, he inspects my irises after a joint, then steps back and keeps looking until I blush.

'Your eyes are naturally blue, Skye.'

I blink at the unforeseen diagnosis. 'It's true — my mother says they were at birth. But for as long as I can remember they've been dark brown like my father's.'

'The brown's caused by a build-up of toxins.' Miles looks at Zane who nods.

'If I detoxified my system, would my eyes revert to blue?' I ask Zane on the trip home.

'We could fast for the next lunar cycle,' he says. 'I need to lose weight for a dance performance anyway.'

'If I don't eat for a month won't I get constipated?'

'That's part of your problem. Your fear shapes the future because you hang on to the past.'

'Uh-huh?' And how's his future been shaping up? With shit-loads of fats and sugar. If it helps him shed a few kilos, I'll be delighted to starve. Are these delusions of grandeur, our dreams of changing our forms? Like we could before Lucifer fell from the Tree — of immortal life, says Zane. The Tree that's begun to grow in my aura, under his guidance.

But didn't Eve taste the fruit from the tree of knowledge of good and evil? Weren't there two different trees in the Garden? I don't ask, because Zane loves to complain that I'm hung up on the left side of my brain.

Instead, I imagine my eyes turning bluer than Seraphine's.

When Damian pays his first visit, Zane's out on a house call.

'If I'd known you were coming I'd have made more,' I say as I let him in.

He eyes the steamed spinach and boiled beetroot with ambi-valence. 'What's on the menu?'

'Soup for an elemental fast.' I turn on the blender.

He looks me up and down and says something inaudible, so I lean closer.

'Are you in mourning?' he shouts above the whine of the motor.

I turn off the blender, empty its contents into a pot, and stare back, baffled, then realise my headband, singlet and dance tights are black.

'We wear black to invoke water during the water week, and puree all our food to prepare for a fortnight without any.'

He grimaces as he listens. 'If you stop eating you'll stop shit-ting.'

'Fear shapes our future unless we let go of the past. Have you ever fasted?'

'Not for two weeks straight. Are you fasting from dope, too?'

'Zane's burning incense to the gods, as he says, but I've cut down.'

Damian strokes his goatee. 'So he worships dope?'

'No, all herbs are sacred to him. He uses them to heal with.' Though I'm vague on dope's healing properties, and I wish Zane didn't smoke so often, I respect his philosophy.

But Damian grins as if it's a joke. 'So what's the point of your fast — not weight loss?'

I don't say that's Zane's motivation. 'To purify our bodies and minds — and an expert said that if I can detoxify, I'll have blue eyes. Like yours.'

'Mine are brown deep down.' He raises one eyebrow. 'Like a Tibetan.'

Now I know he's taking the piss. 'That's not what I meant.'

'No, truly — my partner and I practise Tibetan tantra.'

That's the first I've heard of her. He's been flirting with me. Or have I been reading too much into his friendliness? As casually as I can, I say, 'Zane teaches tantra.'

'Speak of the devil,' Damian says, as Zane, black-clad and surly, burls in.

I introduce them, unnecessarily.

Damian proffers his hand, but Zane just stares at the crater in his forehead as if it's a window on his intentions. 'Don't let me interrupt,' he says, sniffing.

'Damian was just talking about his *partner*,' I explain.

Too late, Zane lifts the pot off the heat. 'Is that right?'

'I'd better leave you folks to eat,' says Damian, edging towards the door. 'You must have worked up a hell of an appetite.'

'Sorry I burnt our dinner,' I say, when Damian's disappeared into the dusk.

'That's not what worries me. Fire follows sexual desire.'

'I'll watch out for that in the fire week.'

Zane's not smiling. 'Hole-in-the-Head's hot for you.'

I'm torn between defending Damian and laughing at the nickname. 'He's already got a girlfriend.' Though that didn't deter Zane. I scour the tainted pot, then simmer what vegies remain for a fresh lot of soup.

Soon group members start to arrive for our full moon circle, among them a raven-haired woman I've not yet met, Stella, an old friend of Zane's. At a quarter to midnight, as we walk down the road to the park on the bay, I count fifteen initiates and neophytes. Pearl and the flautist have been fasting too, I see from their weight loss when we're naked. The absence of passers-by while we set up circles in public places goes to show that magic must work — or that we look like wackos who sacrifice virgins.

A bowl of burning incense at the centre of our circle splits into three pieces when we call down the moon, and as we chant the Hebrew names of the spheres of the Tree of Life, Stella's perfect pitch makes me feel useless.

On the way home afterwards, I ask Zane, 'So how do you know Stella?'

'We once had a threesome with another woman, a long time ago.'

Why only once? I wonder. 'Did either of them get jealous?'

'They were close friends so they shared pretty freely.'

'They must've been closer than Teresa and me.'

'In those days we were focused on the good of the group as a whole. Sex amplified the kind of love and healing we shared tonight. A triad's more powerful than a dyad. We should try it sometime.'

'Uh-huh?' I ransack my recent memory for candidates, but can't get past Damian, and he and Zane would never consent. 'Are you more partial to threesomes if they're two-thirds female?' I ask.

His tentative reply defies my expectations. 'That depends.'

Inspired by Seraphine's serpents and spheres, I've been painting parts of the Tree of Life since my psych tutor set us an art assignment.

Zane admires the latest I've stuck to the emerald wall. 'It's the best.' He sits down on the sofa reserved for guests. 'I love you, Skye.'

That black whirlpool's my favourite too. 'And I love you.' I sit down beside him.

'There's something I've been meaning to tell you,' he says. 'I've been waiting for the right time.'

I take a breath to brace myself. Have the owners of the house come back?

'Last week I treated this woman on a house call,' he says, 'and after the healing she went to sleep. But her daughter was in the next room doing her homework, so we hung out together and watched TV —'

'*Home*work? How old was she?'

'Seventeen. And then we made love.'

Not again. My head starts to spin. 'Whose idea was that?'

'She wanted me to.' He smiles rapturously.

'She said so — or did you read her mind?' I'm choking on the knot in my throat.

'She trusted me,' he says in a low tone. 'She was a *virgin*.'

I force myself to swallow. 'Is she pretty?'

'Yes.' He looks contrite.

Stunned as I am, I can understand. It's rare that a man of his age — and weight, regained since his dance performance — can get into a virgin's pants. 'What's her name?'

'Zoe,' he says ingenuously.

'Why wait a *week* to tell me?'

'You've been having a hard time.'

So much for my dreams of life on the land, growing old with Zane — I'm over the hill at twenty-three, while he's regressed to his teens. 'How thoughtful.'

'I didn't want to hurt you.'

'That's a joke.' As I stare at my black watercolour whirlpool, things begin to focus. 'Who else have you fucked?'

'There hasn't been anyone else.'

'You sat on it long enough. Why should I trust you?'

'I want to be honest. I'm sorry, Skye.'

He needn't have owned up, so he must be trying. I let him cuddle me. He's used to women like Stella who don't get jealous. But if he fucks around, why can't I?

Take his friend Miles who looked deep into my eyes, the iridologist. I'd love to fuck him, but until now, out of blind devotion, I haven't dared *think* it. Zane's been hinting at threesomes, and I'd be interested — if the third party's Miles. And we'll see him in less than twenty-four hours, at an autumn equinox party.

When we go to bed I draw reassurance from Zane's searching kisses. But as my tongue finds the roof of his mouth its hardness startles me. He flinches and pulls his head away, too late. That's why my disapproval of sugar makes him defensive.

I wonder if that schoolgirl knows she fucked a man with dentures.

The next night, on the dark moon, we drive out to the coast. My skimpy singlet should give Miles more to look at than my irises. Zane's silence, behind the wheel, leaves me free to dream up a three-way tantric fantasy, to let myself see, smell and feel it. To manifest, he's told us, you charge a clear idea with intense emotion.

But when Miles greets us at his back door, I see how unclear I've been. In the flesh he looks older and sterner than in my memory, and nothing like Damian. I must have confused the features of both men in my head.

Miles ushers us in to a room hung with balloons as round as the spheres of the Tree. I try analysing the clusters. Look for the Tree in all things, Zane's said. He greets a beautiful blue-eyed blonde with a baby on her knee. She seems young to have initiated; far too young for Miles, who can't take his eyes off her. Though his partner's his age — or much older than me — I feel unseen with my unripe breasts. And fasting didn't turn my brown eyes blue. If Miles weren't an initiate, I'd have picked him for a sexist. The magical lifestyle seems less progressive than Teresa and I envisaged. Women with long hair and skirts set out the food. Not a future I'm looking forward to. At home Zane lets me do all the cooking, unless his friends drop by, when he likes to impress them with his timeless specialty, pumpkin pie.

Raspberries and blueberries top the frosted cake, echoing the red and blue balloons. Or the past and future poised at my shoulders, red and blue fruits of the Tree; if they met in my heart, what colour puree would the present be? Among initiates I never know what to say. If they can read my mind, there's no point opening my mouth. If they can't, I don't want to put my foot in it. I accept the smoke they pass around so I'll blend in.

Though the mood in the house has unsettled me, Zane's said the new moon heightens subtle energies. Some junkies died here, someone says; or did they just live here? Either would explain the atmosphere. At-most-fear. Magical intent has made the dope very potent. Miles and his partner grow their own.

As usual, my high is becoming a roller-coaster ride. Once it starts I can't step off until the ride stops. And as each new high reminds me of the violence of former rides, I promise myself I won't risk it again if only I survive this time round. Yet the others don't find it nerve-racking, or why would they get stoned again and again? So I'm back on those rickety rails, hurtling through the loops of my own private hell, while everyone else appears to be having fun.

At my expense, I've begun to suspect. Every word escaping the lips of Miles and Zane drips sarcasm. As if they know, even know that the other knows, about my fantasy. As if they despise me for it, and would rather have sex with the blue-eyed blonde, who's succeeding at being obscenely desirable while suckling her baby.

But I don't want to dwell on that or I'll manifest it. The dope has vastly amplified my powers of focus, an effect Zane knows how to make the most of — so I'll try.

I've been visualising a lightning flash, in between rituals, to strengthen my sense of the pathways connecting the spheres of the Tree. Drawing a shaft of silver light in through my crown, to zigzag down through the planetary spheres until it runs to earth. Then circulating energy via breath. Joining the dots.

I gaze out through the window across the darkening lot. The sprawl of lantana and lowering clouds bode no better than the conversation, most of which keeps going over my head. Lately I've grown impatient to get to initiation. I don't know what all these magicians think about after they've initiated, but they look far happier than I feel. Maybe when I've initiated I'll *know* what they're thinking, once I'm a member of their club.

As I focus, the flow of light flashes through the first three spheres. A rainbow strobe, then white and black balloons, the orbs outside my head — *supernals,* Zane calls the outer planets. Then the charge electrifies my throat. And the circuit blows.

I'm choking on static. The energy's stuck in my throat. The power surge has overloaded my system. Too late, I regret the strong dope. My kundalini feels like it's flowing backwards, a roller-coaster running in reverse. And I can't set foot on the ground yet; the ride is far from over. Dinner is served, a carnival sideshow of tofu tart, tossed leafy greens and hot dishes.

My obsession with Miles since Zane's confession, I'm guessing now, may have sidelined my rage. As if my desire for someone else could make Zane's straying okay. Why are he and Miles looking daggers at *me*? And, compared to my art-school friends who can't see fairies and elementals, and don't sit at the feet of men who tell stories about fallen angels, these women seem detached, unreachable. Is that how Zane wants me to be? Does the sight of my pain offend him? It's like that childhood game of snakes and ladders. Every smile or friendly word is a ladder that lifts me up. Then one look at Zane's eyes and I've stepped on a snake and slid to the bottom. I'm losing the game.

The slippery, snaking roller-coaster plunges me into panic. Zane doesn't love me, Miles doesn't want me, and the only way out is down. Their threesome will feature the blonde, with her smile as sweet as the frosting I scrape off my cake slice. The women's eyes gleam from impassive masks. Laughter flashes like knives. It's a long ride.

When the blonde's baby stares at me and starts howling, Zane says it's time to go. The little girl snatches and claws at my seal, trying to tear it off. Take it, I want to yell, let me out of this fucking magical mirror maze! But the blonde baby's screaming at the energy that's locked in my throat, trapped behind the

60

cloudy silver seal. I'm tempted to rip the damn thing off, but Zane's leading the way to the door.

His friends rise to hug him farewell in turn. He's unconditionally adored. No-one cares if he fucks around. They tell me to take care.

Do I look like I'm the careless type? It's written on my face. I've lost the plot, and in their eyes I deserve to fall from grace.

·III·

The Pit

NINE

Stranger Than Crucifixion

In a department store one Christmas, when I was very small, my mother had a photo taken of me with Santa Claus. Adhesive oozed from the edge of his beard and his breath stank of booze. I hated sitting on his knee and resented my mother for making me. 'He's just a man in a costume,' I told her as we walked away. 'Oh, don't be like that,' was all she'd say as she dragged me off to browse for shoes. 'He's yucky,' I persisted. 'Can't everybody see?' My mother bent down and hissed, 'Stop making a fuss, will you, it's Christmas Eve.'

No wonder I confused Saint Nick with Old Nick as a child; and the unspoken fact that 'Santa' transposed the letters of 'Satan' didn't help. Later, Zane explained that the church had superimposed Christmas and Easter upon ancient solstice and equinox festivals. When he said that Easter had been named after a goddess, I pictured a pagan precursor of the Playboy bunny. I always wanted to know what lay beneath the surface, behind the mask.

And Zane seemed to have all the answers. If I dared to ask.

The more Zane contradicts his own magical handbook, the less I know where I stand. But we resonate the spheres of the Tree by chanting their Hebrew names as we drive north for his five-day tai chi workshop, which will end on Good Friday. While his impulse to share this ritual mystifies me, I'd rather some structure than none. Since we visited Miles seven nights ago, I've been feeling frayed. *Afraid.*

We're intoning the name of the Saturn sphere — at our throats — when the left front tyre blows. Though Zane swiftly slows and pulls over with no loss of control, I'm shaken. And guilt-stricken — the right front tyre's intact. The flat's occurred beneath my seat and magic's taught me responsibility; I can't blame it on coincidence.

At least we've stopped on the outskirts of a town. It could have been worse. As we walk back the way we came, I can't wait to hear Zane's interpretation.

'You'll need to track down your Watcher and banish it before initiation,' he says.

'Is it the same as the shadow in psychology?' I say.

'That's another name for it. The Watcher hides in the Tree.'

'How would someone recognise it?'

'The stress it creates between levels in the psyche shows up as neurosis,' he says. 'Psychosis, in extreme cases.'

I'm tempted to press him for more information, but I need to steer clear of negative thoughts.

Relief overwhelms me when we find an open garage, as if that somehow lets me off the hook. It's Saturday, Saturn's day, a no-turning-back day. We're back on the road before too long.

If I don't pull myself together soon, I'll miss the start of day two of the tai chi. Not wise when I'm such a slow learner. But I feel loath to leave the shade and privacy of the tipi. All the students look up to Zane, in varying degrees, and they all keep urging him to live here. He keeps promising them that he will one day. What happened to 'we'?

A pretty, long-haired teenager kept making cow eyes at him yesterday, as he led the group in his pink stubbies with no jocks underneath. She acts more confident in her sexuality than I've ever felt in mine. Imagining he wants to fuck her blows my concentration, though it seems like a fitting punishment for my having fancied Miles.

I should never have read Zane's comic book this morning. But if this is a conspiracy it's cosmic in its scope. Where were the comics produced? Are all the initiates in on it? One comic dealt with my negative impact on this community, a blue female alien who keeps getting in the way. The bald, blue, invisible alien's an outsider, just like I am.

66

If Pearl was here I'd be tempted to tell her about my suspicions. Of all the people I can think of, she might understand. I remember her describing how ancient tribes would punish wrongdoing. Denied recognition of his — or her? — existence, the disgraced outcast would slink off to die in the wilderness. Once his society abandoned him, so did the will to live. Who'd have thought I'd ever miss Pearl?

While I don't want to accept that the comic might be a sneak preview of my fate, and to pinpoint what alerted me is complicated, I believe I've been chosen for a ritual sacrifice, to be performed on Good Friday. That's when Jesus was crucified, so the notion's not without precedents. Scapegoats have to be sacrificed to keep the tribe in balance. I'm the obvious candidate.

Once I'm gone, Zane can fuck anyone, if he doesn't already, starting with that cow-eyed girl. He won't have to feel guilt over deceiving me, and I won't have to feel bad about cramping his style.

Random words I've overheard from the lips of the resident elders seem to back up the ritual murder theory. One of them said something about a snake. It'd be the perfect weapon — because the murder couldn't be traced. Snake poison strikes me as a painful way to die, but they can hardly nail me up on a cross. And it's not as if serpents don't belong to the Christian mythos. Jesus had an awakened kundalini. The serpent power ascended his spine and lit up his heart and mind. That's why he's painted with a halo, like saints or eastern masters. But I'm no Second Coming; I'm a woman, for starters — like Eve, who succumbed to the serpent of temptation. It all falls into place if it's not taken literally. The fruit she sampled wasn't plucked from some external tree. I'm just waking up to the extent of my naivety.

It's crossed my mind to wonder how the hell they'd get away with killing me. The local police would bust them. But that's silly; in this neck of the woods wouldn't the cops smoke more dope than we do? And most of these people have magical skills. I keep telling myself they're highly evolved, vegetarian, even Buddhist; they can't be assassins unless looks can kill, or unless they make an exception to stop my vibe destroying their peace of mind. But though I turn down all the joints they pass around during the breaks, my fear's rising — growing with the moon, which will be full on Good Friday, the likeliest date for a sacrifice.

When Zane proposes we visit a mate of his down the coast on Friday evening, I'm hopeful. What's the worst that can happen with just us three?

The suburban, fibro house is a short drive from the commune. Howie rolls a joint as soon as we arrive. To my surprise, he looks like an average suburban guy. Big gut, bad posture, flannelette shirt, short hair. Shamefaced, I decline a smoke. Being stoned amplifies my dread. So does watching Howie's blaring TV. To my relief he turns the volume way down. Feedback has begun to follow wherever I go, closing in on me like a net.

No matter how hard I try not to listen, Zane's and Howie's words implicate me, even if they use mostly metaphors. When they mock the insignia of the police force, I know they're analysing patterns in my aura. If they spoke directly to me, I might try to respond, yet while they talk in code I don't dare; I'm scared of seeming paranoid. Idiotic. They *know* I'm paranoid.

Why else would they want to talk about black holes? My ears prick up in spite of myself. Zane says the scientists refuse to admit that they exist. Is he trying to tell me that *I* exist? Howie says *they* — and I think he means me — distrust phenomena that can't be seen. Like a fishhook, the theme of invisibility snags my unwilling attention. They're not hunting for black holes, Howie says then, but for signs of their presence, the warping of space around them. Gravity gone mad, he laughs, they claim nothing ever escapes. The most dangerous entity in the universe, Zane says, a perfect sphere of absolute blackness. His words jolt my whole body. He might as well have spoken my name. A sphere? I thought a black hole was more like a chakra spinning inwards — a whirlpool sucking up energy instead of spewing it out. Unless, says Zane, you've entered a wormhole and exited in another dimension. I flinch. What if that's where I am now?

As if I've voiced the question out loud, Howie stares straight into my eyes. Is he attracted? I try to suck that thought back in so Zane won't get angry — or get ideas. A threesome with Howie's the last thing I'd contemplate. I might have a black hole's psychic mass but at least I'm not overweight.

Across the room the men talk on, indifferent to my stress. Sick of the flickering TV set, I gaze idly through the window. What I see in the moonlight transfixes me. A line-up of golden bubbles as big as human heads, yet perfectly spherical and transparent; translucent, to be precise. I'm staring straight through them to the shadowy garden behind. Floating close together, suspended in the air, five weightless, motionless, shimmering orbs watch me watching them. As they hover at arm's length beyond the glass, and twelve feet or more above the lawn, I imagine they've come for me. Are they in on the sacrifice?

No — I sense they're benign. To my surprise, neither Zane nor Howie shows signs of knowing the spheres are there. I'd expect initiate magicians to be the first to see them. These magical entities are aware of me, yet they mean no harm. It's as if they're checking me out. Relief seeps through me. Humans seem more hostile. Sedately the silent witnesses drift away in single file. After they pass from sight I feel a little safer for a while.

Afraid of Howie's scorn, I don't tell Zane what I saw until we're on the road bound for the commune next morning.

'You must've seen my elementals.'

I don't argue, but my mind is spinning. So, all along, they were hanging about, waiting to do his bidding? I doubt it. In fact, I privately think Zane believes the world revolves around him. But I have to be careful. None of my thoughts are private anymore.

That night I lie awake while Zane dreams, in the deep dark of the windowless tipi. He told us last week that circular structures make the best resting spaces because the dreaming body can spiral up and out more freely. That's fascinating to know — but first I have to go to sleep.

Dawn's still a long way off when, much louder than the frogs and crickets, the tap of click-sticks starts up just outside. My whole body stiffens. Is it time? Are all the tai chi devotees gathering for the sacrifice? Someone's circling the tipi. My muscles tense for flight and my heart thuds like a drum in a chest so tight that I can barely draw breath. My senses feel almost intolerably sharpened. As if the land itself is amplifying my awareness and I can't sink into oblivion because it won't let me. I consider waking Zane, but resist the temptation. Unlike all the others here, I've stopped believing that he's my saviour.

The rhythmic clicking continues and, though I can't hear footfalls or voices, the sound begins to ascend, spiralling round our cone-shaped lodging. That's no human; and if it was Zane's dreaming body I'd have heard it before. As the sound wheels overhead, at least ten feet above our bed, my fear gives way to exhaustion.

When I open my eyes, Zane's rolling his first joint of the day. I mention the clicking.

'You would've heard my elementals.'

Again, I resent his conviction. If he's responsible for every enigma in our vicinity, I might as well cease to exist.

Tomorrow we'll leave early to beat the traffic. I can't wait. Today, Zane wants to visit a nearby commune on the coast. Howie drives us over the potholed road in his ute. As I strain with every muscle to hold my knee clear of his, he offers to loan me a bicycle. It's not something that's been on my mind, so he can't have read it. Yet he's thought of me — I'm not invisible after all. Cycling will make me more visible than I care to feel right now, but I don't know how to refuse. Touched by Howie's kindness, I thank him and, when he's parked and unloaded the bike, ride off down the dirt track towards the beach.

By the time Howie and Zane reach the sand, I've found a broad, flat, wet expanse. Tracing figures of eight with my wheels, I begin to feel bliss unfurling. A vortex of energy links me to the sky like it did in rituals, or in my elemental temple. It's as if I've ceased to exist in a finite form. A consciousness far vaster than mine is pouring through me, drawing lines. The infinity symbol I'm looping through flows into a yin-yang sign, and from its tight curves I cycle into a spiral. Headlands and surf circle around me as the sky unwinds me. Gulls wheel above and the wheels beneath me graze the grainy surface, writing in a code designed for birds or air elementals.

Even from a distance I can see Howie smile at me. Zane's face is harder to read, though his stare grazes my surface. I wish I could pedal faster, spin my wheels fast enough to rise up through the air. I'm clear that my aura doesn't reflect the insignia of the police force now.

On Easter Sunday Christ rose from the dead. Have I been resurrected?

TEN

If the Crap Hits, Share It

Beneath my inferiority complex lay a feeling I learned to call 'shame'. And therapy taught me that feelings shift shape once reclaimed. But where did that one come from?

Long before I fell short of Teresa, I felt inferior to my mother. Whoever dared disagree with her was wrong. I grew up feeling wrong to my core, for we could rarely agree. We still can't.

She's adamant that I was a happy child. Then where are my happy memories? Recalling anything at all from before my teens has been hard work. Hoping my school photos would throw light on the matter, I found them in the NOT FAMOUS *biscuit tin.*

To be happy, doesn't a child — unlike an adult — need to fit in? I was the only kid in kindy not smiling, the only first-grader in a hand-knit, the only second-grade girl with her legs together, the only third-grade girl with hers spread, the only fourth-grader smiling . . . I hadn't remembered not fitting in, but where were some signs that I did?

We come home to a scrawled note thrust under the front door. Pearl's cryptic script rattles me before I can decipher it. Jagged capitals, slanted so far forwards that they risk falling over, forewarn us: the owners of our rented house have returned from overseas. We need to move out '*ASAP*'. I pass the message to Zane.

'That's a hassle I don't need,' he says. 'My patients have just figured out where to find me.'

It's not like I need more hassles either. He did agree to the terms of our tenancy. But that's not the only news. A postcard's arrived from Teresa.

With a trembling hand I pick it up from the table where Zane's tossed it. The reproduction of a painted Hindu god with blue skin — 'Krishna,' says Zane before I can turn it over to read the fine print — could be the male counterpart of my comic-strip alter ego, but for his thick, black mane.

Teresa's handwriting intimidates me. It's as perfect as ever. As perfect as her aspirations with which she now feels at one. She's doing charitable work, having realised *that*'s how to help the world. Art and magic, she concludes, don't foster humility. Is she trying to imply that I'm too proud? I don't think she could even begin to imagine how far I've fallen. She's meditating. Still practising yoga. Oh, and she's had a fling with an older woman. A spiritual sister, she says — they met in an ashram somewhere. I remember her telling me she wasn't gay. Not that she says she is now. Just that they had a heavenly heart connection. I can't believe I feel jealous of a German sannyasin I've never met. I picture them clad in orange — my complementary opposite — and sharing feelings opposed to mine. Joy, courage, hope and trust; her upright script exudes more than enough.

It strikes me, as it's begun to more lately, that I took the wrong fork in the road. Teresa was smart, trained in commercial art, did something useful, and now she's making herself more useful still. I once thought of her as the person I might have been, minus the coke, if I'd taken the right turn in the road; what a joke. Her unrelieved optimism makes me want to curl up and die. She ends her message by asking how I am.

How am *I*? Stuck in a very different dimension, one you'll never enter, it's too dense with fear — a hell realm you couldn't conceive of in your worst nightmares. *Hari Om* to you, too, sweet sister, whatever the fuck that means. Wish you were here!

She's penned an address but I can't reply. What in hell would I say? Though I guess I should write to notify her when my address changes.

'How's Teresa?' Zane asks sourly. 'Has she found the right teacher yet?'

I shrug and hold the card out to him. He'd have read it anyway.

'All my teachers came to me,' he says, dropping the card back on the table as if it's a power bill, not a precious hand-written transmission of spiritual insight.

Tension is mounting in and around me on the day college resumes. Peak-hour traffic and storm clouds pile up and forked lightning acupunctures the horizon. As I walk downhill towards the campus beneath a sky swollen with bile, I feel as if I'm descending into Hades.

On arrival at college I enter the vast hall named after a Nazi war criminal. I've never been sure if its bad vibes derive from the name or if it was named for the vibes. The space is very dim, darker than outside under that green-black sky. My tutorial has begun, so I sit down at the back. Students I vaguely know sit in uneven rows. But they have no auras. They're dead, according to a voice in my head. In fact, since the night at Miles's, the voice keeps telling me I've died. But the possibility that I could be stuck in between scares me more. No-one sees me rise and head for the exit.

As I walk uphill away from the campus, a plan takes form: hunt for a real estate agent. But first I stop at a health food shop. Since Miles's party, whatever I try tastes weird; and sugar triggers energy surges, making the blood roar in my ears.

Dried apricots taste sweet with no added sugar. I place my selection on the counter.

The girl eyes me narrowly. 'Would you mind if I checked your bag?'

Dumbly I show it to her. She didn't inspect the bag of the last customer.

'I'm sorry,' she says with acute embarrassment, as if she's read my mind. 'I don't know why I asked. I've never checked anyone's bag before.'

Her lame excuse for an apology humiliates me more. I walk on down the road, trailing fibres of unravelled logic. I can't hide from the cosmos. It knows my deepest secrets. I'm an energy thief. The safest option would be to stay away from people. Yet

I need to find a home for Zane and me. The storm is a pimple yet to break.

On my right, amid plush green grounds, a mental hospital looms. Flowerbeds and grand old trees blur the edges of bleak brick cells. For a moment, it occurs to me to ask to be admitted; I can't trust myself. Yet I trust doctors even less. They'd tie me up, inject me, administer ECT; I'm in shock already.

Anyway, Zane says he's worked in a psych ward, and tried all the drugs — and their effects appalled him. The price I'd pay for the luxury of others making all my decisions would be my last chance of redemption. No-one emerges intact from those wards.

It's a year to the day since, returning from college, Teresa and I saw a corpse carried out. I smelled the stench, yet felt removed. Death was all zipped up. Concealed. Contained. Yet now its taint's touched every part of my life that's not filled by Zane. The warehouse had a blocked throat chakra, Teresa used to say, her tone insinuating I did too. But lately I'm not so sure I do. Maybe I can hear things because my throat's too open. Electrical wires are singing — screaming — like someone's turned up the volume.

The outer darkness peaks as I reach the next intersection, and one car slams into another, sending it spinning. Out of control, it mounts the kerb in front of me then grinds to a halt. The driver appears unharmed, yet I'm shocked by his baleful stare. He's blamed me. I stumble on past the car as he restarts his engine, averting my eyes. The storm reflects my inner state, I realise. Now my negativity's reached critical mass, others suffer. Accidents are the Earth's attempt to release built-up pressure.

On the way down the corridor to the psych tutor's office, I will myself invisible and pray I won't run into Chris. I haven't seen my former sculpture tutor since my world imploded, and I don't want him to see me like this. But he doesn't appear. Perhaps he can sense my darkness at a distance. I knock faintly on the psych tutor's door.

He doesn't look surprised as he ushers me in to his office, though we haven't spoken privately before. In fact, I've never seen him show any signs of emotion, unlike Chris, who hides his behind Ray-Bans. When the psych tutor wears shades, it means he's hung-over.

He watches me from behind his desk, fingers interlaced.

'I'm finding it too hard to come to lectures,' I begin. Though I feel so small, my voice sounds huge in the uncluttered space.

'Is the third-year workload getting to you?' He's a master of understatement.

'It's more than that,' I say, at a loss for how to explain. I can hardly tell him my Watcher's running amok in my Tree. 'I've been kind of overwhelmed,' I go on. 'Altered states, you know, heightened sensations. Oh, and Zane — that's my partner — says my problem's too much yin.' I try to crack a smile and shrug. 'Whatever it is, it's pretty distracting.'

He smiles back, his mask as neutral as if I've mentioned the weather. That's the biggest speech I've made for days, and I'm hard-pressed to hold it together.

'Have you thought about deferring?' His fingertips form a steeple. 'It's just that dropping out is so final.'

The way he says the word makes it sound like a death sentence. And I don't want to die. Not if there's a chance that I could come back to life.

'Suppose I were to defer,' I ask, 'could I keep doing psychology?' He's the only person who hasn't freaked me out for weeks. Some thread of connection, however slight, might give me the structure I need. I've abandoned all attempts to build the Tree. 'I can still research and write,' I assure him, though I haven't tried — not since late last year when I handed in a paper on ritual magic.

'You can continue with the psychology strand as long as we maintain contact.'

I can't read his expression, but I suspect he's opted to humour me.

'And why not see the college counsellor, too,' he adds, like an afterthought.

'I didn't know there was one.' We laugh; me nervously, he brightly.

'And you never know — an analytic reference frame might help,' he says, 'since the structure of your life has disintegrated.'

Is that what I said?

'And when did the world turn hostile?' asks the college counsellor.

As she scowls at me like a bird of prey from the far side of her desk, her desiccated face framed by sleek, shoulder-length, white hair, I'm afraid that I've betrayed myself by coming here to bare my soul, or what's left of it, to a parched academic.

'After the second time that Zane — he's my partner — was unfaithful.' Hell, I never meant to reveal that. 'Well, I *think* it was the second time.' Soon I've told her about his fame as a healer and a spiritual guide.

She frowns more deeply, if not at me now. 'And how do you experience this *hostility*?'

'Partly through eye contact with strangers in the street.' I look down at her age-spotted, vein-knotted hands and squirm in my seat.

'How so?'

'I think they feel violated by what I see in them.' Revolted by her state of decay, I lift my gaze to her faded eyes.

'And what is that?' She leans back and peers at me over her spectacles.

'Extreme contempt. Bitterness. Hatred. Things that I'm not meant to see.'

'And does Zane attempt to help you?' She leans forwards, her face contorted with what I take to be horrified fascination.

'He's told me to spin a purple flame through my aura but it makes no difference.' If Zane knew how much I'd told this old buzzard, he'd be disgusted.

'Zane is beginning to sound like a bad influence,' she says icily. 'Have you thought about moving out?'

'Yes. Well, no. What I mean is, we just moved out together, and that's put a spin on things too.'

He found the dark, thick-walled, old-style, ground-floor flat: on a main road next to the railway line under the flight path. When I asked how many he'd looked at, he said fuck spending all his money on rent.

'None of this is Zane's fault,' I hasten to add. 'He's very concerned about me.'

'I'm going to write a referral for you.' She uncaps a fountain pen. 'I'd like you to go and see the psychiatrist in the community care centre.'

'*Psychiatrist?*' I thought she'd decided the problem was Zane's. Doesn't a shrink have the power to take my freedom away? To lock me up in a cell with walls even thicker than our new flat?

'Just go and see Alex for a *chat*,' she says. 'That's all I'm suggesting you do. For now. He's very good. He's a friend of mine.'

Her concern, however perfunctory, has given me some hope, as has the prospect of someone else to care if I live or die. But I feel distrustful as I stuff her envelope into my pocket. The idea that talking might help seems too good to be true.

And what will Zane say?

·ELEVEN·

Disparate Remedies

In the interval between losing my mind over Zane and finding my way to Josh, I never abandoned the quest for self-knowledge. I tried every path under the sun or over the moon — past-life regression, flower essences, lucid dreams, trance, dance, even twelve-step meetings — and on the way I compiled a CV of stints as a Cretan princess, priestess, Christian mystic and inquisition victim, while collecting totems, talismans, ambient tapes and strangers' phone numbers. But I never stayed with anything for long. I was afraid of getting stuck and not feeling free to leave.

Diversions, all of it, Josh would say. Devices for dissociating from pain. I'd never seen it that way, thinking my pain burdened others. Zane had said I was addicted to pain, so I'd tried for years to lighten up. Yet when I smiled or laughed around Josh, he'd stare through me, unimpressed, unresponsive. Not until I exposed my fears, or broke down in tears, would he offer support.

We have to leave our shoes at the door of Pearl's ashram. Not that I'll ever think of it as hers again. None of the devotees remotely resemble my op-shop friend. Young urban professionals surround us, and the most beautiful of all gazes down from the walls, larger than life, robed in saffron and glowing with inner knowing. Only the dark sheen of her skin offsets the pastel colour scheme. The whole place is peachy; too perfect for me. I should never have come.

'The chanting will get you out of your head — it gets me out of mine. And no-one here will project their demons onto you.'

Has Pearl read my mind?

I nod, at a loss for how to tell her it's not just *their* demons that worry me. The incense reminds me of Teresa, though I've often smelt it in Pearl's flat, and when we sit on floor cushions and chant in unison I recall Teresa's melodious voice. My own feels trapped in my throat while hundreds of others fill the space. 'Hare Krishna,' we chant, 'Hare Rama', repeating the names endlessly. The nearness of so many others freaks me out. I thought I'd feel relief at being unseen while they were all looking within, but I'm sweating from fear that they may look within *me* if they notice I'm here. As the chant gathers intensity, my temperature rises till I feel burning tongues licking my sides, feel like I'm on fire. The roar in my ears overrides the drone of the chant for a moment and, as the crowd melts away, I'm at the centre of a flaming pyre. I keep mouthing the chant in panic but no sound comes out, and words, even images, empty from my mind. Then, gradually, the room assumes corners again and the heat in my flesh subsides.

After a seeming eternity we move to another room to drink chai — delectable spiced milky tea. Pearl looks different, some-how remote; and when a tall, fair man asks would we mind if he joins us, she grows even more so.

'Anand.' He bends forwards and extends a broad, strong hand.

As I take it, warmth courses into mine. Then he sits down on the cushion to my right — Pearl's glowering on my left — and attempts conversation. None of his questions — Is this my first time? Did I come with Pearl? Am I an artist too? — require me to say more than yes or no. And maybe that's all he needs, to find out what he wishes to know.

'Would you both like a lift? I'm headed back through the city,' he says as I drain my cup.

Pearl searches my face to see if I do — did she think I'd rather take a bus? — then the three of us stand up and go to re-trieve our shoes.

To my surprise — and Pearl's, I gather — Anand drops her home first.

'I thought you lived over the bridge,' she says.

'I do, but I'm not going home yet,' he says.

Alone in the car with Anand, I begin to unwind a touch. For some reason I feel he can see past the part of me that hates myself so much. Yet I'm already dreading Zane's reaction if he finds out a man gave me a lift. Anand talks about his recent travels — to distract me? — until we reach my address. Then he asks for my number and says we'll go out one weekend for a cup of chai.

I thank him sincerely and, with regret and fear, watch his white car pull away. When I let myself in, Zane's watching TV while spooning ice cream into his mouth.

'What did you chant?' he asks as I wriggle out of my coat.

'One was all about Krishna,' I say.

'And did Krishna come to you?' Scorn drips from his sticky tongue.

'I don't know.' I'm too ashamed to ask him why I might hallucinate being burned at the stake.

Five dollars sounded fair for half an hour's work. Not until I've begun the job do I find that fares make a huge hole in my pay, a fact Zane doesn't hesitate to point out. While he's right, he resents my rising early five mornings a week and leaving before we've had sex. I suspect he's pissed off that I can take it or leave it. Not enjoying sex isn't the problem though; not enjoying *anything* is. Sex releases me from fear because I can't feel myself while Zane fills me. I've become an empty shell, a vessel reserved purely for his pleasure; but I pay for the relief in the aftermath when my evil explodes; when stories aimed at me scream from newsstands, radios and TVs, telling the world that I've set off an earthquake, crashed a jet, fouled the sea, felled trees. And the world blames me. I see the accusation in strangers' eyes.

When Zane says my job is a waste of time I never argue, because I agree, and I don't dare tell him I'm not working for the money. Trifling though it may be, the job saves me from feeling worse than useless, and creates an excuse to escape the flat and be on my own. I can face walking up to the station and back if no-one notices me, and the view from the train window's distracting if I can avoid the signs. I used to love reading on public transport when I was studying, but now I can't open a book or look at a billboard without taking it personally.

An Indian man on the office floor always leers at me, but I stare dead ahead and try to finish before he and his coworkers start. Pearl's friend who passed on the job said to ignore him when I checked, through Pearl, that I wouldn't need to speak with anyone. First, I fetch the vacuum cleaner and suck up the tiny circles of paper that sift down from the printers to leave a dusting of ghostly confetti on the deep blue carpet that makes me feel protected because it's my colour. Last, I wipe the computers and desks clean of fingerprints.

It's the biggest space I've hoovered since my teens. To do our whole house took twice as long, and my mother gave me just a dollar. From that perspective, things are looking up.

Ten minutes early, I enter the waiting room with misgivings. Zane would ridicule me if he knew. A lanky man, his faintly familiar face smudged with stubble, slouches in the far corner where I'd rather be. As he seems unlikely to meet my gaze, I try to recall where I've seen him. Aha — playing lead guitar in a blues band. He's a well-known musician. What's he doing here? Why would someone with a cult following seek psychiatric help? Maybe not all of the doctors here are psychiatrists, I conclude.

When a balding, middle-aged man appears and calls my name, I flinch.

'I'm Alex,' he says.

You're obese, I think. He ushers me in to a room that contains a very large, cluttered desk, behind which he sits, pushing his chair farther back from it than I need to push mine.

'What can I do for you — *Skye*?' he says with a genial smile, having glanced at his watch and my freshly created file.

'I don't know,' I say with complete candour, trying not to stare at his paunch.

'Have your circumstances changed in any way of late?' he asks.

84

'Yes,' I blurt. I don't know where to start.

'Do you fantasise about suicide?' He twirls a black ballpoint pen and smiles blandly, as if he's just asked if I smoke.

'Not exactly,' I say. 'But I think about dying a lot.'

'About your own death?' He makes a dent on my file with the pen.

'Yes — but I feel it's out of my hands.' I tell him of the conviction I had that I'd be sacrificed at Easter, and of the burning sensation when I chanted at the ashram. 'And I can't shake the feeling that my time's running out.'

'Have you been seeing or hearing things?' He clicks his pen in a maddening way.

I describe the golden bubbles and the clicking outside the tipi. 'And, though I doubt very much that they were Zane's elementals,' I say, 'it's not like I saw or heard anything that an initiate magician wouldn't. Well, Zane didn't notice, but nothing I've just told you struck him as strange.'

'And what can you tell me about Zane?' Alex strokes his beard with one hand while the pen in the other hovers over his notes.

After extolling Zane's healing genius, I move on to his ideals and their appeal to me and to others. Then, before I know it, I've said that missing out on his mother's breasts is Zane's lame excuse for his impulses to tug and twist mine until they hurt, and that the first milk to pass his lips was condensed and he's craved sugar ever since. But, I tell Alex, I suspect he's trying to make my breasts sag so no-one else will want me — because, once, when he knew I was due to see my friend Damian, he bit my throat so hard that his teeth left purple-black blotches, like a seal of ownership.

'How old is Zane?' Alex cuts in, as if some thought's just struck him.

'Why?' In a fit of remorse I fear I've said enough already. I don't want to give Alex the wrong idea. I mightn't have made it clear to him how much Zane loves me despite his game playing.

'He sounds like a teenager, and more than a little paranoid, but my guess is he'd have to be older to have done all the things you describe. Late thirties, maybe.'

'I don't know.' The heat in my cheeks must be a dead give-away. 'He won't say.' It's only a white lie. I don't know for *sure*, but I *think* he's thirty-six.

When we moved house a horoscope fell out of a book. It had to be his — the sun's degree corresponded to his birthday. But I got confused when I looked up the planets' positions in my ephemeris. On no day this century did they line up in exactly that way. Unless I move Venus forwards a sign. Then it fits. And another piece of the puzzle falls into place. If the chart *was* his, Chinese astrology terms him a rat. That's what Seraphine called him, though it made no sense then. Even now, I can't guess why he'd try to hide the true nature of his Venus, the planet of love — though the goddess has been called vain.

'I'm afraid we've run out of time,' says Alex. 'Come back and see me again next week. But first of all, we'll transfer you to sickness benefits.' He reaches for a pad and begins to write. 'You're clearly unfit for work.'

When I walk out of the building, clutching the note in my coat pocket, the sky seems to be pressing down like the roof of a collapsing circus tent. My guilt feels like it will flatten me before Zane gets a chance.

At my local Social Security branch I fill out the requisite forms. Fluorescent lighting heightens a deathly atmosphere. No-one's aura emits any light in here. I've held off applying for benefits, but my student allowance ceased when I deferred. One of the questions pertains to how much I earn. I consider omitting my weekly income of twenty-five dollars, but I'm not paid cash in hand. If I don't declare it I could get fined. Besides, the form wouldn't ask about earnings if I wasn't supposed to be working. I sign the narrow box with a shaky hand and join the queue. Looking down to minimise the risk of eye contact with other customers, I notice that my signature has changed. It fits entirely within the box now that it's smaller, tighter, more pinched — like the face I saw reflected in the door as I walked in.

When I'm called up to the counter I hand in the forms and Alex's letter. A carrot-haired youth with a crew cut, who looks like an army recruit, checks them over.

'It says here that you're working.' He stabs at one form with a forefinger.

A bayonet could hardly intimidate me more. *Working?* It's a relative term. Things aren't working all that well. When my mouth opens, no sound comes out. I shut it and try to swallow.

'If you have a job you're not eligible for sickness benefits.' He looks as triumphant as if he's just flushed the enemy out of hiding.

'But I only earn twenty-five dollars per week,' I say. So that *was* a trick question? 'If it's a problem I can give it up.'

'It's too late.' He looks down his nose at me as if it's the barrel of a gun. 'This signature proves that you're fit for work.'

Not until I've left the office and walked several blocks do I realise that I never saw him open Alex's letter. But I can't face going back. Tears well in my eyes for the first time since Zane told me he'd fucked that virgin.

·TWELVE·

No Thyself

Who in their right mind would want to remember? And yet I've sought, unassisted, to relive what I underwent with Zane, because the man to whom I'd turned for guidance lacked interest. Josh, who'd urged me to embrace my history, deemed that stage a distraction. He believed it merely pointed to earlier, more crucial events.

Even after years of therapy I can't be sure when I first felt terror. I just know I often felt it as a child. If I woke before dawn I'd freeze and hold my breath in the dark. And nothing ever happened — as long as I played dead. But one night I peered through my bedroom blind. The scene's still etched like an aquatint in my mind. A shadowy figure bolting across the garden from north to south then vaulting over the high paling fence proved that danger hovered nearby.

In fact I'd been terrified, long before that, of a strange man coming to get me at night. And my mother never told me there was nothing to be frightened of. Why did she withhold reassurance?

My parents used to say I had a great imagination when my version of the facts embarrassed them. Yet their versions never sounded right to me. My mother would omit facts while my father embellished them. That Zane did both seemed only natural.

Who are any of us without our memories? When my parents kept denying that they'd done as I recalled, I lost trust in myself.

The voice that asks for Zane over the phone sounds familiar — brassy, husky and brusque — but I can't place her name, the

Sanskrit sort gurus bestow that all tend to sound the same. I'm curious, as they arrange a date and a time. New patient?

'She just wants to pick my brains,' Zane says after he's hung up. 'Some astrologer, friend of a friend.'

The next afternoon, I skulk in the bedroom when she's due, but Zane slips out to the corner store, forcing me to answer her raps on the door.

'I have an appointment with Zane,' she informs me as if I'm the maid.

The woman I consulted has come to consult my lover. When and why did she take a spiritual name? A cloud of scent makes me sneeze, or maybe it's hairspray, and she's painted her finger-nails alternate lilac and grape. Before I can ask her in, she sweeps past me.

'Have a seat,' I say redundantly, as Zane enters behind us with milk and sugar.

She stares at his feet, perhaps because they're bare on a late autumn day. 'It's an honour to meet you after so long,' she gushes.

He nods up at her — she'd tower over him even if she kicked off her heels — and they sit down in the front room facing each other. His saggy old track pants and baggy jumper make her look overdressed.

'Would you like a cup of tea?' It's all I feel I have to offer.

'Do you have coffee?' She directs the question to Zane.

'We did have. Do you know if there's any left, Skye?' He turns towards me, if not far enough to make me feel quite real.

'There should be.' The words come out half strangled. My voice box seems shrunken, perhaps from disuse. 'Do you take milk and sugar?'

'I like it black.' Her gaze remains on Zane.

'Tea with milk and two and a half *heaped* sugars,' he says, like I didn't know.

I'm hoping that, after I bring their hot drinks, they won't notice I'm still in the room. They don't. Zane's done a brilliant job of transforming what was a gloomy flat; embroidered cushions strewn at the edges, drapes smoothing out the corners. I wish I could take some credit for the charm of our living space, but apart from the giant egg on the sideboard there's no sign of me in the place. I've contributed nothing; just my plaster egg from the installation, with a gaping hole revealing it's a hollow shell — like its maker.

The astrologer wants to talk about an undiscovered planet. She seems to think Zane knows where it is. Her deference towards him and her distance from me, I think as I sip ginseng tea, show she doesn't remember reading my chart. Alex might be a fat, complacent shrink, but he treated me like a person. Why doesn't this drag queen recognise me? Am I underestimating how much I've changed?

They call the planet *Persephone*. It fell from the Tree, says Zane, aeons ago. And with that, any benefit gained from talking to Alex flies out the window. Why must everyone in Zane's orbit talk about me? She says I'm somewhere beyond the orbit of Pluto, at the edge of the system. Too far out to be seen — yet I'm perturbing Pluto; she must mean Zane. None of these people ever refer to their feelings. Is that why they resort to code? Society needs new feminine archetypes, she's telling Zane, women are more than mothers and whores or wives and mistresses ruled by the moon and Venus, and though Persephone's more complex than either because she spans two worlds, she's still an undeniable victim.

My face feels as if it's on fire. I don't know how to snap out of it. Persephone wasn't always a victim, says Zane, she went with Pluto willingly in the beginning, he never forced her. And no-one's forcing me to stay here now. They made up that crap about rape, he says, when they needed a scapegoat to carry their demons. Scapegoat? I think of those outcasts sent into the wilderness to die. Pearl said someone can die just from being ignored; but isn't that victim mentality? I feel like I'm juggling a whole lot of balls and I can't relax or I'll drop them all — reactive red, expansive blue, a mauve sphere of contraction — what if they fall? The astrologer says that Chiron, despite being wounded, could never die. So who the hell am I, Persephone or Chiron?

Now she's got Zane started on Lucifer. She says she's seen a horoscope — horror scope? — for the Antichrist, with the sun, moon and all visible planets aligned in the sign of the Water bearer. Though Zane looks singularly unimpressed, relief leaves me bilious. I can't be the Antichrist if I was born three weeks too late!

After the drag queen leaves, oozing gratitude all over Zane in the process, he says she can see the big picture but she's hazy on the parts.

'Am I like that?' I doubt it, but I can't trust my judgement.

His forehead wrinkles. 'No. You're too hard on yourself. You fixate on what's wrong, dig a hole, and fall into catastrophic thinking.' He must have seen pain in my eyes, because his tone softens. 'That wasn't meant as criticism. It's good that you care — but try to visualise what you desire, not what you fear.'

'Have you had any physical symptoms?' Alex asks at our next session.

I mention the shrillness of sounds, metallic tastes and diarrhoea. 'I used to suffer from chronic constipation,' I say, 'but now I need to go at least three, four times a day.'

He looks like he's suppressing a smile. 'Drugs would steady your nerves, you know. Remind me to write you out a script before you go.'

'I don't use drugs anymore,' I say, utterly terrified. My body doesn't feel like my own and I'm damned if I want to hand over my mind. I've heard about the side effects of psychoactive medication, like weight gain, sluggishness and, worse, constipation.

To my surprise he doesn't argue. 'If you ever want something to settle things down, just say the word.' He opens a manila folder to make a note. Not knowing what it says makes me nervous. 'So how was your week?'

I tell him about the astrologer's nerve-racking visit.

'How do you know that Zane and his friends are in telepathic communication?'

'Because they talk about me in code, and the code keeps changing. How else would they manage to keep up with it?'

'But if they use a code, how do you know it's about you?'

I have to think for a minute. 'Because they always say things that apply directly to me.'

When he jots something down I know it's about me. 'Can you think of any examples?' he says.

'They talk about victims and outsiders and entities no-one can see.' To avoid Alex's gaze, I glance over at the window — odd that I never noticed the bars on it last week. When I glance back, he nods for me to continue. I tell him they've referred to me as the enemy — well, as the police or the government.

'Do you feel you deserve to be punished?' he asks when shame makes me pause.

'More often than not.'

'And what do you think you deserve to be punished for?'

'My selfishness.'

He chuckles. 'Everyone's essentially selfish. That becomes apparent in a job like mine.'

'No,' I say. 'Not some of the healers and white witches I've met through Zane. They're working for the planetary good.'

He smiles indulgently. 'And that includes Zane?'

'Not always — but he's saving the lives of patients with cancer and AIDS.'

'There's no known cure for AIDS.' Alex snorts with impatience. 'And I'd say that Zane's as selfish as anyone when it comes down to sex.'

Spurred on by Alex's leading question, I spill all the details I know of Zane's betrayals. I feel like a double agent, but there'll be ample time for guilt later.

'And was your pal Trisha working for the planetary good?' he says, with an edge of what sounds rather like sarcasm.

'Maybe not altogether at that stage,' I say, 'but now she is.'

'Puzzling that your best friend would need to do such a thing.' He raises a bristling black brow flecked with grey. 'Especially if she felt superior.'

'Need to do what thing?' I ask, confused.

'By fucking your boyfriend, perhaps she hoped to prove she was as good as you.'

'I've never thought of it that way,' I say. You don't know Teresa, I think.

'We're out of time again,' he says, 'but we can talk some more next week. And you might want to check out a group that meets here Monday nights. A few recovering schizophrenics attend it. They're all patients of mine.'

'Do you think I'd fit in?' Surely he can't think I'm schizophrenic?

He shuts his manila folder and heaves back his chair. 'I'm willing to hazard a guess that you'll find some common ground somewhere.'

Arms akimbo, Zane eyeballs me, as if to ascertain what I'm hiding. 'Does the group include *men*?' His tone implies men are foul predators, not harmless like he is.

I had to tell him. He won't let me walk out the front door unless he knows where I'm going. And apart from forays to work, I rarely leave home without Zane. Since I've stopped calling the few friends I had, they never call me, except for Pearl.

'It's not a singles club,' I say, 'but I guess it will be mixed, and I hope it's a chance for me to meet others who might have similar issues.'

'You could do another banishing,' he says, as if he's unconvinced.

'Okay, I'll try,' I say, 'but how can it hurt to talk about my problems?'

'That's the problem with shrinks and their patients, they get stuck in their heads, and the way they think reinforces the way they feel.'

While I think he's right, I don't feel I can trust him either. The discord in my head won't let up. Would pharmaceuticals quieten it down?

'Did you know,' he says, 'that there are harmful chemicals in the human brain which can seize control of a person without warning, for reasons no-one understands?'

I stare at him, stunned. It's unlike Zane to admit to gaps in his knowledge.

'Does that sound like a paranoid delusion?' he mocks. 'Because that's what the shrinks expect us all to believe. It's their justification for drugging patients into a stupor.'

But drugs are okay, to judge from his example, if they're self-administered?

'How will you get home from your group?' he asks when I'm ready to leave, as soon as I've made dinner for us both. He likes me to cook sweet polenta and pour cream over his, so I stir in the raw sugar after I've scooped mine out of the pot. The pale yellow blobs make me think of baby food.

'By bus,' I say, though that probably won't be the case. If it's not raining I prefer to walk so I can keep to the shadows.

When I slip into the common room, three fat guys, counting Alex, and a thin one have formed a loose semicircle. One chair stands free.

'Everyone, please welcome Skye,' announces Alex. 'Margot can't come tonight so we might as well get started.'

Each guy introduces himself. I'm so jittery I miss their names.

'Why don't you take turns telling Skye a bit about yourselves?' prompts Alex. 'How you came to be here, where you are now, that sort of thing.'

The heaviest guy, in size and in vibes — though he's not quite as big as Alex — begins. 'I used to suffer from auditory hallucinations.' He studies his lap. 'At first I believed I'd found my calling — I'd come to spread the word of God. That was the highest point. Then *they* started to warn me about a conspiracy.' He nods grimly. 'Without Alex and Largactil, I hate to think where I'd be . . .'

'Or who you'd be,' says the other fat guy, with a sly wink at me.

To hide my blush I look down. Unsmiling Largactil Man has socks on under his JC sandals.

The second overweight guy, more of an extrovert, turns towards me. 'God used to talk to me via my TV set,' he says, chuckling, 'and I'd talk back to him.'

I nod. Zane might need more proof that the man was insane.

'Yep, I fed takeaway to the TV,' he says, 'when things got really serious.'

That sounds quite mad to me, but I can't help wondering what Zane would make of it. He never reduces his patients to clinical disorders; just treats the unique imbalances in their bodies and their auras.

'I've gotten better since taking my medicine,' the takeaway man concludes.

The thin guy seems painfully shy. 'When I was sick I wrote music,' he says in a thin voice. Light from the overhead fluorescent reflects off his glasses. 'It's hard to believe, even now. I've always been a bank teller.'

'Lots of musicians have day jobs,' I say.

'But I'm *not* a musician. The scores were rubbish.'

Though I'd like to ask how he knows, I don't dare. Especially not now I'm starting to identify the rules of this club. I spent hours in the State Library after work today, researching my psychology essay. The peace of a place where no-one speaks or looks at each other gave me solace. Dipping into the writings of psychologists, scientists, scholars, sex therapists, theorists, gurus, even Nijinsky, whose kundalini danced him into a madhouse, helped me to forget about myself for a while. To be creative you have to abandon your ego, one author said. I seem to have forgotten where I left mine.

'Just before I got sick,' says *not*-a-musician, 'I'd tried dynamic meditations with the orange people down the road each morning.'

'They'd jump up and down shouting "Who? Who? Who?" till they couldn't remember who they were.' Takeaway Man chortles and beams at me.

'It's "Hoo! Hoo! Hoo!" like in *yoo-hoo*,' I say, frustrated by his obtuseness. They do it to raise their kundalini, like anyone here could care less.

'Skye, why don't you introduce yourself to the guys,' Alex says.

'Well, I don't hear *voices*,' I tell them, 'but I don't hear things *right*. And I do hear *things*' — best not to say 'chakra' in case they don't understand — 'like, electrical or mechanical noises are amplified' — though so is the pulse in my ears — 'and I've *seen* things. Giant bubbles in the air, a man's face replacing mine in the mirror — but what I think's really changed is the *way* I hear. And see. Everything refers back to me. I feel guilty most of the time because even strangers across the street or at the other end of a bus react to every thought that enters my mind.'

'What sort of reactions do you mean?' JC looks like he might already know.

'All sorts — coughing, twitching, frowning, dusting lint off sleeves — it's not their gestures, it's the vibe. They look peeved or impatient, even outraged at times.'

'Do they look straight at you?' asks Takeaway Man.

'Sometimes. Other times they'll refuse to, and that can make me feel guiltier.'

'How do you know their reactions are connected to you?' asks *not*-a-musician.

'I feel things in my solar plexus.'

'You haven't mentioned Zane,' says Alex.

'It doesn't seem to have much to do with Zane,' I say.

'Who's Zane?' Takeaway Man leans forwards, his hands clasped, confirming my perception that everyone's always more interested in Zane than in me.

'He's my partner. He didn't want me to come here.'

'Why not?' they chorus, all agog.

'He thinks I should be able to resolve this stuff with magic.'

'That reminds me,' says Takeaway Man, 'of turning the TV on, or off, at twenty paces, using my brain as the remote control.'

I look at Alex who smiles encouragingly.

'Don't worry,' he says. 'No-one here will judge you.'

'I practise ritual magic,' I say. 'Zane's been teaching me. He's taught hundreds of others, thousands, even, and he's also a powerful healer.'

'Not as powerful as Alex,' says Takeaway Man, 'or you wouldn't be here.'

While my sense of worthlessness, worse when I'm with others, has slackened its grip a fraction tonight, I'm appalled that anyone would ascribe healing powers to a shrink who's so powerless over his weight. 'It's not like Zane just heals *mental illness*,' I mumble. 'He doesn't see the mind as separate from the body or soul, so he treats imbalances holistically, and he's had great success with cancer sufferers.'

'He sounds like some sort of guru,' says *not*-a-musician. 'Do his followers carry his picture in a locket on a necklace?'

'No,' I say, panicking. I didn't come here to talk about Zane. 'He doesn't expect anyone to kiss his arse. I've met heaps of his students and they seem very independent, and he doesn't charge that much for treatments or classes.'

The men fall silent, as if in unspoken accord. I freeze. It's starting again.

'So how was everyone's week?' booms Alex.

As I reason that he wouldn't need to ask if they were telepathic, a long and lively discussion ensues. JC can't get a job, Takeaway Man can't keep one, and *not*-a-musician wants to leave his but he's too afraid.

'Wait till you meet Margot!' Takeaway Man tells me, provoking hysterics among the others. 'She's a prima ballerina.'

She's delusional,' says *not*-a-musician.

'She never quite made it,' says JC.

'Skye dances too,' says Alex. 'Modern, not classical — isn't that right?'

'I'm not a real dancer.' Blood burns in my cheeks. Is he teasing me? I don't feel real at all. 'I was always a dud in class, and I haven't been back since I got a job.'

'That's too bad,' says Takeaway Man. 'You look like you'd be a good dancer.' The way he smiles, his gaze lingering, makes me wonder if he's flirting with me.

'You don't seem that bad,' says JC. 'Without my pills I'd be suicidal.'

'No,' says *not*-a-musician, 'you don't come across as mad at all.'

'You're not as sick as us,' says Takeaway Man, grinning.

He might as well say, *You're not one of us*. I knew I wouldn't fit in. And I don't know how long I can stand to go on existing in this purgatory.

'There you go, Skye,' says Alex, 'you've made a good impression here at least. We hope you'll join us again — same time, same place — next week.'

His three protégés nod enthusiastically.

'So how was it?' asks Zane in his most cynical voice when I return, warm from a brisk ninety-minute walk.

'They spoke a lot about when they were "sick".' I don't say that we spoke about Zane or mention gender, but he cuts to the chase.

'How many women in the group?'

'Two.'

'What were they like?'

'One's me.' *Damn.*

'And the other?'

'She wasn't there tonight.'

'How'd you get home?' he drawls.

And so it goes . . . Hell stretching into eternity.

'I walked.'

·THIRTEEN·

Easier Dead Than Shunned

Why did I decide to undergo therapy? Why does anyone? I became willing to do whatever it would take to not become my mother — or rather, to not break down again.

Most people whose psyches come undone never get over what's shaken them up. They just learn to step around it, to live in a minefield. At least, that was once true of me. I'd leave a room if I smelled dope smoke, leave a man if he looked at other women, and I strove to lead a life as free of cult figures as possible. Yet I always knew I was treading a fine line, steering clear of an edge — the cutting edge of my own potential for growth. I'd known enough schizophrenics to guess that healing didn't come in a pill, witnessed a girlfriend swerve into paranoia and keep going, and had only just salvaged my sanity when a male dancer I loved went manic and banished me from his heart for ever after.

No-one I knew who'd lost it had deactivated the mines. A few blew up in my face when I ventured too close. I didn't want to end up like those who'd felt compelled to suffer alone, so I chose to seek professional, if not wholly conventional, help.

A disorder that originates from inside someone's psyche can't be cured by outside intervention. Damage control, not healing, is the name of the mental health game. While modern treatments ensure that almost any disorder can be arrested, understanding its source would require a more enlightened perspective. How does one make an accurate map of somewhere they've never been? The psychiatric model holds no more water than the flat-earth theory: don't wander beyond the well-travelled routes, for there be monsters. Don't sail too close to the edge or you'll fall off. Such superstition was roundly denounced by Josh, the healer I found.

101

Naked under swirling cloaks we dance around a cauldron, chanting, '*Isis, Astarte, Diana, Hecate, Demeter, Kali, Inanna . . .*'

Which am I, or are they all in me? Wet with sweat, stoned only on incense and visions and shared body heat, freed from the straitjacket of identity, I watch our shadows merge on the temple walls till we break the circle.

The structure of the full moon rite, despite our abandon, has emptied my head of disordered thoughts. As the group reverts to unstructured interaction, my fears begin to wing back in like bats returning to their cave.

Across the huge, plush living room, a slim, black-haired woman smiles at me. Should I know her? Kali, maybe — Hindu goddess of destruction? As I smile back uncertainly, she stands and strolls over, long locks swinging, goblet in hand.

'I saw you arrive with Zane.' She sits down with me on the deep red carpet.

Unable to think of a fitting response, I just nod.

She sips her red wine. 'Have you known him for long?'

'About a year.' It will be in six days.

'How old is Zane?' she asks, as if it's a perfectly natural question.

It is to me; and everyone seems curious — my shrink was no exception. 'I'm not sure.' If Zane wanted this witch to know, he'd have told me.

She smiles pleasantly. 'How old are you?'

'Twenty-three.'

'That would make you a tiger in the Chinese zodiac, depending on what month you were born. Tigers are creative, passionate and fearless.'

'I am a tiger,' I admit, 'in theory.'

'Tigers tend to get on best with horses and dogs.'

'They do?' That's odd. My mother's a dog; though I think Damian might be a horse.

'Yes,' she says. 'But they clash with monkeys. Zane's not a monkey, I hope?'

'No,' I promptly assure her, 'he's a rat.'

As she smiles more brightly than ever I realise my error. Now she just has to guess if Zane's twenty-four, thirty-six or forty-eight. Satisfied, she rises and glides away to refill her goblet. But before I can panic at being stranded alone, Zane leans over — I hadn't seen him behind me — and hisses, 'Why'd you have to tell her *that*?'

'I'm sorry,' I say, horrified. 'I didn't mean to.'

'That's okay,' he says. 'She was cunning.'

Yet on the drive home he rages. 'Once people know your age they can trap you in the thought forms of their beliefs about ageing.'

'You mean others can make us age?'

'Negative magic works as well as positive does,' he says, 'and that's what kind most people practise unconsciously most of the time.'

'Everyone practised positive magic tonight.'

'A lot of magicians have set themselves up to compete with me over the years, and they always aim for my weaknesses.'

Which makes me fair game, he must mean. 'That witch didn't seem so powerful.'

'She got what she wanted from you in no time.'

'I'm sorry,' I repeat. 'I won't fall for that again.'

'Anyway, you're wrong,' he says. 'I'm not a rat.'

By the time we get home he's unwound. He makes love to me and we drift off. But before dawn I wake with my ribs straining against a dead weight. I open my eyes. Zane's asleep at my side so he's innocent, though I can't hear his breathing. I focus on mine till the pressure subsides. Was that one of his infernal elementals? Like loony bin inmates, they seem to run riot whenever there's a full moon.

'Chris *who*?' I'm confused that the man on the phone isn't asking for Zane.

'Chris Monk from the sculpture department,' he says. 'Are you okay, Skye?'

If words could convey how not okay I am he'd cop a thesis and then some. 'Why?'

'Pearl seemed concerned that she hadn't heard from you when she gave me your number.'

So Pearl hasn't given up on me? 'She's free to ring anytime.'

'She seemed averse to contact with *Zane*.'

'That's her problem.'

'From what I've heard, *you* may have a problem.'

'I haven't been too well.'

'There may be a very good reason for that. A tutor I work with *knows* Zane.'

'He knows a lot of people.'

'This tutor wants to talk to you, and frankly, Skye, I'd listen. Em knew Zane in the seventies, and she says you should give him a miss.'

I'm feeling more amiss by the minute. Not another damn initiate? 'I've met enough people who know Zane from back then. Another can't make much difference.'

'If you're open to hearing what Em has to say I'll pass on your number.'

'Maybe you'd better not. Zane might answer when she calls.'

'Em said he may not remember her after all this time.'

'Then she can't have known him terribly well.'

'How well do you really know him, Skye?'

'Well enough not to buy into rumours — but thanks.'

'I heard about your deferral,' Chris says. 'Don't let things slide for too long. The more ground you lose, the harder it is to regain.'

After he's gone I feel sad; he never called while I was okay.

'So let's see if I've understood.' When not clicking his pen, Alex twists one way then the other in his swivel chair. Each time I catch myself waiting for it to break beneath his weight, I remember what Zane said about my catastrophic thinking. 'You began, under Zane's guidance,' says Alex, 'to send the Earth positive vibes —'

'I'd always wanted to make a difference and Zane knows techniques —'

'Yes, of course, like magic.' He smiles. 'But my point is that you've progressed to feeling responsible for everything that's wrong with the world.'

'That's got nothing to do with Zane.'

'No, of course not, but he's not helping you.'

'He's only responsible for what Spirit calls him to do.'

'And a constant supply of sex and drugs is Spirit's top priority?'

Again, I try to explain that sex and drugs are sacred in Zane's world view.

'What concerns me is your belief that he's always right and you're always wrong.'

'Not always.'

'For instance?'

I'm at a loss. This morning when I cast the I Ching — with three ten-cent coins, for want of old bronze ones — *Po* came up again. Hexagram 23, *Collapse*, or *Splitting Apart*, said the texts: that's my age and a thumbnail sketch. I'd asked if my time had come.

Alex nods encouragingly.

'It's not all in my head, I *feel* things.' I mention the crushing weight on my chest that's begun to wake me at nights.

'That's where medication could help.'

'I couldn't stand the side effects.'

'Suit yourself — but I think you'd find them negligible given what you tolerate.'

I tell Alex what Chris said about Zane.

He laughs. 'It can't hurt to meet the woman, and it's an excuse to get out.'

Like a piece of debris swept along by a churning, grey current of suits and ties, I'm navigating Pitt Street — and I'm in a pit, alright — when I see a tall, fair, golden-skinned woman with a shimmering halo of light. I almost look away, but as we draw close she beams, and her pale blue gaze brushes mine as we pass one another. I flush, amazed she'd bestow her grace on the ashen-faced wraith that glass shop fronts throw back at me. Then I remember where I've seen her. Up north. Zane treated her. That's why she glowed; she's a yoga freak like Teresa.

Did *she* get a sexual healing?

Em's café of choice, a dancers' haunt, looms on the left. I slink to a corner table by the window. Slender beings with luminous faces sit chatting or flit in and out like sprites. Back to the wall, I wait like a lead weight for Em who said she'd wear a red scarf.

A woman smiles at me for the second time today. 'Skye?'

I nod and she hefts herself up on the stool nearest mine. But despite her glowing red cheeks and scarf, Em's not lit from within like the angel was.

'Chris tells me you're an artist,' she says.

'Art *student*. At least, I used to be.'

'So you've graduated?' She sounds thrilled.

'Deferred.' Ashamed, I glance up at the blackboard.

She sighs. 'My shout,' she says, as if she's read my mind.

While I'm wary of feeling indebted, a smoothie's worth as much as I earned today. 'Strawberry soy shake, thanks,' I say.

She places our orders then cuts to the chase. 'Chris tells me you live with Zane.'

'Chris tells me you knew him.'

'Not intimately, but I knew what he was up to. And Zane won't have changed. His type never do.'

'What do you mean?' I say tightly.

'He's into *sex* magic. He's sucking you dry.'

My eyes meet her small, red-rimmed ones then stray down past her florid cheeks and chapped lips to her stubby fingers and Rubenesque thighs. She's no Aphrodite. It's hard to imagine Zane wasting sex magic on her.

'I don't know what you mean,' I finally say.

'Zane's a black magician, Skye. You must get away from him before he uses you up.'

'That's the most paranoid thing I've ever heard,' I say. And I've heard a few.

'He's manipulating you.'

'How long since you've seen him?'

'I *know* Zane. And Chris says you've changed.'

'Were *you* ever with Zane?'

'No, I saw through his game, but plenty of women were taken in.'

I doubt that he'd have let her in. She doesn't look like his type — unless she was once prettier and slighter. She's no initiate either; that last thought slipped right by her. Our shakes arrive, so thick that the straws stand up. Slurps broadcast each sip we take.

'Before you go,' she says when she's paid, 'you must see my studio.'

Though her work doesn't interest me, I feel powerless to say no. While I'm abysmally lonely, I sense she's scarcely less so.

Around the corner we stop at an obscure door, and walk up to the second floor. Em's space is so spotless that I'm scared to enter in case I contaminate it. She lines up several small, square, stretched canvases. They're almost blank. White, with a few lines incised in the paint using a palette knife. I'm thinking she must have sold all her finished ones, but as she holds forth on themes and techniques I gather she's disappeared up her own arse and these are as finished as they'll ever be.

'Art that was inward was outlawed in Nazi Germany.' Is Em talking to me? 'Abstraction and expressionism,' she adds, seeing my blank look. Not unlike college, I think, recalling the deathly lecture hall — was it really named after a Nazi or were all the students conspiring to stir me? — when Em smiles grimly. 'Kirchner suicided after destroying his work.'

I nod, unclear why she's telling me this. It's freaking me right out.

'I never destroy mine,' she says. 'Not notes, sketches, anything.'

Which reminds me: since I burned my diary I've created zip.

'Food, water and shelter are essential,' she says, 'if not necessarily in that order. We can survive for weeks without food and days without water, but exposure can send you mad within hours. Funny, the *lack* of it got to me. Lucky booze made me throw up the pills. I failed at suicide, too. But time's taught me to cherish obscurity. Fame can kill if it comes too soon.' Her smile implies that she knows what I'm thinking.

As spooked as I am, her words make a warped sort of sense. I'd feel safer if my thoughts became secret again, because I'm unsure of how much more exposure I can take.

'Do you need a lift somewhere?' she asks. 'I've got to get to a class.'

'No thanks, I try to walk everywhere.'

I walk swiftly out and downstairs, feeling like Em's told me sweet fuck-all.

The phone rings while I'm gulping a mouthful of midstream pee. Your first piss of the day, said Zane, for a whole lunar cycle. It's tasted sweeter since I've been drinking enough water to dilute it. Though he did explain how it cures cold sores, the details escaped me. No doubt that's why he's the healer and I'm the patient.

By the time I've washed my hands and gargled, the phone's still ringing. Someone persistent. I lift the receiver. 'Hello?'

'Is that you darling?' my mother says.

'Yes,' I say without conviction.

'You haven't been in touch for ages. Is everything alright?'

Zane can't hear. He's at circus training. 'No.'

'Why, Skye — whatever's the matter?'

Out pours my pitiful litany.

'You haven't been smoking that mari-joo-*ah*-na?'

'Not for some time.'

'Oh dear, darling — it sounds to me like you're having a *nervous breakdown*.'

'What makes you say that?' I ask, aghast.

'I had one myself, twenty years ago.'

I burst into tears of sheer shock. 'You've never said!'

'You were only three, you couldn't have understood. And you were a real handful. I couldn't cope on my own. I had heart palpitations and I'd panic sometimes — I ran out of a butcher's once — until the doctor put me on Librium. "You need a hobby," he said, so I learned to sew. I stopped taking Librium when you started school. But the withdrawal was *shocking* — just like breaking down all over again.'

My mother's strict self-control has always repelled me; and hidden her secret well. At last I can sympathise, even feel close to her, in my inherited hell. I recall how she sewed coverlets,

108

uniforms, even my magical cloak, and imagine her panic infiltrating each pinprick, snip and stitch. So I wore her repressed madness to bed, to school and at sacred rites. If I'd sewn my talisman on my own, would everything be 'alright'?

'Skye, before I go, have you seen anyone?'

'I'm seeing a shrink.' I blow my nose.

Once I've hung up, a sense of hopelessness weighs on my shoulders like a cloak. I was already a burden when I was three years old.

In my upside-down state I hear voices through the ladies-room wall. Time to meet with the group. While I was waiting, my chest tightened until I thought I'd expire, but on quitting my headstand I find I can breathe again, so I sneak round to the common room.

No sooner than I've pulled up a seat, Takeaway Man says, 'Uh-oh, that sounds like Margot.'

When she sashays in, she looks as spun out as I feel. And she's no ballerina, just Shakespeare-spouting Mad Margot from the dance studio; who deals with my unwelcome presence by stealing all the attention I scored last week. Craziness is a lever someone who's felt powerless can exploit, Zane told us once when she'd disrupted the dance class. Is that true of me?

Crazy or not, I can't compete with Mad Maggot. In a padded, red jacket with a fake-fur-trimmed hood, she looks like she's just come in from the woods, to the lipsmacking delight of four wolves. Yet she's ugly. Not her features, though she's no beauty. It's her manic vibe. I could pass for a swan in this flock; even Alex waddles like a duck.

'Any auditions this week, Margot?' he inquires.

'And how's the flat-hunting going?' Takeaway Man joins in.

Mad Maggot, whose glaring red lippy has strayed beyond the borders of plausibility, adopts a demure demeanour in her chair.

'It looks as though I'm going to move in with my boyfriend,' she says.

'Well it's up to you,' says Alex, 'but I don't know — do you think that's wise?'

109

She flutters her lashes innocently. 'He says he'll pay the bond.'

Alex mulls that info over. 'It does sound like he's ready to give things another shot — but unless he's stopped stacking mounds of newspapers on either side of the bed, there's always a chance he could start a fire again.'

Takeaway Man shakes with silent hysteria while JC and *not-a-musician* grin.

'You're not the only gal round here with boyfriend problems,' Takeaway Man whispers to me, then, as Mad Maggot shoots him a suspicious look, pulls his head in.

Nonexistent to them again, if not to myself, regrettably, I survey my options while Alex plays Dad and the Three Stooges make like big brothers. Even if Em's bungled overdose hadn't left me in doubt, I've protested so much that Alex might guess if I asked for pills now. Electrocution kills bats; but is it guaranteed? I once picked up the lead that plugs in to the jug with a wet hand. Volts surged up my arm. My grip locked and letting go wasn't easy. What am I thinking? It's too iffy to fuck with electricity.

Mad Maggot's eyes remind me of the sly eyes in Pearl's paintings. Just the thought of painting cuts me up. It was all I thought I was good for, yet I wasn't good enough. Do you cut along or across the vein? I've heard one way doesn't work. I could cut both ways to be certain: a crucifix inside both wrists. Except Zane can't hack martyrs. Cabbalistic cross then? But not at home — he'd find me in time.

'Skye used to dance too,' Alex tells Mad Maggot, who's sending me enough bad vibes to paralyse an entire dance troupe while still pretending, for the men's benefit, that she hasn't spotted me yet.

If I jumped at the last minute, a train couldn't brake in time. But, knowing my coordination, and luck, I might live; with my legs sliced off at the thighs. What are the odds of turning up hexagram 23 four times in a row when I have to throw the coins six times for each question?

'You've been quiet tonight, Skye,' says Alex, after what seems like hours. 'Did you want to say anything?'

110

What's the number of the bus, is all I can think, that goes out to the Gap?

'Next week then?' he says. 'You can tell us about your psychology essay.'

My scalp's stretched as tight as the dome of the sky, my nerves hum like power cables, my eyes devour light, and all the street signs point to the same conclusion. NO RIGHT TURN means it's too late to get off the wrong track; ONE WAY prohibits ever going back; BENT ST accuses me of deviating.

A seagull swoops past the bus window and I imagine flying, arms flung wide, bound for the sea, or the rocks it pounds against. What if I never saw another bird in flight? Would I want to pass over if there were none on the other side? I think of the dense, dark presences pressing down on my ribs at night. Are *they* waiting for me? But I don't want to catch the train back to the underworld and Zane, don't want to re-enter that tunnel with no light at its end. 324, the sign said, or 325, for Watson's Bay; and from there, the Gap's only a stone's throw away.

Om Namah Shivaya, a voice echoes in my head. I last heard that chant at the ashram weeks ago, yet now it's repeating, drowning out other thoughts. *Om Namah Shivaya*. Though I don't know what it means, the mantra calms me slightly. The bus reaches its terminus. I alight on the footpath and halt, undecided.

To my right waits the train track leading back to Zane. Ahead lies the bus route to the Gap. As I waver, a woman steps off the bus. From the om symbol on her tote bag, my eyes rise to her face: an ashram-goer. Now I know how the chant arose in my mind. It's rippling out from hers as if from a round stone thrown upon a pond. The peace of it reminds me of the temple I made of Chris's office. A space all my own, serene, like the zone where the sky meets the sea on a still day; where I want to go. But it's windy here. It'll be blowing a gale on the coast. Will that make it harder to fall straight? I can't fail — Zane would never forgive me. Yet I can't recall ever hearing of anyone living through a leap from the Gap; nor hearing of too many deaths there. If it's foolproof, why don't more suicides try it? I could research the stats at the State Library; wander up there now. But I'm reaching my threshold of tolerance for exposure. If I don't act soon, my resolve will weaken. The thought of another bus ride freaks me.

At the Hyde Park bus stop I sit on the sandstone wall and go through my wallet. The address on my student card's out of date but my name should speed identification. Twenty dollars. I wonder whether to give it to a vagrant. Not that it'd buy much piss — but it'll make less difference where I'm headed. What *will* persist when I'm dead? Supposing I cease to exist? That's the point though: not having to regret what I've missed. Twenty dollars should be enough for a cab fare to the Gap. One's coming. Waving, I run to the kerb. The cab swerves to a halt. I hop in the back.

'Where to?' The driver turns his head with its greasy pony-tail. Enlarged pores stipple his walrus-like nose. He looks about Zane's age.

'Can you take me to the Ga— ah, what's it called, um, Watson's Bay?' I say, panicking. Now he'll know — though that can't be worse than broadcasting my last thoughts to a whole bus-load.

'Sure.' He puts his foot down and we join the traffic flow. I must have made the right decision or he wouldn't be so willing. 'You off today?' he says.

'Am I what?' I say, startled.

'Off work. Is this your day off?'

'Oh, no, I finish early.'

'I'll say.'

I wish he'd shut up. If Zane can recall past lives in China, Egypt and Atlantis, there must be more than just nothingness after death. But I might return as a lower life form, hard as that is to imagine, if I don't learn my lessons this time around. I've heard that killing oneself is bad karma — but why? Isn't the planet too crowded?

'So whaddya do with the rest of your day?'

Good question. 'Just study,' I say, though it's dwindled to nothing — unless the I Ching counts.

'And whaddya study?'

I didn't need to mind-read to see that coming. 'Psychology.' Fucking hell, I've got nothing to lose by telling the whole truth. 'Oh, and astrology.'

'Is that right?' he says, as if he knows what it is. 'Can you see the future?'

'I don't believe in prediction,' I say.

'Then whaddya study the stars for?'

'If you can see what's coming, you've got more freedom of choice.'

'Like a rear-vision mirror, is it?' he says, braking hard at a set of red lights.

I glance up to see his reflected eyes staring straight at mine. 'That's a good analogy,' I say, feeling dense, and look away as the lights turn green.

'So if you can see danger coming,' he says, 'you're free to change direction?'

The amber light turns red just as we reach it. Amber for go-between Mercury — and red for Mars, the war god, warning . . . I wrench my attention back to his question.

'Yes,' I say, 'if you're forewarned.'

'Ever seen suicide in the stars?' he asks, as the lights turn green for Venus and the cab surges forwards.

'I haven't been looking,' I admit, shocked at the oversight.

'Because I've had a few in the last year or two.'

'In your cab?' I almost choke.

'No, they didn't die on me. I don't mean an OD, though I've had enough of those. Christ, no — one deadshit wanted to go out to the Gap at night.'

'Oh,' I say, horrified. But he's talking about some guy, not me?

'What can your astrology do,' he says, 'to help lost causes like them?'

'If someone's having a rough transit the stars show when it'll pass. They just have to hang on long enough.' We hurtle past the first lighthouse. Clouds are massing out at sea.

'I swear,' he says, 'he freaked me right out. They're selfish, these suicides. When I pulled up he jumped out and ran for it. Couldn't be bothered to pay for the ride.'

Now the road takes us very close to the bluff. Stop while you're on top, I think. Or is that, *Quit while you're ahead*? With a start I remember the meter. $19.80 and climbing.

'Stop!' I say, stunned by my certainty, 'I'll get out now.'

'It's too far to walk,' he says without slowing. We're leaving the high ground.

'I've only got a twenty-buck note,' I confess. 'It's best if you just let me out.'

'A twenty's okay,' he says, 'but I'll take you all the way. It's not far for me.'

Why the unprecedented generosity? Is he on a mission to help me off the planet today? He drives down and around to the park on the bay and pulls in to the kerb.

'Let me get you some change,' he says, as I hold out my twenty.

I can't look at him when he hands me a ten. 'That's too much change.'

'You'll need that for lunch and a bus fare back.' He sounds sterner suddenly. 'Have a nice day.'

I mumble 'Thanks' and scramble out, slamming the door by accident, then walk into the park. Once he's rounded the bend I double back towards the Gap. The relief I'd begun to feel has turned to crippling guilt. That driver had faith in me when mine's run out. How can I throw my life away after he gave me the benefit of the doubt? I wonder whether to buy some lunch before I take my plunge — even criminals due for execution eat a last meal — but the lowering sky fills my gut with urgency.

I cross the road and hurry up the path to the bluff. A hush hangs over the surrounding rocks. Even the boom of the waves below sounds muted compared to the roar in my ears. Suppose I shattered every bone in my body yet lived — who'd pay the hospital bills? I can't risk jumping here: I'm not high enough. Yet the ground rises to either side. Should I take the left-hand or the right-hand path? To the north, the wind bends silvery trees. Southward, red roofs crowd in. I follow the fence up to my left. It can't be much more than three or four years since I came here to draw as an art student. On a jumble of rocks at the top, I pause to gaze back over the harbour. Beyond it the miniature

114

city looks almost pretty, but I want to forget it, and lose sight of the insect people beneath, one coming this way, who might see me. I walk on past wattles and banksias, hands thrust in my pockets away from the wind. Finding the scrunched ten renews my guilt, but I can't let some stranger sway my will.

Now the altitude's evened out, anywhere along here should do. And the path ends — a high cyclone fence bars my way. Enhanced with barbed wire, it juts out past the cliff, defying trespassers to enter the military reserve. So this is it. The fence facing the sea wasn't made to keep anyone out — or in. I spring over it easily.

Ever since childhood I've loved heights; it's falling that's unsafe. I gaze down at the ragged white crests flecking the depths, poised to spread my wings. The air feels taut, viscous, as if tensed to receive me. And I see an image of my father. Yelling at me. I guess I shouldn't be surprised that my bowels choose now to turn to water. I jump back over the fence and rush to a clump of dense bushes for cover, then drag my jeans down to my knees and squat. As my gut heaves and I see my mother crying, a terrifying emptiness sets in. Serrated leaves prick my goose-pimply skin. I'm wondering what else to wipe my butt with when a young man appears on the path.

For a moment I think he's followed me, but then he vaults over the fence. What the hell's he going to do — jump? If I don't try to stop him I'll be responsible. But what can I say? Maybe it's my fault anyway — or why would he be here? Yet he acts as if he hasn't seen me. I hesitate while he stares out to sea. Then he removes the satchel slung over one shoulder. Will he leave it behind? But he takes out a water bottle and sips as he sits on the ledge with his legs dangling free. I'm petrified that he might smell me then realise I'm downwind. I can even smell tobacco when he opens his pouch to roll some. Minutes slide by agonisingly, punctuated by fragrant whiffs of smoke, which I resent inhaling less now I'll never have to again. By the time he stubs out his butt, mine's gone numb with cold, and I figure it's been blown dry as he swigs more water. Piss off, for Chrissakes, I think, dying to hitch up my jeans, until it hits me that he might have just smoked his last rollie. I want to shout *Wait!* But my voice box feels rusty. Paralysed — like in my recurring dream when I'm chased by someone and can't outrun him or scream.

But I must do something. I'm just about to stand up, jeans still down, when he opens his satchel and fishes out a sketch-book and pastels. Holy fuck, not a frigging art student! Quietly, I inch my jeans over my thighs — I can't squat here till he's finished — and zip up my fly. Then I rise and step from behind the bushes, not daring to check if he's looking, and take the path back to the road. Big splotches of rain dot the asphalt. One lands on my nose. If I'd waited a trifle longer, Van Gogh might have been inspired to go.

Now I recall the cab driver's words about that passenger. No-one sane would jump during the day. He must have known I'd fail.

'It starts on the winter solstice,' says Pearl, 'a Friday. The train will take you to Blackheath.' If I hadn't come home I'd have missed her call.

Just the name of the place instils a sense of foreboding in me. 'You mean I'd have to stay there for ten days?' I say, under my breath, so Zane won't hear over the TV.

'It transformed my life,' says Pearl. 'I've been back twice.'

'I *can't* go,' I say, half relieved as I remember. 'I can't just not turn up for work.'

'Can you get someone else to fill in?'

'I don't know anyone else.'

'Your life matters more than some shitty job, and vipassana saved mine.' Can Pearl have guessed? 'You need to ring them to say you're coming. Have you got a pen for the number?' I scratch it down, hard, as the blue biro gives up the ghost. 'I'd come too,' she says, 'if I'd finished my performance art essay.'

Before we hang up, she promises to call and see what I've decided.

Nine days of total silence. Quieter than the State Library. Eleven hours of meditation a day. Avoiding others. Yet Zane's jealousy of those I'd meet scares me more than meeting them

116

does. And what if it makes no difference? That's more frightening than the prospect of dying.

Should I do the vipassana course? I ask the I Ching and flip my coins.

Hexagram 24 instead of 23, for a change. *Return*.

A turning point follows a period of decay, the text explains. The time of darkness has passed. The winter solstice brings the return of the light.

·IV·

The Empty Room

·FOURTEEN·

Old Souls Never Die, They Simply Face Decay

When I first found Josh, via word of mouth, he made me feel safe. My wish list had changed since I wrote the 'male order' embodied by Zane. For starters, an absolute bottom line, Josh didn't tempt me sexually. If I was to turn my life around, I needed no distractions.

Each session took place in an office space with a desk, two chairs and a filing cabinet, instead of on a bedroom floor. The hefty fee I paid at reception implied strict professionalism. While pushing sixty, Josh was no ageing hippie. As bald as a Buddhist monk, he wore bland shirts and ties like a typical shrink. Yet he was an independent thinker with diverse modalities up his sleeve.

During the years I saw Josh one on one, he didn't remind me of Zane. He was far too defined by formalities, a fatherly family man; framed drawings done by his daughters lending a personal tone to his office. No crystals, sacred stones or carved Hindu deities. No theatrical props at all. Josh facilitated shifts of awareness, not miracle cures, in his clients.

Yet despite his difference, Josh, too, looked familiar to me at first sight. Just as with Zane, I trusted him straightaway. Unusual. Over the years I'd grown circumspect where men were concerned, consulting one only because female shrinks had longer waiting lists.

From the start Josh left me in no doubt as to which of my issues he cared about: feelings with their origins in my past. What a contrast to Zane, I thought, when Josh disclosed his age the first time I asked. And not only did Josh affirm my art, he encouraged me to keep a diary.

Woken by a gong at four, we dress in the pre-dawn dark then start to trickle out of the heated dorms. On the way to the bathroom, icy mountain air wakes me up more. Soon streams of silent strangers converge and flood a dimly lit hall. No icons or idols greet us — just a few dozen cushions like lifebuoys adrift on a tranquil sea, and stools at the back for meditators who can't cross their legs.

Men sit to the left of the central aisle, women to the right. We'll spend ninety-nine hours afloat on this sea over the next nine days. We've agreed not to speak, read or write between sittings, or eat outside of mealtimes. I suppose masturbation's out — not that I've touched myself since Zane took over, except during that fortnight he left me behind while he taught tai chi up north. Like yoga, tai chi's forbidden here to give vipassana a chance.

The sight of one man up the front facing us, immovable as a carved Buddha, jolts my nervous system with recognition. *Chris?* But no, the vipassana teacher can't also be my sculpture tutor. He's the only person we're allowed to look at, so I don't hold back. The startling likeness must be a sign that I'm meant to be here, though no-one's seen me. They all keep their eyes averted from each other, too — and, despite the chill of the main hall, I feel like I've won a reprieve. Huddled in my blanket like a grub in a cocoon, I can't imagine ever wanting to leave.

Barely more than two hours later, I'm pathetically grateful for the breakfast gong. Witnessing my thoughts has never felt harder. Tapes guide us to focus on the passage of air through our nostrils. Impossible. I long to follow its coldness deeper down into my lungs, or fly on warmer currents out to the hollow space surrounding us. Anything but to observe my shallow breathing with neutrality. Surrender to reality means setting aside distractions, yet every leaden ounce of me resists. *Anapana*, they call this stage of the journey. It's all we'll do for three days.

Lunchtime inflicts another sort of torture. Despite the quiet, I'm not quite convinced that all sixty-nine strangers ranged along the wooden benches aren't shunning me. Their pointed avoidance of each other's eyes doesn't fool me. They could be in telepathic contact.

122

Return to the refuge of the hall where we all face Buddha in his beige shawl gives me a taste of relief, until the tape of my mind starts to rewind or fast-forward. Flashbacks plunge me into selfhatred, thoughts of the future into dread. How will Zane ever forgive me for depriving him of sex for ten days?

After dinner — if that's the right word, we're only permitted fruit of an evening — we tramp back to the hall for yet another sitting, followed by a video discourse. Via a VCR the vipassana guru says we're here due to good karma, and because we've met in a past life. Some nuance in his croak — and he looks froglike, too — prompts me to cry. Goodwill? Kindliness? Compassion? I thought my bad karma would never expire.

During the night I wake to hear the sound of three women's breathing. Mine's flowing more freely than it has at home. I sink into sleep again. And then I'm hurtling down past clouds, faster than a falling stone, and the sea's rushing up at my face. As I smash through its cold, dark skin the gong soaks in to my consciousness, forcing me to surface a second time.

Legs crossed, eyes shut, Buddha sits motionless for hours on end. If problems or questions arise we can see him during lunchtimes for a private audience — the sole loophole in the vow of 'noble silence' we took on arriving. With the second morning dragging, my attention deviates from my nostrils as I grope for a question worthy of such a handsome audience. How old is he? Is he married? How would he make love? Suitable questions elude me. I couldn't wait for a reason to be silent and now I crave an excuse to speak. The goal of vipassana is freedom from craving and aversion, yet each craving and aversion distracts me from my practice. Equanimity, the recording keeps reminding us, is the key. Equa-*knee*-mity. My knees will be the death of me.

Each day the lunchtime queue lengthens outside Buddha's door, but I don't join it, don't dare break my ignoble silence. Ashamed of my sexual thoughts, I fear he'll read my mind. In front of me sits a thirty-something brunette with immaculate poise. Swathed in a blue shawl, she makes me think of icons of Mary, mother of Christ.

Clinging, says the recorded voice. I've clung to pain. *Anicca, anicca,* croaks the frog. *Impermanence.* Arising, passing away. Has three days on my butt bunged me up or is it my distance from Zane? I want to believe that these ten days can change me, return me to him renewed, and that the strain between us will disappear once my attitude improves. Instead of fearing Zane I want to love and trust him as others do — as I used to.

By the fourth day we're deemed ready to embark on the voyage of vipassana: a continuous, systematic sweeping of awareness through every part of the body during which we must strive to detach from any sensations, feelings or thoughts. As moments stretch into hours, my pain stretches into infinity. Electric-hued serpents swirl through my veins; light up my neural circuits like neon. I remember reading assorted accounts of kundalini awakenings describing symptoms 'experts' hasten to confuse with madness, and comparisons between schizophrenic perceptions and religious phenomena; then I remember the form I filled out on arrival, ticking NO when I came to the question on history of mental illness. Where's the dividing line between creativity and madness? Hidden in my brain or writ plain on the pages of diagnostic manuals? That's what I want to explore in my psychology essay. Where's the division between symbolic, magical thinking and schizoid thinking? Have I crossed that line and, if so, can I ever return? Did my Watcher see and, if so, will he/she tell the authorities? Might I have projected my Watcher onto authority figures? I feel like an illegal alien hiding out in this retreat, incognito. Where does open-mindedness end and paranoia begin? Equa-*knee*-mity, says the recording, warning me that I've drifted away.

Protesting muscles and joints jerk me back. Dullness drags me down. My colon feels like a passage choked by the putrescent fumes of a dead Minotaur as the golden thread of my attention unwinds in a blood, bone and sinew labyrinth — a thread I mustn't lose or I might fall prey to the Minotaur aka Watcher.

124

Why did my coming up here piss Zane off, what did he fear I'd find?

I'm dying to talk to the teacher, but I hate myself too much, and each second *not* spent talking or taking action makes me hate myself more. I shouldn't be here doing nothing but breathing, I'm too fucking passive already. Zane was right, as usual, about excess yin — hell, I couldn't raise enough yang to step off a cliff and let gravity kill me.

Having undergone a process of elimination of sorts — letting go studies, friends, privacy, work, sex, exercise, speech and, yet again, shitting — I'm reduced to little more than eating, sleeping, sitting and breathing. Tomorrow, I promise myself, I'll join the queue to see the teacher.

Five students stand in a line outside Buddha's small, private room when I arrive, having bolted my lunch. We're halfway through the fifth day — the midpoint of the silent phase. Will speech break the spell? Damned if I do and damned if I don't. The last five nights I've dreamt about talking and screaming but making no sound, as if I've been turned inside out. Sucked in, and sucking up waste; that vacuuming job gave me away, I'm a walking vacuum, a human black hole with a dead sun at my core. Guilty of hubris, desire, attachment, cravings galore — until my ego blazed so bright it could only collapse in on itself. I try to focus on my breath in case the others read my mind, and when I hear Buddha's door open once more, I realise I've moved to the top of the queue.

After what seems like hours, the teacher ushers me in and offers a chair. Up close he's even handsomer. Dark eyes radiate loving-kindness as we sit facing each other.

'How are you going?' he says.

'When I try to observe my sensations I keep seeing snakes.' Though sweat creates snaking sensations under my woollens, my tongue feels furry and dry.

'Trust the technique.'

'And the snakes?' I cross and recross my legs, trying to stop their trembling. I've brought an apple for you, teacher, but it's

125

rotten to the core. You're the apple of my eye, an otherwise worm-eaten socket. The two of them feel like vortices trying to draw him in.

'Just trust the technique,' he repeats, his gaze benign. No snake shall sway his equanimity. Why doesn't he shrink from me, as Adam should have shrunk from Eve? The serpent's whispering in my ear, hissing through my bloodstream, winding up my spine like it did up the trunk of the Tree of Knowledge. Can't this holy man tell that I came here to tempt him? I search his face for some trace of sin, of eros, of reciprocity. Yet his eyes hold no more lust than those of a newborn child.

'Thanks.' I force myself to rise. *Trust?* I can't even trust myself to keep breathing.

He rises too and, smiling beatifically, opens the door.

Glowing worms seethe and squirm through my blood vessels when I close my eyes — or are they burrowing under my skin and tunnelling through my flesh? Has my subtle body decayed to the point of emitting an astral stench that lures ravening, scavenging astral parasites? I can't shake the idea of myself as an intricate network of wormholes, empty but for the presence of intruders — or am *I* the parasite? During sittings of what the frog calls 'strong determination' we mustn't open eyes or shift hands or legs. I've opened a can of worms by embarking on this journey, but there was never a point at which I could backtrack. At least once every ten minutes, though it feels more like every ten hours, I promise myself that I'll never ever come back. How Pearl could have sat more than one course, let alone three, confounds me.

Not even my dreams yield relief. Hostile crowds of children, art students, initiates and tribesfolk in loincloths abuse me; or, worse, they exclude me. The 4-am gong brings a strange kind of peace.

Each day the tapes guide us deeper into the nature of the illusion of existence. Molecules, atoms and subatomic particles — too subtle for me. I can't slow down my mind enough to keep it in my body. Instead I think of Zane in my body, which, after nine days of no sex, feels surprisingly solid. Almost the reverse of what I'd come to expect. It's as if having Zane penetrate me has reassured me that I exist. Even if all these vipassana freaks believe that none of us exist, I feel more real from keeping myself intact. I'd like to take a break from sex for a while when I go back, but that would really piss Zane off.

There's safety in numbers, at least while the silence lasts. It's lessened my loneliness, if only when I'm awake, knowing that each of seventy of us is alone with our own sensations.

I dread the tenth day.

After our initiation into 'metta' or heart-centred meditation, the veil of silence officially lifts. Dozens of voices rise exultant, while I alone remain tongue-tied. As waves of words swell and break across the lunch table, I try not to hold onto them, even as I drown in a howling sea of ambiguities. Any topic of conversation loses meaning when I don't identify. All my concentration is needed to distance myself. The lunch hour seems interminable. Then a brunette sits down opposite. I recognise her iconic blue shawl.

'You know you're allowed to talk now?' she says.

'I can hear.' The volume of my own voice shocks me. As resonance fills the cavernous space of my head and chest, they no longer feel empty.

'Do you feel like a walk?' she says. 'I've done enough sitting.'

We exchange names. Sophia rises, so I do too. She leads the way out of the marquee and we walk down the slope. Most days I've trodden this path after lunch, among the gums filtering sunlight, seeing others mindful of keeping apart, and wondering if we'd meet. That even one should reach out to me exceeds my wildest hopes.

'Have you been meditating long?' I ask as we leave the track and weave between trees. What I really want to know is whether vipassana could work for me. Sophia seems self-possessed in a way that I used to dream of being.

'I've sat a few retreats over the years. This is my tenth.'

No. I couldn't do this again once, let alone nine times more. My shaky elation threatens to nosedive into the carpet of rotting leaves.

'How did you hear about it?' she says. The grain of her face shows as clearly as lunar craters through a telescope, yet her skin's not coarse. In fact, it's so fine that each pore exudes an unearthly light.

'A friend thought I ought to try it.' As Sophia's eyes meet mine I feel them mining into my core. If I don't tell her, she'll see the truth like veins of gold in ore. 'I think Pearl might have sensed . . .' I don't know how to end the sentence.

'That you'd lost your way? Many paths promise perfection,' she says, 'but they emphasise will, not surrender. Vipassana offers release from the bondage of craving for perfection.'

Bonds enchaining Zane, for whom I could never be perfect enough. But, basking in Sophia's luminescence, I can begin to believe that the last few months will soon fade like a dream, and life might even receive me back into its bosom, now I've found the right teaching — until the harsh cry of a raven nearby shakes my delicate faith; sounding, with its croak so close to speech, like it's saying that nothing could be right for me, that it's only a matter of time before it swoops down with others to pick my bones clean. *Anicca, anicca.* This too will pass, I just mustn't attach to anything . . . and the gong to go in reverberates down through the bush.

'It's been great to meet you,' I say to Sophia, then fear that I sound like I'm clinging.

She draws her blue shawl around her. 'These retreats happen regularly. And you can come up to sit between courses. I sometimes do. Maybe I'll see you here?'

I nod eagerly, wishing there could be a way for me to catch up with her in Sydney.

As the train descends from the magic mountains that gave me a broader view, I watch my fears mass like thunderclouds; I don't want to descend too. Yet I feel lighter than I did after rituals or fasting, the vapour trails of my thoughts vanishing faster into the blue. Buddha recommended we sit for an hour mornings and evenings back home. I've resolved to try; he's supplanted Zane as highest authority in my eyes. Somehow I'll have to maintain my mountain outlook, the inner light I've accrued. But as the land flattens out and the bush gives way to boxes and borders, ominous signs begin to intrude. Rooty Hill, root chakra, base chakra, debasement — going down — to Blacktown, black holes, or how about black magic? Mort Street, think mortality, mortification, change trains . . . and then it's Terminus Street, end of the line, final sign, dead meat.

I step off at my station and into what feels like a war zone. Low-flying planes rend the smog-stained sky as I cross the road, turn right and head home; cars screech, trucks rumble and trains rattle past, sending vibrations up through my feet. I focus on my breath flowing through the gates of my nostrils, and cop a lungful of fumes. Then before I reach the front gate Zane emerges to meet me. How'd he know I was coming? As we walk towards each other I see him in a new way, much like when I tripped on mushrooms. But now I don't see a rainbow aura surrounding his holiness like divine rays. Instead I sense long, sticky fibres as if his subtle body has strings attached. I'm walking into a web. What a shock — I never saw it before. It's too late to evade the spider and his eyes signal his intent. The light I won back through those hours of agonised effort is his food and very soon he'll syphon it off me, suck it inside a black hole.

At his greeting — a slight nod, an intense stare — despair clamps hold of my heart. The pressure is on: to prove I love him in the way he needs.

Energy-hungry, lusting for a feed, he draws me back in to his lair, where he touches and fucks me until he's gorged on the light that redeemed me and I'm in the dark again.

·FIFTEEN·

Nothing Neutral Under the Sun

Unlike most men I'd known, Josh felt that I spent too much time alone. 'You need more contact with others,' he'd stress. Group therapy seemed like a logical progression. It got to the point that whenever I mentioned a failed encounter he'd say, I only see you one on one — I'd need to observe you in a group to know how you push others away. And it didn't take much to convince me that I needed help with intimacy.

'I was tongue-tied when I was young,' I told him during one such discussion.

'Shyness is a symptom of shame.' He opened my file. 'Did your parents hit you?'

'I'm not sure anymore.' But he'd reminded me. 'Years ago I made the mistake of playing a taped consultation to them. I'd forgotten what I'd told the astrologer.'

Josh wrote an illegible note on my file. 'So you leaked family secrets?'

'About my father spanking me while my mother watched. They lost it when they heard the tape. My father swore he hadn't and my mother called me a liar.'

'That's a very defensive reaction,' Josh said. 'No wonder you live in fear.'

'I'm not sure what you mean,' I said. 'What gave you that idea?'

'When you walk into my office I often feel fear. I have to remind myself that it's yours.'

I tried and failed to decipher the scrawl on my file. 'How do you know it's mine?'

'Because I'm not feeling it until you walk in.'

Too bad I never taped my sessions with Josh. Not to play back to my parents, just to vindicate my own sanity. Taping

group therapy sessions might have proved even more enlighten-
ing. And yet, in the diary Josh had sanctioned, I began to dissect
his and Zane's similarities.

Pumpkin pies have never been my specialty. But Zane's left one
in the oven and it smells as good as done. My mother used to
test her cakes with skewers but, finding none in the drawer, I
borrow an acupuncture needle that's lain on the sideboard since
we moved in. Twice the size of a hatpin, it slides out clean so I
kill the gas. Seraphine's coming for dinner. She and her man
will stay the night.

Zane said that Luke might drop by too — the cherub-faced
bass player. I don't know who's visited while Zane's had the flat
to himself, but it's as if my absence has moved him to renew old
friendships. Despite my nervousness — I've hardly socialised
for months — this turnaround impresses me as a good sign. If
Zane opens up to the pleasure of being with his friends, he's less
likely to mind me seeing mine, all of whom I can count on the
fingers of one hand. No, make that a thumb.

Pale, gaunt Seraphine, hair down to her hips like her partner's, grins wryly at me as they glide in — because she knows
how much she's changed, or because I have? The barber clipped
off my copper locks, leaving a mousy crop, around when I
began to hide inside looser clothes — to lessen my sexual guilt;
not to look, as Zane accused, like Pearl. She used to follow me. I
guess some role reversal's occurred.

After sharing a joint, which I decline, Zane goes to the
kitchen to fetch the pie. Leaving the others by the fire, I follow
him out to find forks and plates. With solemn ceremony he
divides the golden disc into twelve, reminding me of a
horoscope before the planets are drawn on it, then serves five
slices with sour cream. Our guests seem unduly impressed. You
should have seen what we got to eat on my retreat, I think.
Vegetarian feasts that leave tonight's dinner for dead. Out of
practice at eating dinner, I don't touch my dollop of cream.
When was the last time Zane ate anything green?

After another joint — I suppose there's more than one way of taking in green — Seraphine and Zane discuss her treatment. I didn't realise she'd undergone surgery. Zane talks as if he's got it sussed, but how come he couldn't cure her cancer? And should she be mixing conventional medication with home-grown dope?

A knock at the door makes my heart thud. Coping with two visitors seemed like enough. But when Luke steps across the threshold, I swiftly adjust.

'I hear you've been away, Skye?' He squats down by the fire.

As if some faint phantasm they'd only sensed before has materialised, the others spare me a more lingering look.

'Yes, I attended a ten-day meditation course.' For the first time tonight I have everyone's attention. Four pairs of eyes; the most I've attracted since the schizos' therapy group. I feel intensely exposed.

'You're looking lovely. Radiant. It's clearly done you the world of good.' Luke beams. 'When did you get back from your retreat?'

'Yesterday,' I say, and soon I'm telling him all about it. After ten days of holding in words I must have stored a few up.

He listens so attentively that I almost forget myself. Yet I wind down, not from lack of words but of nerve. My perceptions sound naive, even grossly obtuse, to me. Meaning charges the merest words of others without touching mine. And so we gravitate to the others' conversation, which translates to the four of us listening to Zane.

Later, before leaving, Luke turns back to me. 'Honey,' he says, 'it's been wonderful to bask in your ambient energy.'

I smile bashfully, hoping Zane won't get jealous.

When I've tried to practise vipassana for the prescribed hour each morning this week, Zane's rolled towards me drowsily, murmured and leaned into me. This morning, sick of being distracted, I slide my blanket off the futon, taking care not to wake him, and slip out to the tiny sunroom. But before I can even begin he fills the doorway, hair mussed, face flushed, rubbing sleep from his eyes.

'What're you sitting out here for?' he bawls. Stripped of all clothes and the grace he possesses in more conscious states, limbs stubby and tummy tubby, he looks like a disgruntled toddler. Before, he vented resentment when I went out to work. Now I'm not even allowed to venture from bed.

'I didn't want to disturb you' — what a crock of shit; why must he disturb me? — 'and I need to concentrate.'

'Maybe you'd be happier if we lived apart, Skye' — he heaves a huge sigh — 'but I just don't know if I can trust you.'

'Zane, I love *you*.' The words sound false to my ears. As long as I hate myself, how can I love anyone else? Sex with other men is the last thing on my mind.

'It's Stella.' Leaning away from 'it' as if it's likely to bite, Zane holds out the receiver.

Bewildered, I take it from him. 'Hello?'

'Luke said the two of you spoke the other night.' The tone of her low, melodious voice is loaded.

I hold my tongue, unsure. While Zane's jealousy's routine, Luke's partner can't be as insecure?

'Ye-es — a little.'

'We should talk privately, Skye. I have a proposal for you,' Stella says. 'Is there a time I can call you when Zane's not around?'

'Ye-es.' I don't need eyes in the back of my head to know he hasn't left.

'Is he still in earshot?'

'Yes.'

'How's later today at, say, two?'

'That's alright. Thanks. Bye,' I say.

'I'll explain then,' she says and hangs up.

'What did she want?' There's no way Zane's X-ray eyes wouldn't detect a lie.

'I don't know.' I might be transparent but at least I'm safely empty.

134

'She wants something,' he says, yet he seems satisfied.

When he goes out to rehearsals just before one, I meditate for an hour. Trying to practise on waking has proven futile. He throws a tantrum if I leave the bed, blows up if I edge away. And I can't find any peace of mind while he's touching me. He's threatened by my trying another teaching, I suspect. But it's more than that, hard as it is to admit. I can't quite dismiss the feeling that he's stealing my energy. It doesn't make sense; he's got more than enough of his own. But after meditating beside him, I've felt worse than before starting. As I sit in the sunroom alone, my mind begins to slow down slightly.

When the phone rings at one-thirty I spring up and run to answer it.

'Skye? This is Anand. Remember me?'

'Oh, hi.' My throat's choked up with what feels like my heart.

'Sorry to leave it so long. When would you like to go out for that chai?'

'Um — Saturday would be fine,' I say, praying that Zane won't be home at the time.

'Would it suit you if I pick you up around one? Let's visualise a sunny day and we'll go somewhere outdoors.'

I agree and we leave it at that, but Zane's not going to like it. My mind's revving so fast that I've spun into orbit.

When Stella doesn't ring at two, I'm disappointed — and relieved. The possibility that she'd want to know me had me all keyed up. But I shudder, remembering Em with her needs disguised as a desire to 'help'.

The phone rings at 2.22. An omen, I want to believe. Two's a psychic number, Pearl told me once. I've got a few in my DOB.

'Are you alone?' says Stella as soon as I answer the phone.

'Yes.' Words can't convey to what extent.

'Let's talk then. Zane was teaching you magic, but that's fallen through, I gather? Okay, here's what I propose. I'm at a stage in my own training where it'd benefit me to take on a student. You're the ideal candidate. So — what do you say?'

'I'm honoured,' I stammer. And ambivalent. One Skye felt released when all the ritual fell away; she has an aversion to magic if it means wilful attempts at control. The other Skye's lost without signposts; she craves the guidance Stella's offering. Torn between the opposites of craving and aversion, I surrender to the other Skye. 'Leaving the work unfinished didn't feel right,' I admit. I'm drifting in limbo, so throw me a lifeline, give me something to cling to, I think.

'Does that mean you'll consider it?' Stella sounds exultant.

'I'm willing if you are,' I say.

'You just want to fuck each other.' Zane shoots me a filthy look at five to one on Saturday afternoon.

'We just want to talk to each other.' That's crap too. I've told Anand zero, hardly spoken. He's done all the talking, and if he does again, today, hopefully it'll distract me from the paranoid movie produced by my brain.

'And what do you two talk about?'

As I try to imagine an answer that won't inflame Zane more, I realise he's heard scarcely a peep out of me since the equinox or before. Since he fucked that seventeen-year-old virgin.

'Meditation,' I finally say.

Zane looks disgusted. A white car turns in to the driveway.

'There's your white knight,' he says, as the driver's door swings open.

The two of us watch a bearded blond giant stride up the path wearing an outgoing smile. The two of us — and the two of *me*, one of who feels drawn to this warm-hearted man, while the other wants to run as far and as fast as she can.

'Well, go on. Open the door for your *date*.' Zane jerks away as I reach for his hand. I hadn't thought of Anand as handsome but he must look like a Viking to Zane.

I fling the door wide. To look either of us in the eye requires Anand to look down. Something in our faces makes him frown. Then he offers a hand to Zane. I feel like I'm introducing a prospective boyfriend to my mother.

'This is my boyfriend Zane,' I manage to say. It sounds un-natural.

Zane takes Anand's huge hand, but his eyes appear to grow smaller as I go to hug him, and he backs away.

I walk down the path with Anand, leaving the other Skye behind. She can't enjoy herself without Zane's consent. But *this* Skye's damned if she'll pass up a chance to be let off the leash.

'We'll go to the teahouse in the Garden,' Anand says.

The Garden where the Tree of Life grows? Think serpent, the Fall and original sin. But he must have meant *Gardens*. I envision him as a guardian spiriting me away, furled in the white wings of his chariot.

On the way he speaks of his last trip to India — of mystics, sadhus, swamis, gurus and miracle-working holy men who produce ash, and objects, out of thin air.

'Zane's kind of like one of them,' I say, as Anand pulls in to a park opposite one of the garden gates.

'Who, that guy I just met?' He nearly runs into the car in front. 'It never fails,' he says more soberly, backing up. 'I visualise a space on the way to where I'm headed and one's always waiting.'

We step out onto the footpath and pass through the gate. 'Zane's got amazing control of his bodily functions,' I say.

'No offence, but he looked a little bit unfit to me.'

'Not his weight, I meant his internal organs. He stopped his heart once, during a train ride, for so long, his lips went blue.'

'Were you with him?'

'No, that happened before we met.'

'Then how do you know what colour his lips were?'

'He saw his reflection when the train went through a tunnel. That's how he knew he had to restart his heart.'

'And what else can your friend do?' Anand's lost his sceptical tone, as he leads the way to an outdoor table. We're bathed in green.

'Well . . .' After a moment's hesitation — would Zane mind me saying? — I decide that he can't overhear. 'I've seen him regurgitate food at will.'

Bushy, blond eyebrows meet in a straight line. 'It sounds as if your friend could use some professional help. I don't mean a

psychiatrist — most of them are quacks — but a psychothera-
pist, maybe. Hypnosis might alleviate that.'

'Zane's perfectly healthy,' I argue. 'Animals can throw up at
will too.'

'How about I go and get us a pot of Earl Grey tea,' says
Anand, 'and how about some cake?'

I shake my head. He returns with a tray from which he takes
a teapot, a milk jug, two cups, two forks and a dark wedge on a
plate. The heartbreaking blue of his eyes confounds me as he
hoes in to the mud cake. If toxins truly do turn eyes brown, how
does he neutralise his?

'Sure I can't tempt you?' he asks, mistaking my interest.

'No. Oh no, thank you.' Sugar still takes me precariously
high. The more pleasure I risk, the more potential for pain. If it
worked in reverse I'd have some reserve of pleasure stored up.
'Sweetness doesn't agree with me,' I say.

'It's not what you eat,' says Anand, 'it's the way you eat it, I
believe.'

I nod because that sounds right to me, and remember early
days with Zane; how he'd do a flow with his food, make it part
of his being before consuming it. I haven't seen him do that for
ages. The fact is, I've grown disillusioned with Zane; but so has
he with me. He doesn't always walk his talk, nor can he heal
everyone, least of all Seraphine; but I know how much of a
burden I've been, going through what he calls 'a hard time', and
he wouldn't act so possessive if he didn't love me. This isn't
where I ought to be, I think suddenly, why am I hurting Zane?
This isn't me.

Anand, sweet man, is talking about his production company
now while I just nod rather than stupidly ask what exactly they
produce, but I don't feel connected to him the way I do to Zane.
I can't — he's too materialistic. No way could I ever merge with
him. Despite Zane's fears. That's the best thing about sex with
Zane — it lets me disappear. He's an open door or gate — if not
an open book — through which I can fly, leaving ego behind.
Reaching out to touch the cosmic mind, to follow the path of
tantra.

I think Anand hopes to inspire me. Fair enough. I don't have much to say for myself. It's understandable that he'd seek to fill the empty space, but I don't want to be Anand's doorway.

'Zane's into tantra,' I say.

Anand looks at me, his train derailed. 'Ah — the plural of *tantrum*?'

'No, I meant he teaches tantric techniques.'

That sets Anand off on a new, more abstract track — his life philosophy. I'm feeling overwhelmed again. The longer I'm gone, the more pain I'll cause Zane. And the angrier he'll be.

'You've gone quiet,' Anand says at length. It took him long enough to notice.

My attempt to smile back feels strained. The other Skye *didn't* stay behind — or maybe she's brought Zane?

'I'm still coming down from a vipassana course.'

'Don't sink too low,' Anand says.

'What I mean is, I got used to not talking.'

His interest in my mountain sojourn soon sorts that out. I catch myself not wanting to go home. But shadows have begun to sprawl across the gardens. As we wander back up the path, every leaf, though in shade, throws out its own halo and I feel like I'm floating in the green aura of Aphrodite. Could a few sips of tea have made my head so light?

Driving back across town, Anand says we must meet up for tea again. I agree, surprised that he could have enjoyed my company. Before I climb out of his chariot, he kisses me warmly on the cheek. I wave him off. And feel the bottom drop out of my stomach. It's reverted to the bottomless pit it is when there's nothing but fear to fill it. Anand breathed life into me and now it's drained out.

When I try to let myself in, Zane bars the doorway. So much for tantra.

'You were gone a long time.' He glowers at me. 'Did you fuck him?'

'No! We talked and drank tea.' It can't have been much be-yond two hours, certainly less than three.

'And what'd you talk about?' His face is a mask of disbelief.

Shame and guilt compound my fear. 'Anand's travels in India, philosophy, his production company . . .'

'Maybe I should let him read my script,' mutters Zane.

'I'm sure your ideas would impress him,' I say.

Zane snorts. He's still blocking my access, arms folded, raspberry-cheeked. I try to push past. With the graceful precision that years of practising tai chi has given him, he unwinds and hurls me across the room. I lie breathless on the cushions in the corner where I've landed, almost relieved at this loss of control. I don't feel bruised, just confused. Still, he wouldn't have done that, I remind myself, if his dope supply hadn't run out. Well, three days without getting stoned must be a record for him. I've never known him to go even twenty-four hours with nothing to smoke.

A call from Pearl breaks another record. Three for me in one week. I'm glad Zane's not about. She's booked a return flight to India. 'I need someone I can trust,' she says, 'to mind my flat for four months at least.'

'We've got a one-year lease and it's not even half up.' No point saying that only Zane signed it. I can't begin to consider Pearl's offer.

'I don't need an answer today. But tell me — how was the retreat?'

Soon becoming absorbed in recollection, I realise it's the only news of my own that I've had to tell for months. The last thing I say is that I'll get back to her.

I'm stitching press-studs on a doona cover when I hear a knock. I'd always hated sewing, so I don't know why it's calming me. Of course there's far more to dressmaking than just joining up two big rectangles, for which I need only to feed seams through the machine in straight lines. Yet Zane did say that I've become my mother. Not because of the doona cover, which he said he could really use, but because he takes my distrust of him as a criticism. As if I trust anything.

'Is Zane in?' asks a pretty, young brunette when I answer the door. A low-cut, clinging bodice displays her full breasts to perfection and her raised eyebrows imply that she wasn't expecting me.

It's mutual. 'No, he's not.'

'Would you let him know I called,' she says with a petulant air, as if to the maid, and turns to leave without revealing her intentions or even her name.

Though he's already denied it, I wonder yet again if Zane saw other women in my absence. Not that it makes a difference to what I've decided. But as for how to tell him, I feel divided. *I'm moving into Pearl's flat because she can't find anyone else to mind it.* He won't believe that. *I need to escape before you sap what's left of my life force.* That'd get a reaction.

'You had a visitor,' I tell Zane on his return from some house call. 'Big tits, quite pretty, a bit surprised you were out?'

'Oh, that would've been Shakti,' he says after furrowing his brow for a minute. 'I have no interest in her,' he assures me, 'if that's why you're looking so worried.'

'No,' I assure him back, 'that's not an issue.' I brace myself for the impact, but it means I won't have to explain about Stella. 'You know how you've been saying maybe we should live apart? Well, I'm willing to try it for the next four months.'

·SIXTEEN·

A Time to Shriek and a Time to be Violent

Why had Josh waited so long to initiate me into his group? He said it was best to get to know clients first. Not everyone who consulted him was ripe for group therapy. And after all the dramas I'd been through, his circumspection reassured me.

Yet the past keeps coming back to haunt us. Josh's group featured the same types as Alex's had: an unrealised musician, a manic man who lived on takeaway, even a depressive, whom I secretly dubbed 'Morrie Bund'. An ageing, out-of-work actor rivalled Mad Margot's antics. Doesn't every compulsive liar possess dramatic talent? If Maddy could be believed, she'd been through more admissions than auditions. I couldn't decide who pretty, blonde Zoe reminded me of. But Josh assured us that everyone would, at some stage, play the role of our parents.

Apart from a few art prints on the walls, the group therapy set lacked magic. Props included tissues, pillows and a punching bag that had split at the seams. But I knew we didn't need candles, incense or essential oils to banish toxic shame and invoke intimacy. The claustrophobic, air-conditioned office did the job, just. There wasn't room to swing a cat. Yet we all took turns with a baseball bat. 'I have a right to be angry.' WAP! WAP! WAP! Witnesses held their heads to shield their eardrums from the impact. The thwack of that bat triggered more rage in me than I had time or space to release. 'It's okay with me that you're angry,' we chorused — we had to if we wanted validation. The process gave me headaches. But Josh reinterpreted our frustrations.

'Why can't we share the time more fairly?' Morrie Bund grumbled one day, while Maddy screamed into a pillow because she'd been overlooked. 'We all pay the same.'

143

'Morris has raised an important issue,' Josh informed us. 'But making the group too predictable would defeat its purpose of helping you to deal with the real world.'

'Doesn't that depend on which part of "the real world" you frequent?' I said.

Josh peered at me through his spectacles. 'How would you run the group?'

I stared at the starry sky in the Van Gogh print behind him. 'That's beside the point,' I said.

'Not if your struggle with my authority isolates you from the group.'

I shrugged. My head had begun to feel tight. 'I'd give everyone equal time.'

'That notion comes from your past,' Josh said, 'and your fear of competition, while I facilitate this group through intuition. The others don't have equal needs each week' — the shy musician nodded at this — 'but you'd impose equal time on them just because you've got unresolved trust issues.'

How could I disagree?

The circle was the only part of Josh's system that made sense to me. Though we sat on chairs, not cross-legged on the ground, the circle felt familiar. And, like I'd once done after rituals, I recorded highlights in my diary.

Sleepless late one night, I walk to the open window of Pearl's first-floor flat and lean upon the sill in the dark, peering out at a deeper darkness. Since the move my depression's lifted — I've even begun to paint, tentatively — and I look forward to seeing Zane. This evening he seemed preoccupied, though, and took off an hour ago. His refusal to stay the night, like he did before we lived together, makes me think he comes round just for sex. I'd dared to hope that my progress might impress him, but he acts like he resents having to go out of his way to get laid.

The heady, heavenly scent of jasmine on the spring air inspires me to try to count my blessings for a change. Though I'm restless now, I've been catching up on sleep. The neighbourhood's peaceful: no lorries, trains or planes. Beyond the back fence I can just make out a lane, and beyond that, a small park illumined by streetlights. As my eyes linger on a pool of shadow in the lane, they begin to adjust to the dark. I almost scream. Beneath a frangipani, against the paling fence on the lane's far side, a man stands staring intently up at my window.

'Zane!' I call out, trying not to sound suspicious. 'What're *you* doing here?' But with my mood of gratitude shattered, my tone lacks the ease I intended. His surveillance of me at this ungodly hour puts his earlier distance in doubt. 'Do you want to come back up?' I ask, not wanting him to, yet hoping he will, if just to reassure me I still mean something to him.

Without so much as a word, he lets himself in the back gate. Darkness is his element, he moves so fluidly through it. My whole body trembles as I walk downstairs to unlock the door. Why was he hanging about outside? Did he think that, if he waited long enough, another man would arrive?

'One's lover shouldn't be one's magical teacher,' Stella says, as we drink tea at a round table in her front room.

I hesitate, reviewing what Zane told me about her. 'Who taught you?'

'Luke.'

'I thought he *was* your lover.' Now I'm really confused.

'It's different with me and Luke.'

No wiser, I let my eyes wander over her mythical menagerie. Carved dragons hold candles and coil up table legs. Engraved faeries and airbrushed unicorns adorn all available wall space. Assorted quartz crystals — aligned in an intricate grid, I'd assume — sparkle from every flat surface in the room. I feel as if I've stumbled on a treasure-strewn, subterranean cave inhabited by an ivory-skinned, ebony-haired sibyl.

She gives me a list of tasks — 'Best if you start with a clean slate' — so first I must make a new silver seal. 'You can burnish back the old one,' she says. 'Just inscribe it again. And you'll need to work your elemental cards every day.'

I wonder if that's really what I need, as I take notes. To lose all sense of myself and become one with a flat, abstract shape —

to experience existence from the point of view of a yellow square?

'You can't neglect your homework.' Stella must have sensed my doubt. I feel like I'm back at school except my teacher's wearing a long, black dress and a gold pentagram at her throat.

'By the way,' I say, when I'm leaving, 'I caught Zane spying on me one night.'

'So he's *still* being a naughty boy? We'll work on banishing at your next lesson.'

I walk home from Stella's more excited than scared, for a change. My new teacher sounds as if she knows how to beat Zane at his own game.

On Zane's second-last night in town we make love with Pearl's guru looking on from three sides of the room. As the force of Zane's orgasm surges up my spine, my skull flowers into the sweetness of a thousand-petalled lotus. Like a newborn, I lie curled within the curve of his arms, the unfurling of my subtle anatomy turning the universe into a womb.

When I wake in the morning he's by my side. Though he leaves tomorrow to go up north to teach for two weeks, I feel closer to him than I have for many months. I want to believe he believed me when he came back that night and I said — eternal refrain — that it's him I'm in love with.

In the afternoon, when I tell Stella, she says it's a 'guy thing': wanting more than one fuck at a time. Literally, I think, recalling the threesome Zane told me they shared; there's more than one way of looking at existence from the perspective of a triangle. This morning when I meditated on my fire card, I tell Stella, I felt a circuit flowing between my third eye and both knees, and then I lost all sense of my body, became pure energy.

Stella sounds pleased, and guides me through the business of banishing anyway, but I don't feel as if I'm going to need to use it on Zane.

The evening before he's due to leave, Zane brings me a letter that's arrived from Teresa. I set it aside, wanting to give him all

146

my attention. But he doesn't seem amorous tonight. I'm tempted to ask about his day — he went to treat a new patient this morning — but can't find anything to say that won't sound insecure. Instead, I regret missing my new yoga class because he slept over, and promise myself I'll make up for it while he's away.

He stays the night again, but doesn't hold me in his arms. I want to pretend that his spirit has flown north already, but my gut tells me that geographical distance isn't the issue.

Once the hum of his engine fades, tears begin to flow. He's promised he'll call me when he gets back but I know he'll call someone else first. I recall the way he smelt, the way I felt, that other time — but it made no sense until I learned, one whole week late, that he'd fucked that girl.

Which reminds me — Teresa may have penned a reply to my letter. Hopeful that news will make me feel better, I retrieve it from the futon where Zane left it — a blue aerogram with a purple stamp depicting some mythical bird on one side, return address on the other: an ashram, in Rishikesh this time — and rip it open.

Teresa's been subjecting herself to 'austerities' — her tone says, *You* wouldn't know about those; and if she means swallowing then regurgitating numerous yards of bandages, give me the bliss of ignorance — and she's been subject to 'illusion', by which she means *ganja*, not *Ganga*, Hindi for Ganges, though she's begun to learn Hindi. She's sat through some twenty-day retreat — so she's twice as strong as I am? — and the word 'duality' rears its head heaps; she refers to her 'split personality'. One side wants to serve Spirit; the other's purely self-serving. Oh, and she's begun to fall for a charming Indian swami, with whom she plans to open a hostel to feed and heal the needy, and her spiritual mentor who means to wed her (picture a white silk sari?) is so evolved, she writes, that he's transcended the need for sleep — simply sits stock-still all night in a lotus pose — though, if she's still attached to pushing up Z's, I wonder how she'd know. Yet his sexual prowess sounds impressive, the best ever (read: better than Zane's), and she feels she's really met her ultimate soul mate.

147

She congratulates me on my deferral from college — 'another illusion' — and asks me how my cleaning job's going, calls it the yoga of service.

I let her aerogram fall to the bare, wooden floorboards. The flow of my tears gathers momentum, swelling to a torrent. I feel inferior, trivial, useless, worthless and supremely unlovable in spite of Teresa's extravagant Hindi salutations and blessings. Everything has come together for her while my life's falling apart — as it has been, at an accelerating rate, since *she* had sex with Zane. 'Moving right along' sums up her philosophy; maybe it ought to be mine. But how can I move towards where I want to be until I know where, let alone *who*, I am?

Walking home from the shops, I run through my wardrobe in my mind. Yesterday a redhead at yoga asked me to come to a party tonight. She's my age, but I have no idea who'll be there. I'll be grateful for the distraction once I can decide what to wear. I haven't been to a party since that fateful night at Miles's, and if the redhead hadn't suggested we go together I'd be too shy.

I cross the road to turn in to the lane that leads to my back gate and, too late, notice who's coming the other way. Please don't recognise me, I pray, but I've been feeling less invisible lately.

'There you are!' Mad Margot calls out, her eyes zeroing in on mine. 'Do you happen to have a needle and thread?'

'Not on me,' I answer, hoping the truth will placate her.

'Can I come home with you?' she says instead, eyes wide with alarm, and lifts up an arm as if it's a broken wing.

Now the problem stands revealed, how can I refuse? The seam of her outsized cheesecloth blouse gapes from elbow to armpit to waist, exposing a matronly, bone-coloured, underwired bra. I look away, aghast.

'Please, I can't let *them* find out,' she says under her breath. 'It won't take a minute.'

'Okay,' I say. 'We're almost there.'

She falls into step alongside me. We turn the corner into my lane. The basket she's toting makes me think of Red Riding

148

Hood again. She follows me through the back gate, up the path, upstairs, and sits down on my floor while I ferret out needles and cotton reels. When I turn round she's pulled her blouse up over her head, hiding her face.

'Help! I can't breathe!' she shrieks. 'I'm stuck!'

I hold my breath too, afraid to step closer and more afraid not to, wondering if she needs asthma medication and whether to upend her basket. *The path to liberation is selfless service*, I hear Teresa say, and somehow I find the presence of mind to check Margot's blouse for loose threads and liberate it from the clasp on her necklace.

'She nearly *killed* me,' Margot says, her voice grown coarser.

I jump back, almost falling onto the futon. 'Take your pick of these,' I offer.

She chooses one of the larger needles and a bone-coloured spool. I gather my psychology notes to prepare to work on my essay. It seems rude to recline on my bed while her butt's pressed against hard boards, so I sit down, back to the wall under the window, opposite her.

'I'm so *sorry*,' she whines in a higher voice, minutes later, 'for spilling all that blood.'

I look up. She's still trying to thread the needle with a frayed, wet piece of cotton.

'Let me.' I trim the end, poke it through, then give it back doubled, ends knotted, but now I doubt her ability to mend. 'Are you okay with that?'

She nods and bends over the blouse, head bowed, tongue protruding slightly. From the corner of my eye I can see she's making headway, so I return to my notes and the problem of how to work them into an essay.

When a person experiencing a kundalini awakening receives negative feedback, I've written, *from society at large or the inner pressures of early conditioning, stress arises not from the process but from interference with it. This evolution can be catalysed by specific techniques or may occur spontaneously in an unsuspecting individual. As the symptoms tend to mimic schizophrenia, such individuals are at risk of being misdiagnosed.*

'Who are you trying to fool? You never wanted her.' The gruffly masculine voice makes me start. 'It's not my fault' — she's reverted to the coarse voice — 'that *she's* such a slut!'

I wonder in passing if the authors of these texts on spiritual emergency have spent much time studying real-life examples of their theories. Why's Margot roaming the streets in her state? Hasn't anyone noticed? What happened to Alex?

'Ouch!' she squeals in the high-pitched voice. She's pricked one of her thumbs. 'Leave her alone,' says the gruff voice, 'she's been punished more than enough.'

Since I've got about as much hope of cobbling together an essay out of my snippets as Margot's got of restoring her op-shop blouse to normality, I don't feel I need added distractions.

'How's the sewing going?' I venture, terrified of who might answer me.

'We're nearly done,' she says in what I take to be her normal voice. She falls quiet for the next few minutes. Then, 'Do you need a mirror?' she asks.

'Do I *have* a mirror?' I ask, nervously. 'Downstairs in the bathroom.'

'*Don't* give her a mirror,' says the coarse voice. 'She's too full of herself already, don't encourage the little trollop.'

While I'm striving to maintain a sense of myself as an innocent bystander, I don't feel fully confident that none of these voices are addressing me. If only Margot would get dressed and go.

'Why don't you try it on?' I say.

'*You're* the whore around here,' says the gruff voice. 'It's never fitted *her*.'

If this process truly is 'schizophrenia', we will all become schizophrenic before evolving to higher consciousness, I read, wondering what made my handwriting change, and if 'we will all' includes Teresa or Zane.

'I think I will try it on,' says Margot, sounding more like my idea of her. She hauls the blouse on, slipping one arm through at a time. There's no sign of a split in the side, or of her right hand. Peering at where it should have appeared, I see why. She's sewn the sleeve into the seam, converting her blouse to part straitjacket. She struggles to force her hand into view but the stitches won't give. Now, heaven help me, she'll need scissors.

'Not to worry,' I say unconvincingly. 'We're getting there.' If only the prick of a needle was all I needed to wake from this nightmare.

When Margot's departed at last, I have to eat and dress for the party. I pull on a clingy black blouse with long, flowing sleeves, tight jeans and red leather boots, then gel my spiky hair back. *Fuck you, Zane*, I think, *I don't need you!* I imagine him using his tantric tricks on some hippie-trippy chick in a tipi tonight and, for the first time since he fucked that teenage slut, I know I look better than alright. I apply highlighter and eyeliner, neither of which I've worn since before he fucked Teresa, slip into my velvet jacket and skip out of the flat. The redhead's waiting down the road at the wedge-shaped café and we walk to the bus stop together.

Loud music spills through the open door of a two-storey terrace when we arrive; Elvis Costello, an album I played to death in the warehouse studio. No sooner than we've stepped inside, we're dancing amid a human tide.

'He lives here' — the redhead gestures — 'and him, and' — she glances round — 'her.' Then she stalks over to dance alongside the first guy she identified. Someone takes Elvis off the turntable and puts the B-52s on, and the dancing grows rapidly more unhinged as they scream about a rock lobster. The grungy vibe harks back to pre-Zane days, songs long missed lull me into a daze, and sweat plasters my flimsy sleeves to my skin as I thrust my breasts and shoulders and hips. The flatmate of the guy the redhead fancies has his eye on me, I could swear, as he edges away from the dancing and lights up. I watch, not least for the novelty of seeing a cigarette smoked for its own sake — the smokers I've known of late shake out the tobacco and use it to stretch their dope. He's long, lean and pale like his cigarette, wearing tight jeans like I am. And his gaze doesn't waver. I start to feel wet between my thighs. Then the girl flatmate asks him for a light, eclipsing my view. After she moves on I manoeuvre to keep him in sight.

When I remember to look for my red-haired friend and can't find her, I gather it's late. The dance-floor crush has thinned and someone's turned down the hi-fi. My lean, lanky tempter stands at the foot of the stairs, and stares. For hours he's been teasing me, dancing where I can see him yet never up close. One Skye wonders whether to call a taxi right now. The other Skye says it's cheaper to take a bus — in the morning.

'Do you want to go to bed?' he finally says, when we're the last two in the room.

I follow him upstairs, stunned yet compelled by what the other Skye's doing. We undress in the dark, then fall onto his mattress — the springs make a fun change from a futon — and he springs on top and his hips start swinging. He's slightly less well endowed than Zane is, but each difference only excites me more. I move my hips too and moan and groan — like I've never done at home — and soon he's come and he's snoring while I'm working out when my period's due, something I don't need to do with Zane who seldom spills his semen, and then only because he knows I'm not ovulating, or so he says. Satisfied that I'm due to bleed in a day or two, I respond with no less ardour when Long-Limbs stirs from his dreams with a renewed hard-on. Then he's asleep again and I'm worrying whether he has any STDs. Yet Zane doesn't use condoms; he always knows his lovers are disease-free. If he can trust his instincts, why shouldn't I trust mine? When my new lover wakes at dawn — reminding me of Zane in one way, with yet another hard-on — I don't hold back. If he's at risk of transmitting anything, chances are I've already contracted it.

Despite my daily bids for Stella's approval — by trying to become a red triangle on a green background or some other elemental symbol — the grunting, panting exertion reassures me that I'm still human. I'd forgotten how good sex can feel with a mere mortal, unless I'm just finding out.

When we wake a third time, to the glare of morning, my conversational efforts fall flat. Lover-man doesn't care to discuss his plans for what's left of Sunday. The last thing I see as I leave is the redhead making toast with my bedmate's flatmate.

After a week of thinking of little other than my latest lover, and rehearsing opening gambits in my head, I ring the number my red-haired yoga friend gave me. Maybe she's dialled it already.

'This is Skye,' I say, as if I ever told him my name. 'We met at the party at your place last weekend.' That's the only come-on I know — unassuming understatement.

'Oh, hi.' His tone implies that he remembers me — just.

'I was wondering if you wanted to get together?' I've failed to sound casual. Maybe I should have rehearsed out loud.

'I don't mean to be rude,' my now undeniably one-night stand replies, 'but I don't think we've got anything in common.'

'Fair enough.' The redhead did say he's a mathematician who gets off on gambling.

After spending the first week of Zane's absence mooning over a casual fuck, I spend the second dreading his return. And knowing he's not returning to *me* is no longer my main source of concern.

Zane's flat looks just like it did when we shared it, if a trifle tidier, confirming that I wasn't deluded about my invisibility. A male friend of his has moved in to what was the healing room, so I guess he's treating patients in his bedroom, as before. I drink tea while the men share a joint and we end up retiring late.

'Did you fuck anyone else?' Zane's waited until we're alone and ready to snuggle down under his doona in the cover I've sewn. After our two-week break, a 'How are you?' might have been more heartening.

'Yes,' I confess, fulfilling his expectations in the one way I've learnt how to.

'Get out,' he roars, his crazed face thrust into mine, 'I never want to see you again!' An almighty slap knocks me off his futon, into the abyss I've feared for far more than a fortnight.

'But you fucked someone else too,' I shrill. 'You fucked them first!'

'That's beside the point,' he says, not bothering to lie. And why deny it, now we're no longer together?

'That's not fair!' I say, scrambling up, breathing fast.

But then when was it ever?

·SEVENTEEN·

Love Will Grind Away

Group therapy bewildered outsiders. When I recounted random highlights, they'd express shock. What a crock of shit, they'd say. Who needs that? Yet knowing what I needed had never been my forte. Josh seemed subtle compared to Alex; professional compared to Zane.

Not that Josh and I always saw eye to eye. But I provoked our first really serious misunderstanding by questioning his habit of handing out antidepressants like candy. No-one, as far as I knew, had begun the group while medicated. But as the months went by, those taking drugs outnumbered the rest of us. Though Morrie Bund defended his pleasant childhood memories, he, too, ended up with a prescription. Something about the therapeutic process was proving depressing. Not desperately so, but the level of complaints increased — the length and detail of testimonials of emotional pain. Josh called it 'coming out of denial'. Nor was I denying mine. But why pop pills for what I'd begun to address, at substantial expense, through therapy?

Then Josh began to talk about medication as part of the process.

'Drugs should be a last resort — at least that's what I've read. I hope I'm under no obligation to take any,' I said.

Josh peered at me over the tops of his spectacles. 'I hope you'll keep an open mind.'

I glanced around to see gazes as neutral as those of hypnotic subjects. Compared to the others' minds, mine seemed clenched like a fist in the face of Josh's pill-osophy.

'I thought the group was supposed to support us to feel our pain,' I said when Josh wrote the manic guy a script at the end of the session.

'That's right.' Josh's face was a picture of patience. 'Medication won't make the pain go away.'

'Then what's the point of taking it?' The manic guy sounded so disenchanted that I privately dubbed him Take-it-away Man.

'By protecting you from getting overwhelmed,' Josh explained, 'it helps you stay in touch with the pain.'

'It does?' Take-it-away Man looked even more alarmed, yet he left for a chemist after checking we'd wait for him at our regular coffee bar.

As we queued up to order, Zoe nudged me and said, 'Are you okay?'

'Yes,' I said, 'and I plan to stay that way. Do I look like a guinea pig?'

'Have you reacted badly to medication in the past?' she asked.

'No,' I said, 'and I don't want to in the future. What could be more overwhelming than side effects like brain damage?'

'You sound like you've had some sort of drug problem.'

'Dope made me insanely paranoid — but it just brought out what was buried.'

'Bring out your dead!' she said, and we laughed till our eyes watered.

Except for Morrie Bund, whose charm screamed ulterior motive, blonde, blue-eyed Zoe seemed friendlier than the others. Or maybe just more familiar, if Josh's insights could be trusted.

My yoga teacher makes each pose look so natural that I never know whether to love or hate her. Corpse pose, always the last, is my favourite — a reward for attempting the others, most of which may forever elude me — and Mel likes to leave us in it for ages. Yet this morning I can't enjoy lying flat on my back with closed eyes, because I'm enraged.

I don't know if Zane can stop and start his heart the way he said he once did, but he can turn love off and on like an engine, and hormones, it seems, are the key. He came around — days after saying he never wanted to see me again — and smugly said, *So your casual fuck rejected you?* I shouldn't have asked about his. He's 'in love' with the only woman he's ever met who's got 'prepubescent hormones', even though she's twenty-six. I asked why he'd come by. I still love *you*, he accused.

Mel tells us to roll onto our sides and take our time to get up. Before rising, I open my eyes. On her feet already, Mel's a walking ad for yoga. Toned, tanned and slender with large, full breasts and limpid, blue eyes, she could sell anything: mascara, with such long, lush lashes, or lipstick, with those sensual lips, not that she ever wears it. She's the essence of effortless beauty, a blonde version of Pearl's guru.

'Skye, can I talk to you before you go?' she says, as I lay my mat on the stack.

'Sure.' I walk back to get my things. Everyone wants to be near Mel. What could she want with me? It crosses my mind that she might think the class is too advanced for my needs. Yet the reason I came, besides avoidance of Zane, was my failure to keep up with the dancers. I slip into my sky-blue kung fu shoes, prepared for the worst.

She's waiting alone by the door. 'It's hard to know where to start,' she says, and I swallow and inhale deeply, hoping she'll suggest somewhere else I can go. 'Oh, hell.' She laughs, flashing flawless white teeth. 'I know Zane left you for me.'

'*You* —' I burst out laughing too, from nerves and shock.

'I felt terrible' — the lashes sweep down, obscuring her baby-blue eyes — 'knowing you were still with him —'

'He *told* you that?' Now I'm really surprised.

'Well, I left my partner when I fell for Zane. I don't believe in two-timing.'

Prepubescent hormones? She *does* have a little-girl voice.

'The way men play women off against each other makes me so angry,' Mel goes on. 'I never meant to hurt you. And I feel bad for breaking my partner's trust, too . . . I've decided to go back to him.' She looks relieved.

'Does Zane know you have?' I can't help cackling, and not because I might get a second chance. 'He said he's in love with you,' I say, spurred on by her openness.

'He'll get over it,' she says. 'I just hope my partner does. I've missed him so much. Shall we go for a coffee?'

Why Mel, almost a goddess, should open up in this way to me, as we sip lattes in the café where everyone goes after yoga, I don't know. But it's good for my ego.

'I hope Zane doesn't think he can just come slinking back to me,' I say, 'now the source of prepubescent hormones has abandoned him.'

'*What* hormones?' she says.

When I try to explain, and tell her about the teenager, Mel looks thoughtful.

'Lucky I broke it off when I did,' she says. 'He turned out to be really weird.'

I lean forwards, more intrigued to hear any insight of hers than I ever was, waiting for Zane to shed light on the secrets of the cosmos. 'For example?'

'Well, one time we camped overnight in a tent in the bush down the coast,' she says, 'and I heard these strange noises right outside. Something that sounded kind of like a humungous cat and I know feral cats can grow very big but it sounded bigger than that, maybe as big as a panther. I was petrified. In the end I couldn't stand not knowing if it was dangerous, so I woke Zane. And he said —'

'That it was just his elementals?'

'No way,' she says. 'He told *you* that too?'

'They must be pretty sophisticated shape-shifters.'

'No shit,' she says, 'that's outrageous. By the way' — she hesitates, as if she's afraid to betray someone — 'did he ever hold his breath during sex?'

'All the time — *and* flex internal muscles *and* suck back his cum *and* shoot each orgasm up his spine.'

'The first few fucks were incredible,' she says raptly, 'but then I began to wonder where he'd gone. I'd always wanted a partner who knew everything about tantra, but I ended up feeling alone. My boyfriend's just an ordinary guy but at least he wants to *be* with me.'

That strikes me as wildly desirable: an ordinary guy. 'I know what you mean,' I say, and sip my latte. It's grown cold.

'Oh, and Zane seemed kind of young,' she says, 'to have lost all his top teeth.'

Walking home via the local shops, minus one essay and plus a phone number, I could kick myself for not sussing out if Damian's still taken. Now *he*'s an ordinary guy, if only by my standards. I'd just handed 'Kundalini, Creativity and Psychosis' to my psych tutor when I ran into Damian, who's urged me to drop around. He's convinced I'll dig his flatmates, especially the Tibetan Buddhist who's into astrology. It seems the world's full of people who want to know me, now Zane doesn't.

'Hi there, Skye,' says a deep voice as I step off the zebra crossing.

'Oh, hello.' It's a miracle I haven't crossed paths with Alex sooner, living down the road from his rooms.

'Haven't seen you for a while,' he says, with his jovial, paternal smile. We pause on the bustling street corner. 'How's life treating you — now that I'm not?'

Feeling a twinge of guilt that I vanished from his group with no trace, I tell Alex I'm generally saner these days, and that I no longer see Zane. He nods approval, as if it's no loss, so I shrug to hide my pain. Alex has gained even more weight since we last saw each other, I notice. I tell him I've gained some friends. No need to mention magic, he'd label Stella delusional. Still, as I stand, chatting with him in a relatively rational state for the first time, I can't deny that the magical dictum of 'Do what thou wilt' makes more sense to me than the medical practice of stifling psychic phenomena with pills.

'Well, I'm pleased to hear that things are looking up, I always knew they would.' Alex beams as his gaze strays from my eyes down to my thighs and back up. 'You know, Skye, I always had the hots for you.'

Heat rushes to my face. I don't know what I'm meant to say. Fragments of comments he made in private come crashing back into my mind as my solar plexus tenses like a fist. Shuffling flashbacks I can't quite decipher make me feel faint and sick.

'Got to run, sorry. So long, Alex.'

As I hurry away, the voice of one Skye in my head — or is it my mother's? — says we ought to report him for that. But the other Skye swiftly silences her with the thought that no-one would believe me.

In the café, each weekday after yoga, I'm slowly growing acquainted with Mel. It's slow because, since that wild first revelation, we haven't been alone again. A wiry, young dancer with a round, handsome face, Ramon always joins us, while a cast of extras comes and goes, most of them actually actors who work as extras, too, when they're not washing dishes and waiting tables.

This morning I shyly tell Mel and Ramon that I've bought a motorbike.

Surprise flickers in Mel's eyes. 'Cool. You've got a licence?'

'Not yet,' I say, 'but a neighbour's ex is going to teach me to ride it.' I reel off the advantages that the neighbour who sold it told me about: loads of fun, economical to run, easier to find parking spaces . . . The factor that decided me was fear of being alone again. I've felt desolate since my latest rift with Zane.

'So' — Mel looks less sceptical — 'it was an impulse buy?'

I nod ruefully, though I'm delighted to have an excuse to warrant attention.

Ramon's dark eyes light up. 'It was love at first sight. *Love on the rebound*, Skye! You'd been missing the presence of a powerful, throbbing machine between your legs.' He's shared enough laughs at Zane's expense to know I won't be offended.

'That's it,' I agree. 'To see Zane as a machine's more or less how he saw me.'

'What is your will, master?' Mel drones, arms outstretched like a robot.

'Give me *head*,' Ramon commands. 'You can keep your *soul*.' He leans back and taps the ash from his cigarette.

'My will is thy will,' I intone, and feel a strange thrill, though Ramon must be gay. Not only is he the friendliest guy at yoga but the most attractive.

'Can I have a light?' Mel asks him, a poor ad for her naturopathic practice.

'Let there be light,' Ramon declares in the masterful voice, then, taking the cigarette she proffers, he lights it from his own. 'And so there was light.'

The intimacy of the gesture confounds me. Not for the first time, I gather they're flirting, and can't help feeling jealous.

Whether a male is straight or gay, Mel steals all the attention. And the low self-esteem her charms provoke in me is compounded. For days now, I've been as constipated as I was before I met Zane.

When we leave the café I'm startled to find that Ramon's headed my way.

'I hope you don't mind me saying, but I always had my doubts about Zane,' he says as we turn in to Oxford Street, and he imitates Zane's penetrating gaze, contriving to give it an absurd intensity. They've crossed paths in countless dance classes. Despite Ramon's wicked mimicry, I sense his empathy. 'Not that I can't see what you saw in him — I can, really, but he's too old for you.' He titters. 'Let's see, who can we line up for you — someone from yoga, maybe?'

We gossip about who's hot, who's single and who's not, as we walk down Oxford Street — that is, Ramon fills me in. Apparently he's been unattached for an unspecified while.

'I'd love to have a sexual relationship with a woman one day,' he says; the last thing I'd have expected to hear as we pause on the corner where he turns off for work.

Yet I look into his dark, flashing, thick-lashed eyes and smile encouragingly.

The beautiful, childless guru gazes down on me with no judgements as I lie on the raft of my futon afloat on the sea of Pearl's rough wooden floor. I'm lost, devoid of a compass, and I never looked to the stars for guidance, or I'd have seen it coming: a soul in search of a vessel to board. I'd ask Mel which herbs to take to abort if I thought it would have no affect on her karma. As for mine, raising a child alone would be tough if I had enough money. But a child needs stability. My mother could have sunk me. I'm unfit to be a parent, let alone a single one. Still, I guess I should consult the father. Though I'd never intended to ring Zane again, or not without a damn good excuse, I can't deny that the other Skye, behind my back, has been looking for one, hoping he might be open to me now that Mel's moved on.

161

'How could you,' he explodes over the phone, shocking me with his savage tone, 'get yourself pregnant to another man? I don't want anything to do with you!'

'How can you be so sure it's not yours?' I feel sick, a familiar sensation of late. The chance that the father is the gambling mathematician proves he was spot on about our lack of common ground: gambling and maths are not among my strong points — unlike my memory. 'You ejaculated the last time we had sex,' I point out.

'I knew you weren't fertile,' he says smugly. 'I never ejaculate when you are.'

'How can you tell when I'm fertile?' It didn't seem important while he was around, but the information might come in handy now I'm on my own.

'By the smell of the hormones you produce.'

'Ah.' Not prepubescent ones, obviously.

'How are you otherwise?'

'Okay.' Best not to mention the motorbike. He'd want to know what man's teaching me to ride it.

'Well, take care,' he says. 'Bye.'

When I've stopped sobbing I call the feminist clinic that Damian's flatmate swore by and take the next available appointment, at 3 pm on Christmas Eve.

A whole month to get through, alone. Yet I think I'm waking up to my hormones. Out walking amid summer scents or practising turns on the wide, dead-end road by the water, I feel more at one with each moment than I ever did while meditating. Even the sheer physicality of nausea and dizziness brings a kind of relief. Perversely, I feel reconciled with the life force. Life is budding within me.

Damian's Buddhist flatmate, who's waiting outside, said I'm brave to opt for a local instead of a general, but I don't want to miss the passing of the being that's lodged in my womb so briefly. As the doctor scrapes and vacuums it out, she retains a coolness that I find more painful than the procedure. Her female attendants stay silent too, so I pray for the evicted soul. There

162

was never any question of being able to keep it. Soon Pearl will return and I'll be ousted too.

The Buddhist shows surprise at seeing me reach for tea and biscuits as soon as I'm settled in the recovery room. 'I've always felt sick after mine,' she confides, and I recall the counsellor's caution: abortion's no substitute for contraception.

'Have you heard of a "lunar phase"?' I ask her on the drive home. 'They said we can ovulate whenever it comes around.'

Back at her house we consult an ephemeris. As near as we can figure, my baby could have been a magician as easily as a mathematician.

'It depends on whose sperm found the target,' she says. 'We know Zane's is viable because he's fathered a child already.'

'The other guy did send in three squadrons,' I counter.

'That doesn't mean he had the most able semen,' she says. 'You might have to accept that you'll never know.'

She's made up her bed for me to crash in but I crave company — so, after Damian and she cook pasta for three that I barely touch, we all head out to a party.

They introduce me to lots of their friends while I drink lots of punch, which soon numbs me pleasantly all over. My scant bleeding ceased before I left the clinic, but my womb's ached dully since the local wore off. Emotionally anaesthetised, high on the dope that's going around, I abandon myself to dancing in a room crisscrossed with tinsel strands and strings of tiny, blinking, coloured lights. A lavishly bedecked plastic tree stands in one corner; a consumerist travesty, it strikes me in my stoned state of mind, of the Tree of Life. Or am *I* the travesty — shimmying, swaying, and grinding hips that flank a ravaged womb while the Christian world celebrates a virgin birth?

Damian dances near me, singlet stuck to his glistening chest, arms whirling, eyes far away. The Buddhist told me that he and his girlfriend split up due to diverging life goals. I want to reach out to console him, but he doesn't seem to see me. Not till 3 am when we're back at his place, slumped in armchairs with cups of tea.

'My bed's all ready for you, Skye,' says the Buddhist. 'You must be wasted by now. I'll just go round to my boyfriend's.'

'No — thanks so much for everything,' I reply, 'but I think I'll go home.' I'm starting to feel like I'll never stop crying once I'm left alone.

'You can't walk home in your state,' she fusses.

'It's okay,' Damian says. 'I'll take her.'

'What, not on the bike?' she says.

'I've been dancing all night,' I say. 'I can ride pillion for five minutes.'

'She'll be alright, I promise, Mum,' Damian says, grinning.

Unconvinced, she hugs us and retires to her clean, fresh sheets, leaving Damian and me to discuss our end-of-year assessments. He got an A for his philosophy essay. I tell him my psych tutor liked 'Kundalini, Creativity and Psychosis', but said I'd copped out on the creativity bit. Damian wants to know what mark I got. B–, I admit. He asks if I'll resume my course next year. I tell him I doubt it. We finish our teas.

'Looks like you could use some sleep,' says Damian. 'You look shattered. Maybe you'd better just climb into my bed.'

'Where will you sleep though?' I say guiltily.

'On the other side.' He flashes his wickedest grin. 'I hope you don't snore, Skye, not that it matters when I'm so damn tired.'

We take turns using the bathroom. I crawl between his sheets first, after peeling off all my clothes; because they're sticky with sweat, I justify to myself, though so am I. Then Damian comes in and kills the lamp. Enough light seeps beneath the curtains, once my eyes adjust, for me to see his torso tapering down into red briefs. He slides in on his side of the bed without so much as a little toe touching me.

'Night-night,' he says, back turned, and straightaway he's breathing peacefully. Unlike his flatmate, he didn't give me a hug.

Wide-awake, I lie on my back, aching to be held. My need for affection feels almost unbearable. I glance at his clock. 4:44. I try to focus on breathing. Next time I look, the red digits read 4:45. Damian would have taken me home if he didn't want to deal with me. I edge across the inches between us and press my chest into his muscular back. He stirs and murmurs in his sleep,

164

but doesn't move away. Heartened, I lay my belly against his lumbar spine in a partial embrace.

'Wha—?' he groans and a spasm jerks the length of his slumbering form.

I pull back, mortified. 4:55. Birds call and chatter outside. I lie motionless, eyes tracing the rose-shaped cornices on the ceiling until 5:05. What am I doing? I just want to be held, I tell myself. I've slept alone for the last seven weeks. And the last person I lay beside didn't cuddle me once, though he shot his load into me three times. The thought of going back to Pearl's unfurnished flat, her bare monk's cell, to spend Christmas Day feeling empty in a new way, doesn't appeal. If Damian held me *and* we ended up making love . . . But I've been warned off intercourse for two weeks. 5:13. I nestle my cheek into his shoulderblade. He promptly rolls over.

'What the fuck, Skye?' he says. I'm too ashamed to reply. 'I don't want to fuck you, okay? I'm still getting over a break-up, like you are. You of all people should be more sensitive to the fact that I'm grieving and I need some time out.'

He seemed happy mingling with his stoned, drunken friends last night. What's so wrong with me? 'Sorry,' I mumble into the pillow.

'It's okay,' he says. 'Get dressed, and I'll take you home.'

I fall onto Pearl's futon at 5:59, fresh off the back of a bike twice as powerful as mine, and manage at last to snatch a few hours sleep.

The burr of the phone cuts it short.

'Erghh?' I say.

'Merry Christmas, darling,' my mother says. 'Listen, are you alright?'

'Yes,' I lie, as the mother of all hangovers begins to kick in. 'Why?'

'Zane rang us late last night, wanting to know if we'd seen or heard from you. He sounded very concerned that you hadn't answered his calls.'

'I haven't seen or heard from *him* for weeks,' I say through my teeth. I feel as if someone's performed a termination on my brain.

'But you *are* alright,' she says, as if I must be; now I'm no longer with Zane.

'Sure. I'm just fine.' I wish them a happy Christmas and promise to visit soon.

Within half an hour the phone rings a second time.

'Where on earth have you been, Skye?' I've never heard Zane so stressed. 'I've been worried sick that you'd go out and get yourself pregnant again.'

'It's not safe for me to fuck for a fortnight,' I say. 'By the way, if your sperm had lasted five days they might have made my lunar phase. Though not all sperm are that vigorous, are they?'

'If I'd known it was my child,' he says, 'I'd have wanted you to keep it.' How dare he; until I can care for myself, what do I have to give someone else? Yet behind his reproach, he sounds profoundly sad. 'I've missed you, Skye, more than I've ever missed anyone. I don't suppose you'd want' — his tone grows hopeful — 'to catch up tonight?'

I hesitate. What would my new friends say? And yet he must still love me, or why try to find me? I don't need a lonely Christmas night after my solitary day. Maybe the time apart has changed him too?

'Alright.'

166

·EIGHTEEN·

Hysteria Repeats Itself

From the outset the group felt incestuous to me. Yet no-one else in it seemed to notice; perhaps unsurprising when at least half were incest survivors. They'd call each other daily, between group sessions, and Josh urged me to join in. I held back, wondering how the hell they afforded their mobile bills. Once I answered my phone to hear Take-it-away Man whine, 'Hello — who is this?' He'd worked his way down a list, I presume, and lost track of who he was up to. I was tempted to think that Josh had got his medication wrong.

Anyway, the group had begun to invade the rest of my week. I had to field calls at all hours. Morrie Bund rang me the most. Worse, the blurred boundaries theme infiltrated my dreams, like the one with Zoe hanging out washing on my balcony after I asked her to leave.

Then, at the next therapy session, she said, 'I feel hurt that Skye never calls me.'

'Try telling Skye directly,' Josh said in his gentlest tone.

'You remind me of my mother,' she told me, 'when you won't let me in.'

'Aren't mothers meant to push us out?' *I said. Though forceps had pulled me free.*

'I was premature,' Zoe said, her lower lip tremulous, 'and it's left me with an unconscious fear that women will reject me.'

'Accepting someone doesn't mean being joined at the hip,' I said.

'I haven't noticed Skye rejecting Morris,' Zoe told Josh.

I waited for someone to call her on her passive aggression.

'I've been waiting for someone to comment on their special bond,' Josh said.

'It's not like I'm keeping score,' I said, as my head began to throb, 'but while we're on the subject of "special", why does Zoe get to talk more?'

'Zoe asks for what she wants,' Josh said. 'I'm not a mind-reader. If you can't get your needs met in the group, you'll never get them met in the world.'

'That would be true if Josh ruled the world as well as the group,' I told Morrie Bund when we dissected the session over coffee with Zoe trying to eavesdrop.

That night, in a dream, as I walked through a park with Damian, Zoe came between us. Midweek, the nightmare Zoe moved into my house, and wouldn't shut up. Before the week's end, she'd wormed her way into my bed and resisted removal by force. Even if I'd wished to accept her, I stood no chance during REM sleep. But I documented the dreams along with group dialogues that I found no less surreal. Did no-one else keep a diary?

At the next session Morrie Bund missed out on a turn. He jiggled his knees and tapped his feet but Josh didn't respond till the end, when he said, 'Morris, would you care to tell us what you're trying to crush with your heels?'

'I've been wondering,' Morrie Bund said, 'if another therapy mightn't suit me better?'

'That's an excuse people use when it gets too hot in the kitchen,' said Josh, 'but you'll never get well if you run away.'

Morrie Bund pouted. 'How much longer will I need to stay?'

Josh's eyes narrowed appraisingly. 'Why would you ever want to leave?'

I stared at his dead-straight face, expecting to see his tongue stuck in one cheek. What hope did we have of healing if he wouldn't let us leave him? As I thought about my mother's difficult labour, it hit me: Josh wasn't a father figure for me, as he was for the others. Gender notwithstanding, the man symbolised my mother.

On Boxing Day I wheel my motorbike out of the shed, eager to ride via backstreets down to the bay. Guy, my friendly instruc-

168

tor, said I'm ready to venture out solo if I steer clear of traffic, viable on a public holiday. The ache in my womb's let up and my hangover's gone, but I've got a pain in my backside, courtesy of Zane. If I'd been turned on, it might have felt okay; Ramon's probably never tried it any other way. But I shouldn't have let Zane force me, and in the back of his car. I'd told him my vagina's off limits, but . . . any port in a storm. Then he turned shitty when I whimpered and resisted, and dropped me off with no mention of future contact. Good riddance.

I swing the back gate shut, kick-start my bike and cruise down the lane. The breeze tongues my throat like a lover and the sun's deliciously warm through my T-shirt. Why sacrifice this independence for the bondage I've thought of as 'love'?

I stop at the corner, putting my foot down before I turn; but to my shock the bike topples, taking me with it, and lands on my left knee. I kill the ignition and manage to wrench my leg free. Thankfully my butt's gone more or less numb, but I can't right the bike, I'm too weak. After trying for some minutes during which no cars pass by, I decide that I'll need to ring for help. Damian lives closest, but I'm too ashamed after yesterday.

Instead, I limp up the lane to the flat and call Guy. Miraculously he's home and says he'll ride straight over. While I wait, lying prone, knee throbbing, I shed my first tears since Christmas Eve. The abortion's taken more out of me than I'd realised — or Zane has.

If only I hadn't weakened. Initially, I couldn't resist his art — an exquisite, painted angel on a handmade Christmas card, propped against the tarnished biscuit tin by my futon where I can see it. The angel stands with one foot on earth, the other in a flowing stream. His wings, from tops to tips, describe the shape of a heart as big as an aura. Behind him, a road winds to a horizon, to vanish between blue mountains. Zane's sense of perspective and proportion shine within the card's confines in a way they didn't on a larger scale. If not for the bright gold hair and snub nose, it could be an idealised self-portrait. The face looks as peaceful, gentle and kind as Zane's did when we first met. The subtlety of the shading recalls the nuances of Zane's touch.

His words — of life, love and light — in his delicate script make me miss him so much that I lift the lid of the biscuit tin half full of mementoes and drop his card in.

Despite my feeble physical state, I feel strong enough now to live without Zane. My loneliness, while crippling, was far worse when I lived with him.

Once Guy's replaced my bike in the shed and determined that my knee's intact, he whisks me down the road in search of a café that's open for coffee and cake. He and his girlfriend, my neighbour from 1A, are separating; so I guess he's lonely in his own way.

When Pearl lets herself in downstairs, Guy and I are drinking tea; so we have a few seconds in which to adjust before she's aware of either of us. And maybe a strange presence in her home is unexpected. Such are my attempts to guess why she seems so displeased to see me as she hefts off her backpack and slings it down by the futon.

'I thought you might've found somewhere to stay by now,' she says, the starkness of her shaven head in keeping with her greeting. 'I need some peace and quiet — so I want to settle back in today.' Shadows under her eyes bear out her claim.

'You said to stay while you were away but not what date you'd be back,' I remind her. 'I don't suppose you've met Guy?'

'No, I haven't,' she says, bristling with ambivalence.

'Yes, you have,' he says, 'when you came round to 1A to borrow a ladder.'

She regards him warily until the penny drops. 'Oh, you're *that* Guy.'

'Can I make you a cuppa?' he offers.

'No thanks, I can't spare the time.' She rummages through a side pocket on her pack and pulls out a string of glass mala beads. 'There — I thought of you, Skye. Now I need to get cracking and make some changes round here.' Her gaze sweeps the room that I've grown quite attached to; scours the walls of my symbolic womb. 'This space feels too enclosed.' She strides into the kitchen and yanks out some drawers. 'If I'm going to

170

live here I'll need to open it up.' Then, to Guy's and my surprise, she begins to swing a hammer, smashing holes in the partition between the main room and stairwell.

As Guy and I exchange looks, I don't need telepathy to guess what he — a down-to-earth electrician — must be thinking. Pearl's acting more like she's spent time in a padded cell than with her guru. I slip the necklace over my head and wonder whose roof I'll sleep under tonight.

'Can I give you a lift anywhere?' Guy asks me.

'As soon as I collect my things — and my wits,' I say.

'I'm opening up a space in *me*,' Pearl chants as she hammers away, uncovering raw wooden beams beneath the fibro layer.

While I gather my scant belongings and stack them into milk crates — sketchbooks, paints, pastels, brushes, clothes and magical tools — I ponder whether Pearl's ever been any less volatile. Did I miss the signs? I hope I don't have too many more spaces like this one lurking in *me*.

'Oh, Jeez, folks! I hate to be a wet blanket' — Guy's sober tone startles me and Pearl stares blankly — 'but that panelling's lined with asbestos. Now it's exposed you can't stay here, in fact, we should all vamoose a.s.a.p. — you mustn't breathe the dust. It's carcinogenic.'

'Come down to the clinic at closing time,' Mel tells Ramon, 'and I'll work on your pressure points. It won't stop you smoking, but it'll help.' As she tips two sugars into her latte I cringe — though where did I get the idea that naturopaths should set an example?

'You're a godsend, Mel!' Ramon inhales smoke savagely, as if to hoard some for the withdrawal to come. 'You're so lucky you never started,' he tells me, sounding in awe of my purity.

'She's just sensible.' Mel lights up too, as if to imply she'd rather die of cancer than of boredom.

'So you've moved in with a *witch*?' gloats Ramon.

'A good witch,' I say.

'Skye used to live with a sorcerer,' says Mel somewhat dryly. 'In theory, that makes her a witch too.'

'The sorceress's *apprentice*,' I qualify, to Ramon's raucous glee.

Until Pearl's return I'd been unaware of Stella's spare bedroom upstairs, so I guess I'm lucky — but there's a catch. Since I moved in, the training's become more intensive, necessitating daily meditation on geometric shapes, and my working of a series of planetary rituals. I often wonder what Mel and Ramon would think if they could see me standing in Stella's empty back room tracing pentagrams or cabbalistic crosses in the air while chanting archaic Hebrew names. Rhythms do more for me, I'm reflecting over my cappuccino — why pretend to prefer lattes, like the others, if not smoking sets me apart? — when Ramon spontaneously invites me to a daytime dance class.

Delighted that we've found common ground where Mel can't follow, let alone lead — she's not a dancer — I leave the café with Ramon. Once Mel's gone he's a most attentive companion. Plenty of passers-by smile at us, and what a pair we must make; he wearing a striped sailor's jersey and long johns, me with my mohawk, leg warmers and tights.

'Farrell's had the hots for you for ages,' he teases as we traipse down the hill from Oxford Street. 'Haven't you noticed, Skye?'

'He's made eye contact once or twice, but I haven't seen him lately.'

'Maybe he's given up,' sighs Ramon. 'I think he only came to see you.'

'I don't believe that,' I say, feeling no less thrilled that Ramon seems to, 'still, he *is* kind of cute.' Freckled, fair, tawny-haired, very short, no flab anywhere and about my age or a touch older. 'Not exactly tall, dark and handsome' — like *you*, though I don't dare say that — 'but he's the most attractive *eligible* guy at yoga' — or at least the little dick *acts* hetero — 'so,' I conclude, 'what should I do?'

'I'll give you the magic number.' Ramon claps his slender dancer's hands — two fingers of one are stained yellow-brown, I note with regret — and reels it off.

I scribble it down, wishing Ramon would give me his instead, but he can't afford to get a phone connected.

172

The Skye who delays calling Farrell is the same one who opts to, at last. We know Ramon's the one, she says, so why chase red herrings? He's out of the question, I argue, what do you think he gets up to — or *up* — at nights? But within the week she agrees to ring Farrell one evening, to humour Ramon. Maybe he'll get jealous and realise his true desires, she whispers.

'*Hel*-lo.' The fact that Farrell's answered — he shares a house with other actors — assures me of my intuitive timing. 'Come on over,' he says.

'*Now?*' What'll I wear?

'Make hay while the sun shines,' he says.

By the time I ring the doorbell of a large, rambling old terrace, I'm trembling. I feel self-conscious and awkward as Farrell ushers me in to his room. Ironic — I'm wearing designer jeans and a slinky white T-shirt, Stella's hand-me-downs — in contrast to his pyjama pants.

'Have you tried rebirthing?' he asks as he closes his bedroom door.

'No.' Surely that can't be what I'm here for?

He sits down on the bed but doesn't invite me to take the weight off my feet.

'The woman who rebirths me is unreal,' he says, looking straight past me. 'Since I've begun to do sessions with her my throat chakra's clearing.'

'Cool.' In theory, that should activate truthfulness, trust and telepathy, enabling Farrell to see past my monosyllabism to my complexity.

'You should try it,' he says. 'It would open up your voice.'

What's wrong with my voice? Nothing, I realise, that he'd know about. I've hardly opened my mouth yet. Unconvinced, I avert my gaze.

Below a framed, professional portfolio shot of him, propped against the wall, crystals arranged on the floor before it as if to stake out a makeshift altar, a large-lettered message proclaims, *I LOVE YOU, FARRELL*, in his handwriting, I presume. Embarrassed, I glance about the room and suddenly he's standing in front of me. As he draws my T-shirt up and off, I notice the lack

173

of furniture. Is that why we need to fuck kneeling on the floor? He seems more aroused than me and I wonder if he can see his photo over my shoulder. The yoga poses we shared promised more than this premature physical closeness.

And that's not all that's premature.

'Sorry to ask you to leave,' says Farrell within minutes of his solitary orgasm, 'but I need my beauty sleep.' He hitches up his pyjama pants. 'Don't forget to call my rebirther, will you?'

'No.' Why did that word elude me fifteen minutes ago? I feel numb as he hands me her business card and opens his bedroom door, stunned as I let myself out the front door, dazed as I wander along backstreets.

When I get home, I can tell Stella's out. Luke's mulling up at the dining table.

'Hey, honey,' he says, 'how would you like to learn to fly?'

'I'm still getting the hang of my vroom-vroom,' I joke, assuming he's using a metaphor — unless he's referring to astral travelling?

'Never mind that.' He smiles widely. 'Hang-gliding requires different skills.'

High from my first flying lesson, though I never left the ground, I call Farrell a week after our failed first encounter. Ramon assured me Farrell was just *acting* casual. That's what guys do, he said, and he's more qualified to know than I am. My instincts tell me Farrell's probably gayer than Ramon, yet dares not admit it to himself. But my instincts were wrong about Zane, who made a far better first impression. At the risk of making myself feel worse, I decide to see if I can't reverse Farrell's first impression of me.

'Just thought I'd give you a call to see what you're up to,' I tell him casually.

'I'm in love with someone else now,' he says with even greater casualness.

Someone else, I think, as distinct from *yourself*? 'I've lined up a date with your favourite rebirther,' I say, trying not to sound like I've been kicked in the gut while I'm down.

174

'That's a good move,' he says. 'She's sensational.' Maybe he's in love with her? 'Look, gotta go, I'm busy running through a script.'

When isn't he? 'That's okay, gotta fly.' I don't give a flying fuck, I tell myself, I had nothing at stake beyond showing Ramon that I gave it a go, so he'll be less likely to guess that I'm falling for him.

'You've got a great voice,' he said this morning, after we'd sung 'Stand By Me' together while he strummed a battered guitar in his poky kitchen. 'It's so deep,' he'd enthused, 'and *powerful*!'

Encouraged, I rang the rebirther the moment I got home.

A middle-aged woman with long, straight hair and a loose, orange robe lets me in to the plush suburban mansion and leads me down the hall, past much bigger photos of her wild-eyed, white-haired guru than the one swinging from her mala beads. The warm colour scheme makes me more aware of my hair, dyed blue by Stella for my twenty-fourth birthday.

Soon I'm lying on my back, eyes closed, in a quiet, dim room, with her voice guiding me to breathe deeply and evenly.

After several minutes my hands begin to contort into curled-up claws. Have I regressed to the foetal stage already? Connecting my breath as she suggests feels like an effort. My impulses tell me to hold it, to revert to my old shallow pant; or to leave, to alleviate the tension.

After some time — I can't tell how much since it seems to be slowing down infinitely — my insides begin to ache: my womb, to be precise. Then that sensation fades and another replaces it.

My left knee's playing up, still bruised from the bike, but when I look down on it inwardly, I see a blood-soaked gash in the knee of the Levis I wore at thirteen. Whooshing down a steep, unlit slope on a friend's skateboard at night, wielding an umbrella to deflect the driving rain, I felt poised on the verge of flight until I dived into wet bitumen; and as the pain shifts to the base of my spine, I recall I used to love jumping from heights. As a small child I'd jump out of trees and off the roof of the

175

garden shed, until the time I landed astride the handle of a wheelbarrow. If I'd had longer legs I mightn't have slammed my coccyx so hard, but as I shot up I climbed taller trees and stayed aloft, obsessed with birds.

As the moments trickle by, the pain in my tailbone begins to dissolve. Each breath flows through my body, unobstructed by gross cellular memories. And then I'm flying, defying gravity, swooping over sand dunes on man-made wings, arms braced, feet dangling in air. That's how I felt last week, under Luke's tutelage, blissfully freed from the ground plane. I never wanted to glide back down.

Too bad. My head starts to ache. The stress centres in my brow, yet grips my skull like a vice. I try to exhale the crushing pressure but it only tightens its hold.

And the rebirther's calling me back. 'Open your eyes when you're ready.' Is my time up? 'You need to get up and dance around to ground yourself,' she instructs.

Though I've never felt less like dancing in my life, I struggle to my feet. Swaying clumsily to the recorded beat, I shake my head but it still hurts. If only I could rest on the mattress for a while. A twinge shoots through my knee. I tell her how much it hurt during the process.

'The left side of the body's ruled by the right, lunar side of the brain, and knees absorb shock,' she says. 'So your feminine side feels unsupported.'

And Farrell thinks this tangerine midwife's some sort of genius? Taking my thirty dollars, she sends me on my way. No follow-up is mentioned. So I'm fixed?

Light-headed and disoriented, I wander in search of a bus stop; tread upon clouds instead of paving slabs as my thoughts scale precarious heights, predictable preludes to a fall. Overhead a dead bat dangles from the wires — until a second look reveals just an old pair of runners, laces knotted. Yet it might as well be me — left hanging, discarded, unable to stand my ground. I can't regain my footing, nor sense myself as distinct from anything. I've flown too close to the sun again, melting the wax on my wings, and my feathers aren't held together by a solid framework of logic. I'm lighter than the air I breathe, yet leaden with fear as I cross the street. To escape the stares of passers-by, I hide in a burnt-out bus shelter. Like me, it's charred. Gutted. Black inside.

I'd hoped a rebirth would break the spell of the last thirteen months, but I'm reborn into a new hell, reduced again to nothing.

·V·

The Yoga Household

·NINETEEN·

No Fling Without Wings

Transference, it's called, when a client projects desires onto a therapist. And then there's counter-transference — an even squirmier can of worms. While Josh devoted more time to clients who'd been interfered with in childhood, those who'd missed out on paternal attention of any sort suffered compound neglect.

Josh would probably put it down to my father projection, but I'd swear he lit up at the mention of sex. And Maddy appeared to share my perception. After she'd been forgotten once too often, she began to remember being molested by assorted male relatives.

When Josh called for feedback for Maddy after her latest strategic confession, I said, 'You repressed those memories for so long that I'm questioning if someone messed with me.'

Josh nodded. 'With your relationship history, it's a strong possibility.'

But my failure to follow up with details relegated me to the sidelines.

'My first lover was twice my age,' Zoe told Maddy, 'so I can relate to your shame.'

Josh glanced sharply at Zoe. 'Maybe you'd like to share next?'

Of course Zoe would, despite her resistance. Josh had to urge her on while the rest of us faked interest, except for Take-it-away Man, whose interest was confined to how to get into her pants. As usual, the subject of sex made her coy.

'So how did you meet the guy?' Josh probed.

'He was a friend of my mother's.'

'Was he her lover?'

We knew Zoe's father had played up, but this promised to be a new revelation.

'I think so.' She'd closed her eyes.

'Look at us, Zoe. We're here to support you.'

Her lids fluttered open. We all smiled reassuringly. She gulped in conditioned air and sighed.

'You just think so?' Josh prompted gently. 'I'd say you'd know.'

'Well I knew they'd been lovers but I thought they might've stopped. Otherwise I'd never have let him do it with me.' She screwed up her eyes and began to rub them with balled fists.

'Stay with us, Zoe,' Josh exhorted her, 'come on, don't go away.'

'He'd been keen on me for years,' she squealed, like someone locked in a bad dream.

'And how old were you when he tried it on?'

She sniffled. 'Seventeen.'

That's not so young, I thought, as I fought to pay attention — the recycled air was stifling me and I'd missed my turn three weeks running — but then my first fuck hadn't been the one who'd done my head in.

'Do you want to tell us what happened?' Josh coaxed Zoe.

More tightly squeezed eyelids and strangled sobs meant she wouldn't miss telling us for anything. 'He'd just given my mother a healing massage on her bed, so I knew she was stoned, and I was in the next room doing my homework with the TV going —'

As Zoe paused for breath, I feared there wasn't enough to go around. When I tried to breathe into the knot in my guts, the impulse got lost halfway down. He could have been anyone, I reasoned, Zoe hadn't identified him, so why did I have to leap to conclusions? Please, I prayed, don't let the paranoia start again.

'Stay with it, Zoe,' said Josh, 'keep breathing. What happened then?'

'The usual, we just watched TV at first. Zane liked cartoons.'

In my bedroom, on a morning when Ramon is bound to be sleeping soundly, I set up a circle with my cards. Luke told me, step by step, what to do when I said Ramon wanted help to quit smoking. 'Can't Stella show you some healing spell?' he'd said, half joking, after Mel's techniques failed him. He praises my 'good influence', turns to me when guilt follows his debauches, yet appears to have more fun with bad influences like Mel. Won't he be tickled pink, even awestruck, if this ritual works! He and Mel acted pleased to see me — I hadn't been to yoga for weeks.

I greet the four elements symbolised by my cards. The backlash from the rebirth hit me pretty hard. For a while I scarcely spoke to a soul apart from Stella, and then only to tell her I'd done my homework. After I saw a butterfly materialise on the edge of my air card, she said I could give the elemental meditations a rest.

I request the blessing of Kwan Yin, goddess of compassion, and summon Ramon's body of light to banish the quarters with me by tracing flaming pentagrams in space. Air feels constricted, so I exhale tightness. Blocked anger taints fire; I tell the heat to go. Sorrow fills the water quarter — I will Ramon's tears to flow. From earth I banish the shadow of his father's violence.

Luke said this ritual ought to heal the issues behind the smoking; and from stray reminiscences of Ramon's, I've gathered what those might be — a brutal father, a cowed mother and sister, and a scared little boy sucking fire into his lungs instead of screaming out red-hot rage.

Next I greet the archangels, use the mudra — or gesture — Luke showed me, and recite a healing mantra. Last, I thank Ramon's divinely graceful body of light, visualise it merging back into his sleeping form, then exit and break the circle, having thanked everything including Kwan Yin.

Mel sounds concerned on hearing about my new casual job. 'So there'll only be you and this painter alone in his studio, with you starkers?'

'He teaches at college and his oils sell for five-figure sums.'

'I might be able to get you work three days a week, not just one afternoon. What're you like at massage?' she asks.

Guy once said I had healing hands after I'd massaged his headache away. 'I've never been trained,' I say, 'but —'

Just then, Ramon walks into the café looking distraught, so I guess we're about to find out why he hasn't shown up at yoga for days. Not since I performed the healing ritual. To my surprise, he strides over to me as if he hasn't noticed Mel.

'I haven't smoked all week, Skye, and now I've got the worst case of shingles.' He lifts his tank top to expose a blistering, red rash encircling his torso. 'It's ruined my sex life,' he moans. That, I'm aware, consists of picking up strange guys down at the Square. He hasn't had a steady boyfriend since we met.

'It's a healing crisis,' I reassure him, feeling a prick of guilt at my secret. 'You know how snakes shed their skins? Well, it's like a rebirth.'

'Giving up cigarettes sucks,' he complains, sitting down on a spare stool beside me, 'but not having sex is the *pits*, Skye. I feel like I'm going insane!'

'Trust the process,' I say. Though tempted to mention the ritual, I don't. It might be best to wait until he's through the withdrawal. 'Emotions tend to flare up when we don't use addictions to hold them down.'

'I'd like to nail them down and bury them under six feet of dirt.' He glares at me as if he suspects I might be one of them. I've never seen him so angry and scared.

'If you want to come back to my place,' says Mel, 'I'll give you something for that.'

He turns to her gratefully and orders a short black.

Why do men prefer Mel to me? I wonder as they yak, and come up with a list of reasons longer than my legs, fairer than my hair and bigger than my breasts. I'd hoped my attempts to help Ramon heal himself might bring us closer, not push him away.

As I extract myself from a party one night, a man on his own edges towards the door too. Though his face is sharp, not round, he reminds me of Ramon, and the pain of feeling unwanted, which made me switch classes, kicks in again. Then I remember

184

lingering after a class once, entranced, as this lean loner improvised.

Yet his dark eyes don't mirror recognition. 'Are you on foot too?' is all he says.

We talk as we walk, and somehow stumble upon the subject of vipassana. He's sat three retreats, I learn, by the time we reach the corner where our paths diverge.

'I'd like to sleep with you.' He's unabashed by the admission.

'I'm *Skye*.' I'm over anonymous sex, thanks to the nameless mathematician.

'Ash.' Instead of shaking my hand, he takes and grasps it lightly, and we walk the rest of the way back to Stella's holding hands.

The masks arrayed on the walls perplex him. 'These aren't yours?'

'No,' I say, and tell him a little about Stella and our rituals.

'I didn't think you'd made them. They look vacant.'

His compliment could hardly be less direct. 'They're *neutral*,' I say, appalled that I'm blushing, 'or they'd be human, not divine.'

'If they're supposed to be neutral,' he says, 'why do they *all* look feminine? I bet they're all self-portraits of Stella.'

'You're taking them at face value. Each one has its own energy.' And yet I suspect he's right, and that her view of herself is idealised.

Ash plucks a silver mask from the wall and, before I can protest, puts it on. The ibis-feather trim hides his hair like a helmet.

I feel a guilty thrill. If Stella walked in now, she'd kill us. But she won't; she went away for the weekend.

'Hermes, I'm at a crossroads.' If Ash can improvise, so can I. 'And to know which way to go, I need a sign.'

'A path only has meaning if you follow it for your own reasons.' The black and white feathers wave as he cranes his neck, ibis-like. 'Never forget that your body holds the keys.'

'That's given me plenty to think about, Hermes.' I wait for him to take off the mask, but instead he unbuttons his shirt and sheds it, then starts to unbuckle his belt.

Rising to the challenge, I fling off my blouse and unzip my jeans. All his clothes soon hit the carpet, revealing a body as divine as the mask, and I don't need to see his expression to notice he likes what he's seeing through Hermes's eyes. I feel exposed with my face naked but he misses it, kneeling to kiss my navel. Ticklish, I fall all over him laughing until we're half under the table. When a key turns in the front door he's poised above me, blissfully unaware.

'Sorry to intrude.' Luke slips past, beaming. 'Don't mind me.'

Ash freezes. 'Who was that?' he says as the back door shuts on a stifled giggle.

'My magical teacher's soul mate — and teacher.'

'He seems relaxed.' Ash flexes his hips deliciously. 'Can *he* teach you?'

'He's been teaching me to hang-glide.' I tilt my hips and we find our rhythm.

'At least that's. *Practical*. I'd say. Vipassana. Gave you. More than. Magic has . . .'

We reach our destination, the same one for now, simultaneously.

Over the next few days, inspired by Ash's observations, I conceive of a mask for Venus with a pout like Mel's; and Luke's disappearing chin would distinguish Jupiter. Ramon's cheeky grin eludes me — maybe it would look good on Pan?

I'm sketching ideas for Demeter when Stella brings a fat letter upstairs. I rip it open. *My dear friend*, it begins. Tears prick my eyes. It's been so long since she gazed into them, has Teresa forgotten my name? But no, she wrote it on the envelope. And soon she'll address me to my face. Next month she flies home. Just as well that my life's back on track and she'll never know how low I fell. She's shacked up with her swami — been there, done that — but there's a catch: because he's worshipped by so many students and devotees, tradition demands that he live like a priest. *As you know, I abhor deceit*, says a scrawl slightly more flawed than formerly, *and masquerading as his student has wounded my pride, but the flow of rupees and his reputation depend on me living this lie* . . . Which she justifies by enumerating the virtues of her husband-to-be. But I sense compromise between each line. And she called Zane a charlatan. Furthermore, though the dude still scorns sleep, he won't let his star pupil snooze either. He's dispensed with his lotus pose and spends all night trying to get his lingam inside her. That should test the selflessness of her desire to serve.

Nowhere does she say she looks forward to seeing me. *How's the motorbike?* is her parting shot. My reply will keep. Her letter's taken six weeks to arrive and she'll be back in less. Then I'll tell her I sold the bike because dancers can't afford to endanger their knees. But what I really want to tell her is that I've found a gorgeous new lover, a grounded, spunky, creative, intelligent *equal* — not some pseudo-spiritual, sex-crazed, self-important cult leader — and that I've got *two* initiates guiding me, not one con man who's spread himself too thin. For once, I don't envy nor see her as more aware than me — which must be as close to enlightenment as I've ever been.

Probably only a miracle could have reconciled Ramon and me. So it's lucky Mel needs us to lead the yoga while she studies overseas. It'll be a stretch at best. We're far from adept. Between us we can do almost as many poses as Mel can, if none half as well; so we take turns leading and fill in each other's gaps. Then we do coffee, catch a modern class, and ramble back to Ramon's, a dingy flat that he's tarted up with theatre posters and props. None of the others came today; so, though the demon tobacco's reclaimed him, he makes an effort to ration himself for my sake.

'You ought to try a vipassana retreat,' I tease. 'You'd have to quit for ten days.'

He looks at me curiously, dark brown eyes round in his moon-shaped face. 'You did one of those, didn't you?' he says in a hushed tone.

'Just the one,' I say and blush, unsure of where to look. He's begun to listen, really tune in to me, now Mel's gone for six months.

'Do some meditators do *more* than one?' His eyes grow rounder still.

'Sure. I had a lover who'd done four.' After four nights with Ash I was looking forward to more. And he introduced me to his parents. My black and white hair — dyed by Stella, who likes to improve upon me however she can — didn't faze them. But Ash hasn't called around for weeks. 'Three,' I correct myself. 'That's all he'd done.'

'*Three?*' breathes Ramon. 'Do you really think I could do one?'

'You don't have to spend a cent unless you want to donate at the end.'

'So it's *free*?'

'Well, yes. Unless you feel inspired to give. Like, if you reaped some benefits.'

His frown of concentration deepens. 'How often do they hold these retreats?'

'Regularly. The next one starts straight after Christmas. Boxing Day, in fact.'

'That's almost four months away!' he says. 'What're you wearing tonight?'

'Who knows? Kali might be fun to go as.' I rummage through my bag for bells, and buckle them onto my ankles.

'Skye with bells on!' Ramon claps his hands. 'Who did you say Kali was?'

'I didn't. The Hindu goddess of destruction.'

'Oooh.' He shivers delightedly. 'And what do you do with those?'

I stamp out a few routines from my beginners Indian class, scaled down to suit his cramped kitchen.

'It's not so different to flamenco.' Ramon leaps up and breaks into a rhythm.

My heart leaps too but I stay seated, awed by the speed and sureness of his feet. Suddenly he's a man, not a boy; straight-backed and dignified, exhaling fire.

'Come on, Skye, I'll show you some steps.' He holds out a hand.

I try to mimic the pattern he raps out on the black and white chequered lino, but end up inventing something less staccato.

'You're a natural dancer,' he says when we sit down to catch our breath. 'Don't worry so much about which form to follow, just let yourself find your own.'

That's what attracted me to Ash. 'What will you dress up as?'

'I'm not in a party mood. I might just spend a quiet night at home.'

This doesn't sound like the Ramon I know. 'Are you feeling alright?'

'You're so good for me, Skye.' He looks soberly into my eyes. 'I don't have any other friends who see my spiritual side. Do you ever wish you could be, you know, part of a spiritual community?'

With a pang, I recall those fantasies featuring Zane. 'I am, in a sense. My home's so harmonious. You'll have to come visit sometime.'

'Ooo-ah.' The glitter of fear and excitement returns to his eyes. 'I'd love to, one day when Stella's out. I don't want her casting a spell on me, turning me into a toad.' He giggles maniacally.

'You'd have to wait in a well for a prince to kiss you,' I say. Or a princess, I think.

'*You* could undo a spell though, couldn't you?' He looks at me ingenuously.

'I'm still just a beginner,' I say.

'But you told me about how you wrote that list before you met Zane.' He flashes me a smile that radiates faith. 'You couldn't have manifested him unless you'd had magical powers already.'

'No-one can work voodoo on you if you don't want them to.' Now might be the right time to tell him about my ritual. 'Healers were all most witches ever were —'

'Let's make a start on your costume,' he says, contorting his face with distaste, and the moment for intimate revelations slips away.

At long last I'm ready to leave Ramon's in a black sheath we made from a large garbage bag, ankles jingling and dozens of cardboard-cut-out skulls wreathing my neck on a string. 'Kali would wear a hundred and eight,' I say, 'but the idea's what counts.'

'You look beautiful,' gushes Ramon as we walk to the corner to dial a taxi. Extravagant, but I don't care to ride a Saturday-night 380 like this.

Back at his flat, Ramon draws a black dot over my third eye with a laundry marker. When the horn honks, we hug goodbye, and he kisses both my cheeks. While I'm disappointed he chose not to come, I've resolved not to pick up anyone.

A dark sea broods beyond the window as I sip red wine and squint at a horizon shot with lightning. I can't yet see anyone I know, as I prop up one wall of a rambling old flat, my black sheath rustling whenever I so much as breathe. But I know most of the archetypes circulating the floor, grazing assorted nibbles or milling at the bar. There's Anubis, wearing a giant, black jackal head; Christ bearing a spiky tiara; Poseidon with dreads, a trident and wetsuit; women draped in ringleted wigs, satin slips and spangled veils; men sporting capes, makeshift togas and loincloths. Someone sticks Bananarama's 'Venus' on the turntable. There's no shortage of versions of *her* here tonight. The pungent smell of a spliff drives me out onto the balcony, where the salt air inspires me to want to live near the sea. Not unlike I did when I longed for a man, I start to compose a wish list for a flat: ocean view, lots of light, space to paint, peace and quiet . . . I glance down. Trees and a garden, even shared.

Then I see him; walking up the path all in white, feathered wings quivering. Did someone slip something in my drink? But this is no hallucination. I consider fleeing via the balcony, but in my get-up I might regret it. What would Kali do? I step back inside.

When our eyes meet, it's as if no time has elapsed since our first — or last — encounter. But Zane no longer looks like that

190

brash little boy. He's shape-shifted into the Temperance angel he painted on my Christmas card.

'Kali,' he laughs. 'That'd be right.'

I choose to ignore his sarcasm. 'You look great in white.' What I mean is, you looked like a slob before, who'd you lose weight for?

A smile lights his whole face, transporting me back to our honeymoon phase before my instability frightened him. 'You look great too.' I guess that means he fancies me even in black polythene. 'So . . . how've you been doing?'

I mention yoga and dance, but not how lonely I've been, or Luke's flying lessons — Zane might get jealous. 'And Teresa's due back.'

'So she didn't find what she was looking for?'

'She sort of did. I think she's just visiting.'

As he nods, his eyes grow misty. 'Skye, I'm sorry for everything. I fucked up with you seriously, and I'd undo it if I could.'

'It takes two, so it's not like I blame you.'

'You look so happy,' he says. 'That's good.'

'I'm happy to see you.' If partly because I felt insecure with no-one to talk to. 'You look happier too.' That's crap. Contrite, then? Whatever it is, I like it.

He mentions his latest projects, but humbly, as if he acknowledges limits. If I hadn't let him project his limitations onto me, things might have been different.

'You know,' he says, 'I keep wondering how things might've been if I'd trusted you more. I kept jumping to assumptions because I'd been hurt too often before.'

'I know.' And because of side effects associated with dope smoking? Yet his remorse makes me feel like hugging him, feathered wings, rustlings, skulls and all.

'Skye . . . could I call you sometime, take you out for coffee? Would you mind?'

For a moment I'm too stunned to reply. I never expected to see Zane tonight, let alone to get asked on a date. The mere idea strikes me as potentially dangerous. Yet unless I give him another chance I won't know if he's changed.

'No —' I flush. 'I mean, no I wouldn't mind. Do you have Stella's number?'

TWENTY

A Lie for a Lie and a Truth for a Truth

Though the session drew to a close just after we learnt who'd deflowered Zoe, I said that her history shed light on mine. Josh said he'd look forward to my next share, but to make lots of calls in the meantime. I shrugged. Two decades had passed since Zane's deceit. My side of the story would keep for a week.

For once, Josh didn't interrupt when I finally spoke, and the others all listened for a change instead of sneaking downstairs to smoke.

Josh looked rapt. 'I wondered when we'd hear about your emotional breakdown.'

'It wasn't just emotional.' I wondered when he'd last opened my file.

'I meant as distinct from a mental breakdown.'

'Which part of seeing and hearing things wasn't clear?'

'You've never referred to delusions,' Josh said, his tone grown stern.

Despite his alternative style, he was a registered psychiatrist. Framed certificates hung on the walls. I didn't need labels when I already felt like an outsider, so I racked my brains for a less loaded term. 'But I must've referred to altered states?'

Josh nodded. 'It's normal for survivors of sexual abuse to report out-of-body experiences.'

'Why?' Maddy was, I suspected, conducting research for future performances.

'To rise above the shocking things being done to your body protects your psyche. Whether you stay to watch from a distance or fly far away, shock propels your consciousness up and out. That's why,' Josh said, 'many victims forget what happened — they weren't there — unless they regress through hypnosis or some accidental trigger.'

'I've never had an out-of-body experience,' Zoe complained.

'It's not something you'd ever want to have either,' Josh told her. 'Feedback for Skye?'

'I imagine you felt abandoned by your father,' Maddy said.

'I get that your mother was very competitive,' Take-it-away Man said.

'In case you think I was competing, Zane never said he had a girlfriend.' Zoe transfixed me with a gaze she must have imagined was intimate. 'I feel joy that you've begun to let us in.'

Her joy seemed as premature as her birth had been. Baring my soul hadn't enabled what Josh called 'into-me-see'. Instead, I felt negated by the group's simplistic view of me.

'How are you feeling, Skye?' asked Josh.

The accusation implied by 'negated' wouldn't win me sympathy, while 'despair' might suggest clinical depression and the need for drug therapy. A vague, jaded umbrella term would be safest. 'I feel pain.'

Zane once said that the media uses negativity to attract attention, and that's what we do in this group, I mused, as I recalled the beauty of Zane's: intimacy with the earth, moon, stars and trees, our shared visions for the future. Now, the past obscured all else. But I'd come here to give the past its due. Why had my father avoided me? My eyes blurred and I blew my nose.

Josh noticed. 'Do you need attention?' he said, but I shook my head, so he turned to Zoe.

I missed sharing a magical vision of the web of life. Instead of sensing connection through planetary cycles and seasonal rhythms, we were intimately implicated in each other's neuroses and schisms. I glanced across at Morrie Bund who'd nodded off. Like my father during my mother's tirades. And then I remembered a quarrel with Zane twenty-one years earlier. You sure gave your old man an eyeful, he'd said. Come off it, I'd said, he was out to it. He was staring right up your crotch, said Zane, didn't you notice the smile on his face? I don't know why I'd gone to my parents' with nothing on under my skirt. Had Zane been feeling me up in the car? But while my mother nattered I had seen my father smiling — as dreamily as if he'd drifted *away. That's insane, I said, he can't even look me in the eye. Your old man's more cunning than he lets on, said Zane.*

I'd thought he was projecting. No man, however distant, escaped Zane's jealousy.

Scrunched oil-colour tubes, spent glaze-medium tins and torn rags strew the paint-spattered floor, interspersed with Coke cans, crumpled paper bags, odd socks and Mars Bar wrappers. I recline undraped, as they say in the business, on the rumpled drape hiding an ancient foam mattress as dust motes cavort in the sunlight spilling through grimy windows. Jake crouches over mammoth sheets of weighty acid-free paper, the knees of his jeans worn through so oils and pastels encrust his knees, as well as his nose, knuckles, forelock and fingertips. He smells of mineral turps and sweat and a sweet yet sour musky mustiness. So *this* is a famous artist, the fabled beast I once longed to be? I can't help but feel that I could paint better, and with a lot less squalor and fetor. What's the big deal? He's just working bigger, using artists'-quality pigments. When I was at tech, males tended to paint on a larger scale. As a rough rule of thumb, the less articulate the man, the vaster the canvas. And Jake went to tech. We had some of the same teachers, most of them men. It seems Jake's found success by following in their footsteps. I've often wondered what it might be like — to be a man.

And a few nights ago I had what amounts to an insight. Zane and I went to the cinema to see a kung fu flick — he's most partial to martial arts, animation and sci-fi — and during the screening he started to touch me, which felt fine at the time; I'd long since lost the plot, due to indistinct subtitles. Anyway, what happened next blew my mind. Somehow our polarities swapped places. A masculine urge throbbed between my thighs. I'd never felt so one-pointed, powerful, uncomplicated. And Zane became wholly receptive, like a socket as opposed to a plug. The reversal persisted even after we left the cinema and strolled, hand in hand, through Chinatown. When I tried to talk about it he said he'd experienced it before, but not in a very long while.

When I try to describe the sensation to Jake, he doesn't discount it, yet I sense he's jealous. He says Zane's using me. I retort that I'm using Zane. Why try to explain that I'm still in love? Even Zane doubts it.

Each Friday at two when I enter Jake's studio, it's the same. I stand on the small semicircle of uncluttered floor beside the mattress and shed my shoes first, then my jeans and knickers. Before I can even unbutton my shirt, Jake begins his preparatory ritual. He kneels in front of me as I strip off, plants his mouth on my crotch and tongues my clit. The first time he did it I freaked and resisted; until I realised he had his own limit. So now I just lie back, thrust my hips forwards and fantasise until I come, by which time Jake's ejaculated into his old, paint-stained Levis. Once that's done, he's ready to load up his brush and express pleasure on paper. That his work's self-indulgent goes without saying; at least, not to him. As long as his dealer keeps dropping by to take away those that look finished, he has just enough space to stretch more canvas and explode his ego all over it; and I'm paid enough, with the massage job I scored via Mel, to not need the dole.

Sometimes I feel guilty. Jake's wife has no idea what we do. Still, my role's very different, as his muse and confidante; I'd never dream of trying to fill her shoes. I prefer being worshipped, though it's not really *me*, but Jake's ideal of Woman. None of his paintings ever bear the faintest resemblance to me.

Zane, on the other hand, wanted to take some shots of me for his 'altar'. A contrast to Farrell, that narcissist who'd enshrined his own image. I hadn't known Zane could take photographs on top of his other talents and, as it turns out, he can't. He just took nude polaroids — asked me to part my lips: 'Your fanny's so pretty!' — which turned out far from flattering. The centrefolds in the magazines flanking Jake's toilet look better. But I guess I should be pleased that Zane chose to use pics of me. Not that I've seen his altar. There's stuff we don't share now. We agreed to respect each other's freedom by not asking too many questions. Zane said he's not sleeping with anyone else and I said neither am I. Jake and I don't meet outside work so it wasn't even a white lie. I'm not in love with Jake, nor he with me. To

196

tell Zane that a paint-smeared, cum-stained art-world star likes to go down on me routinely would make it sound more significant than it is.

I haven't even told Stella. Only Ramon, who thinks it's a hoot. The more I can show him that other men find me desirable, the safer he'll feel (when he's ready to explore that hetero urge he once confessed to) desiring me. I didn't say it's *him* I fantasise about while Jake's eating me out.

'We need to talk,' says Stella, when I walk in, 'about your training.' She's seated at the round table, sipping a cup of tea, her long, black hair plaited and coiled about her head like a snake. The masks on the wall all look as implacable as their maker.

I agree, feeling as if Mum's just sprung me sneaking in from an illicit date.

'You've let your work slide lately, Skye. You should have advanced more by now.' She shakes her head and shrugs. 'At this rate you can forget about initiation.'

I glance up, at a loss. Why would the gods and goddesses give a toss about Stella's schedule? Don't they come when I need them?

'I'm sorry.' Indeed. Sorry to be Stella's only pupil. Not only is it lonely; she seems to expect so much. Which reminds me: Teresa's due back soon.

'What do you want to get out of magic?' Her tone's short and sharp.

Terror-struck, I search for a truthful response. None that leap to mind seem acceptable: psychic self-defence, something to push against, a sense of belonging.

'Self-knowledge,' I say, 'and tools I can use to help heal the planet.' That's where I was at when I first met Zane — profoundly inspired. But by the time Stella arrived on the scene *I* needed help to heal. If she'd offered to teach me braille — or morse code or Martian — I'd have agreed.

'Maybe you'd make more progress,' she says, 'if *you* had a student.'

My eyes dart to the assembled masks as if they could speak on my behalf. 'I don't know if I'm ready for the responsibility.' Nor if I'll ever be.

'That's one of your problems, Skye.' She sighs. 'Always underestimating yourself. That's what I thought when I met your last date, what's-his-name. Yes, Ash. I'm sure it was for the best that he shot through. His energy was quite dark. Now you've got him out of your system perhaps you can concentrate again.'

Perhaps I could if his wisdom hadn't rung truer for me than hers does. 'Working three and a half days a week,' I explain, 'leaves fuck-all time to do rituals.'

'You'll have more time without the distraction of flying lessons.' She smiles as I stiffen. 'Didn't Luke tell you? He won't be coming around for a while. It's a trial separation. And as for ritual, it can only enhance your work. So that's what we'll do. An invocation. We'll ask Borus to help you find a job that gives you responsibility.'

Whatever you say, I think. Let's invoke the north wind — and I'll ask Borus to huff and puff and blow you away.

'Do you want to stay the night?' Ramon invites.

We were wending our way home from a party when rain began to fall, so we're sheltering under a rotunda roof.

'Okay,' I say, feigning casualness. 'It'll save taxi fares, I guess.'

'It'll be fun!' He reaches for his ghetto-blaster. 'A pyjama party!'

Talking Heads's 'Psycho Killer' blares out into the night. Despite having danced for hours already, I whirl and twirl to the beat. Ramon's rapt attention lends wings to my feet. When the rain lets up we wander back to his flat along wet streets.

'How's it going with zany Zane?' he asks, once we're cosy in bed; he on his sprung single mattress, me on the sofa cushions, inches away.

In such close proximity to Ramon, the last thing I feel like discussing is Zane. But I end up relating a conversation as we lie side by side in the dark.

'He says, "Are you seeing anyone?" and I say, "Not exactly", so then he says, "So you *are*", so I say, "Just Jake, who I model for", and he says —'

'Did you fuck him?'

'No, I told you, he just —'

'I know what you told me,' Ramon says, 'but I'm doing Zane, okay?' He clears his throat. 'Did you *fuck* him?' he says in a rougher, gruffer voice.

'No,' I say. 'I'd only fuck you. He just eats me out before he paints me.'

'Well alright, then,' Ramon concedes. 'As long as he knows his place.'

'He knows how to bring me off,' I say, 'and that's what turns him on.'

'Is *Zane* seeing anyone?' Ramon cuts in. 'Anyone *else*, I mean?'

'No, he'd been seeing a woman my age called Jade, but now they're just friends, he said.'

'So apart from the interrogation, it's okay?'

I'm unsure of how to answer. Not wanting to deter Ramon if there's half a chance of romance with him, I settle for, 'Better than before, now we're seeing each other less' — it's true — and we wish each other sweet dreams. I can't tell if Ramon's gone to sleep, though his breathing sounds peaceful. The temptation to edge across onto his mattress suddenly seems irresistible. But without even a trace of a come-on, I can invent no justification. Maybe I learned my lesson from Damian?

Yet I feel madly aroused. And Ramon can't be unconscious; his breathing's too quiet. So I don't dare masturbate. Instead, I resort to an exercise Stella taught me: reviewing the day's events in reverse. Undoing karma, she calls it. I get as far back as sneaking a peek at Ramon taking off his tank top.

When I wake, to a fine, warm spring Sunday morning, he's propped on one elbow, watching me.

'Time to do our yoga,' he says, running a hand through his tousled hair.

His dedication impresses me. I never do any outside of class. We spend less than an hour tying ourselves in knots, but linger for longer than usual in corpse pose. Then Ramon puts the kettle on and starts washing up.

'Have you noticed yet' — he's standing at the sink in his singlet and long johns — 'that I haven't had one cigarette since we left the party twelve hours ago?'

'And how many seconds?' I joke. The yoga's teased out the kinks those cushions put into me, but I'm looking forward to brushing my teeth.

'Skye, don't you get it? I'm a different man around you.'

'You're good for me, too.' I explain that Stella's getting a bit militaristic.

'I've got a great idea,' he says. 'Why don't we set up a yoga household?'

'You mean *live together*?' Did I die in my sleep and go to heaven? How much karma did I undo?

'We'd need two or three others to keep the rent low, non-smokers and vegetarians, but we could teach yoga at home. With a big enough front room,' he enthuses, 'I could teach dance, too. And you'd have a permanent exhibition space.'

'You haven't seen my art,' I say.

'I've seen you dance, and you're inspirational. We could do group meditations to heal the world. You could lead them. Just imagine! All of us visualising peace and the ozone layer healing and enough clean water and food to share around.'

My mouth hangs open. Just as Zane's become more feminine in my eyes, Ramon's begun to sound more like Zane. What's going on? Have they swapped polarities?

'So are you in?' His grin's almost manic. 'To begin with, we need a goal. Let's set up our yoga household when we get back from vipassana.'

'That's only three months away.' What'll I tell Stella? But I'm stoked that Ramon's decided to come. I doubt I'd have gone on my own again.

'My lease here runs out before the retreat starts,' he says. 'Maybe we should find a place earlier.'

'Maybe.' Though I still can't believe he wants to, if we do that he'll be living with me by the time Mel gets back. Won't she be surprised!

200

'You're my guardian angel, Skye.' He gazes solemnly into my eyes. 'With you nearby I feel clear and strong. At times, I can almost see myself living the lifestyle of a celibate monk.'

I will myself to smile, but it feels false. That's not what I want to inspire in Ramon at all.

The sun's setting and the moon's rising over the sea when I join the others spread across the grassy slope of the headland. To avoid running into Ash on my own, I'd hoped to bring Ramon, and I thought he might enjoy an outdoor performance. But he's been partying hard. Perhaps the reality of the retreat, now less than six weeks away, has hit him. He's been looking like shit at yoga in recent days.

I hadn't seen Ash since he vanished without warning weeks ago. And yet here I am — along with most of Sydney's dance and theatre fringe. I scan the crowd for familiar faces. Down to the right, an attractive blonde catches my eye. She looks to be about my age and vaguely familiar. There's Zane, further down, to the left. I wonder idly if he's dancing much, and how many of the assembled women he's fucked. Not that I'd ever know, even if we were still lovers. Which we aren't; not since I let Jake fuck me one day, a few weeks back. Have you fucked your painter yet? Zane had asked when we'd seen each other that night. Yes, I'd told him defiantly, to hide my fear. *But it didn't feel right.* You're so destructive, Zane had accused, what'd you want to do that to him for? Due to frustrated lust stirred up by being close to Ramon, and resentment at you, Zane, even revenge, because you want to own me — not that I dared say so; nor did I object when he disowned me yet again.

Ash dances in a loincloth, his body painted red all over. Not for the first time, he looks like some pagan god, if a different one. I'm unsure of what I covet more, his affection or his freedom of expression — but twenty minutes later, when the applause and the light have died, I decide to ask him why he withdrew the former.

He's pulling a shirt and trousers on over his red skin when I approach.

201

'Hello, you,' he says as he sees me. Has he forgotten my name already? 'I can't stand and chat, I'm running late for an engagement, but I'll give you a call.'

'You don't have my number,' I say, too late. He's rushed away, still red-faced and red-handed.

Feeling abandoned, I join the straggling throng drifting down towards the beachfront. Beside me walks the blonde who sat near me on the headland.

'What did you think of that?' she says, and I realise that, like me, she's unaccompanied.

'Hard to pin down,' I say, 'still, maybe that's his appeal.' Though I'd like to skewer and roast the arsehole, out pours my grudging admiration.

'You dance too?' the blonde says, and we chat about improvisation until we find a side-street café where other fringe dance aficionados have gathered.

'I'm Skye,' I say as we slide into a booth.

'Not the Skye who Zane was seeing?'

'Yes.'

She grins. 'I'm Jade.'

'No!'

'Fraid so.' We start to giggle.

'Do you still see him?'

'No. Do you?'

'No. When did *you* stop?'

'A few weeks ago. He got jealous of another man in my life.'

'How often had you been seeing each other?'

'Three times a week, four max. You?'

'Same.' We nod in unison.

'Were you lovers?'

'Yes. You too?'

'Yes. He swore you weren't.'

'Funny. That's what he said about you.'

We order coffees, then move on to some serious cross-referencing of the discrepancies in the stories he's told each of us. Next, we target his possessiveness, control tactics, sexual style and reputation. Disbelief and anger alternate as we bond.

We're laughing riotously over our coffees when Zane walks by outside. I see him first and nudge Jade.

'What'll we do — hide?' I say.

'Why not confront him?' She's staring at Zane when he looks in and spots us. Jade nudges me back. 'Let's just laugh at the prick.'

As we throw back our heads and guffaw, I see Zane clench his jaw, turn away and speed up.

Guy laughs along with me as we start on a new pot of tea. Stella's away and I haven't seen Luke for days, so the flat's all ours tonight. Now the motorbike's no longer our focus, I feel like I'm starting to get to know Guy. He's a hardcore sci-fi fan, and knows stuff I'd only ever heard from Zane's lips; which makes me wonder how much of Zane's arcane wisdom comes from science fiction.

Stella keeps intimating that Guy might like to be more than my friend. I haven't told her I'm stuck on Ramon or that I plan to move in with him, but her matchmaking's maddening, so I said Guy's too straight for me, too down-to-earth and ordinary. That might be just what you need, Skye, she said, an ordinary guy.

'We hit it off straightaway,' I tell Guy. 'Jade's not just pretty, she's witty and funny. That's one good thing about Zane — his taste in women.'

'So I've gathered' — Guy smiles at me over the table — 'and I've only seen one example.'

'I've met a few.' I blush. Does Guy desire me? I'm surprised that the possibility's never entered my mind. He's strong and handsome in a stolid sort of way. Yet I desired Zane because he's not chained to the 'real' world — he took me beyond it when our paths first crossed — and then I clung out of fear that I'd get lost on the other side, or even just find myself stranded here without a guide.

'Zane lacks the knack,' Guy says, 'of compartmentalising the facts of his life.'

I glance at him sharply. *The facts of life?* Was that a sexual innuendo, or are compartments breaking down in my mind?

'It's all relative, I guess.' I sniff and the air flows in like syrup, viscous and dense compared to the lightness of my head. As Guy jokes about us having relations, I hope he means kin, not sex, and wonder why I feel stoned when we haven't smoked. It can't be the tea either, I made it myself; though didn't I leave the room for a moment? Now my thoughts have begun to resemble my mother's.

'We're all related,' I say, taking some of the onus off my mother. Air trickles thickly from my nostrils. 'All descended from Eve.' Does that sound sexist? 'And Adam, naturally.'

'And it doesn't stop there if you buy the theory of evolution.' His languid inhalation assures me the air's transforming to treacle.

'No.' I hope he doesn't think I'm a closet bible-basher. 'We'll never stop evolving.' As I gaze into his eyes, the gap between us begins to gain substance. Or have I begun to lose mine? Before I can ask if Guy knows why empty space might start to solidify, he rises from his seat and steps towards me. That seems like some sort of answer, so I stand and go to him and our arms simultaneously reach for each other.

So still we hover, within our embrace, not a ripple beyond pulse and breath. Inhaling then, face to Guy's shoulder, I move into my breath, become it: nothing but wind whooshing through a tunnel until I soar out into light; bright blue, overarching sky. But I'm flying instead of falling.

Riding air currents high above a plateau, I see every stone, any movement in each shadow, with the eagle eyes in my feathered skull. Three pyramids lie below me, one far larger than the others, and as I breathe again I'm sucked down into darkness. Though no light defines the end of the tunnel through which I'm flung, hieroglyphics line the walls and I glimpse a painted snake with three heads.

When a voice says, 'Why don't we go to bed', I find myself in a room with a round table and a piano, in the arms of a man I no longer know.

'Okay,' I say, though I'd rather return to where I've just been. As I lead Guy upstairs, I decide to give my thin futon a miss and share Stella's waterbed. No sooner than we've fallen into its rocking, rolling swells, I'm back in some subterranean passageway face to face with a black panther.

All night Guy embraces me as I shift shapes, times and spaces through a stream of unending dreams in which I sense his unseen presence, and when I wake at dawn — to lose consciousness of that fluid immensity — he stirs in the bounded realm of the waterbed too.

I'm wondering how to raise the subject of where we went and why, when the nudge of Guy's hard-on against my thigh raises another question entirely. We've just shared an awesome mystery, beyond the visions Zane triggered in me, and all without the interference of sex. But what did Guy experience? Did the earth — and the heavens — move for him? Or did he just hold me all night, holding back his desires, out of politeness?

I hug him one last time and pull away.

'Aw, you can't get up just *yet*.' His persuasive if playful caress leads me to guess he never left his body.

'Sorry' — I make waves as I sit up — 'but I've got to work today.'

TWENTY-ONE

Too Much of a God Thing

The time had come to ask myself again: What did I want from therapy? I'd been struggling just to get my barest needs met. What therapy wanted from me seemed uppermost on the group's agenda.

'Skye, we haven't heard from you for weeks,' Josh said one day. 'You seem preoccupied. Is there anything you'd care to say?' He made it sound as if I'd excluded him and not the reverse.

'Well,' I ventured, 'something happened on my way here today.' I'd been cutting across Hyde Park when a vagrant beckoned to me; yet as I passed his bench I saw that, though unshaven, he was no bum, but Ash, the dancer who'd abandoned me two decades ago. He was sorry he'd left me hanging, Ash said — sheepishly, because he'd just been left, and his ex refused contact unless he entered therapy.

To mention that he'd asked if I knew a good therapist seemed unwise; the group might react to my denial. I said that Ash's heartache brought home to me how far I'd come — to have found my life partner — and yet his performance-art career had soared, unlike mine.

'So you finally got closure,' Josh said. 'How do you feel?'

'Envious of Ash's professional success.'

'Never mind that his personal life is a mess?'

'Why do jerks who keep hurting others succeed?'

Josh sighed. 'They don't hurt us as much as symbolise those who abused us in childhood. Out of habit we go for the devil we know and struggle to change it again, but real change only occurs to the extent that we feel our old pain. Working with symbols can free us. Recognition, like Ash, has eluded you until now. But recognition's empty without intimacy.'

'I wouldn't knock it back,' said Morrie Bund. 'Why can't we have both?'

'Or either?' said Maddy. 'Isn't that what we're here to find out?'

'I don't see how I can resolve that here,' said the muso, who, like me, had been quiet for weeks. 'I want to quit work and pursue my music, but that'll mean I can't afford therapy.'

'The more you feel driven to leave,' Josh said, 'the closer you are to buried treasure, the gold of denied, repressed, old feelings. That's why it's crucial to stay when the urge to escape becomes obsessive. It's no use succeeding at music if you lose yourself in the process.'

The muso reddened. 'I've thought about that.'

'And?' Josh prompted.

'I'm ready to leave the group.'

'Are you?' Josh blinked. 'I disagree.'

'I thought as much.' The muso's face had contorted. 'But I always did feel unsupported in this group, so it's no surprise you won't support me to leave.' He stood up, strode to the office door, and let himself out with a slam.

'I feel shock,' said Maddy as his footsteps faded away.

'I feel angry,' said Morrie Bund. 'Why should he get out of paying?'

'I feel he must've held onto resentments,' said Zoe. 'He kept so quiet.'

'That's not a feeling,' Josh said. 'It's a judgement. What's the real feeling behind it?'

'I think I'm feeling abandonment pain,' said Zoe. But not for long — as usual, she'd commandeered the group's focus.

If she'd been my client I'd have sent her away to do vipassana in silence for ten days, but no-one was asking me.

'Do we know of anyone who's got better?' Morrie Bund asked.

Tell me a story, Daddy, the others' faithful eyes seemed to say.

Josh laughed. 'So you want to see my references?' He waved a hand around the room. 'Here they are. You're all getting *better. But this work requires a lifelong commitment. It can't be rushed.'*

Morrie Bund looked unimpressed. 'I get that no-one's in a rush.' Having joined the group before I had, he, too, appeared to be taking his time.

Therapy, it struck me, was not unlike a drug, Josh's prescriptions aside. You tried it, hoping to enhance your life, but it soon took over, until you couldn't function without the consent of your inner child. I felt tempted to follow in the muso's footsteps. But I didn't want to leave any loose ends.

'My flatmates are so self-destructive, Skye,' moans Ramon for the umpteenth time, 'but when you move in we'll turn the TV room into a meditation temple.'

As we rattle along in a nonsmoking carriage bound for the Blue Mountains, I try to dismiss my resentment that he went and rented a house without me. He's saved me the upstairs bedroom with a balcony overlooking the street. I can hardly wait to get back and see it. At least his ditzy flatmates won't be joining us on the retreat. Not that I've met them yet, but they smoke cigarettes as well as dope. Still, they helped Ramon pay the bond. With his old lease about to expire, he ran out of time to consult me.

'If you last the distance,' I promise him, 'you won't know yourself.'

He grins at me uncertainly and I wonder how well he knows himself now. 'Those poor wayward girls.' He sighs. 'What they need is a positive same-sex role model like you, while they're still so impressionable. They're only twenty-two.'

'How old are *you*?' I ask, though I know. On his last birthday he said he'd turned twenty-three.

'Twenty-*four*.' He makes it sound ancient.

Strange. Did he lie before? 'Like me.'

'Your spiritual influence will transform the whole household,' he goes on. 'We can even do some exorcisms or healing rituals.'

'Ten days of no smoking, drinking or drugging will give you more spiritual influence,' I tell him. Now might be the right time to own up, while he's a captive audience. 'I did a healing ritual to help you stop smoking,' I admit, 'more than six months ago, just before your shingles broke out.'

Midafternoon, midsummer sunlight beats down on the bush rushing past the window. Yet cold beads of sweat collect in my armpits as I watch his face cloud over.

He searches mine like he's waiting for the punchline. 'Are you serious?'

I nod. Has he forgotten he asked for my help?

'So it was you who brought that on?' His eyes and jaw have hardened and the red blotches dappling his face because he's hung-over have darkened.

I feel as if I'm seeing him in a new light; or is it the other way round?

'I didn't give you the shingles, if that's what you're thinking,' I say. 'That was a stress-related symptom of resisting your feelings.' I wish he'd stop looking at me that way.

'Time to spend a penny.' He jumps up. 'I'll be right back,' he says, seeing my dismay.

I watch the shadows of low-slung clouds sliding over tree-covered slopes. What's he up to, one last fag in the WC? He can't really think I've hexed him? Okay, so he missed sex for a few days. In a way, the rash did him a favour. Zane called me names for humouring Jake, but compared to Ramon I'm a vestal virgin. I've had no sex in weeks and there'll be no scope where we're going.

Here he comes. No, he's chatting to some guy at the other end of the carriage, and beckoning me to join them. I'm sorry to lose my window seat, yet relieved that he's still speaking to me.

'Skye, meet Vin,' says Ramon. 'He's headed our way.'

I greet a short man with long, wavy locks and a violin case at his side.

'Vin's done *thirteen* retreats,' Ramon says and flops down opposite him.

'I keep coming back for boosters,' Vin says. 'It's harder to practise at home.'

210

'I know. So many distractions.' I sit next to Ramon, facing backwards.

'So you're an old student,' Vin says, grinning.

'Veteran of one course, but it saved my life. Really.'

'Let's hope it saves mine,' says Ramon.

'Vipassana's not without its dangers,' says Vin, and proceeds to regale us with stories of meditators who didn't make it. 'I've never heard of students dying, but one freaked out after five days and crawled away and got found beside the railway line.'

Ramon shivers. 'Skye never mentioned the risks.'

'It's as safe as any process can be,' says Vin, 'unless a person's unstable.'

Ramon rolls his eyes back into his skull and contrives to laugh kookily. His red-blotched skin and darned, white pyjama shirt conspire to enhance the effect. As the three of us laugh together, I forget to mind sharing Ramon. Two charming men beats one, and soon I might meet dozens.

'Please cover your shoulders,' a course facilitator whispers in my ear as I walk from the main hall to the marquee. 'Bare skin will distract other meditators.'

I'm wearing just a sarong, a contrast to my last spell here. Despite the retreat's discreet dress code, I'm sexually aware of every meditator, but none more than poor wild-eyed Ramon, who looks like he's climbing the walls. Would they have put him in a men-only dorm if they knew how distracting he'd find it, or confined him to the male side of the hall? Yet he appears, from the corners of my eyes, to be applying himself; so I feel, besides shame at craving and clinging, as if he's secretly mine.

Scenes flood my mind, growing ever barmier in the balmy heat. One features Ramon in his tuxedo pants and best shirt, clicking his castanets, with an altar behind and me beside him in a ruffled white dress and a lace mantilla. Red and white flowers (roses, tulips and lilies) surround us, while the song we once sang together — 'Stand By Me' — plays at our wedding.

If he's meant to be into men, how come he hasn't found a steady?

211

I've resisted the possibility that Ramon could be my soul mate, believing Zane must be, because we'd shared visionary highs. But after the mystical trip with Guy I'm questioning my definition. Ramon, more than anyone, has faith in me, and doesn't just want me for sex. That he seems not to want me for sex at all might change in time. In a short time from now we'll be living together — perhaps happily ever after.

Speaking of time, there's the gong and I haven't begun on anapana.

Over the next few days I notice Ramon roaming up and down looking stir crazy, but after the fifth he's still with us so I know he's going to stay. At times I pray for each hour of silent suffering to bring us closer together, but mostly I just pray for equanimity. How perverse — my desire to find freedom from desire.

Wandering through the bush after lunch once, I find a chunk of quartz, red at one end shading through to white at the other. The quintessential symbol, I think, of my existential dilemma — lust vs. chastity, risk vs. blank canvas, desire vs. neutrality. I put the bipolar rock in my pocket as if it could magically balance me.

The next day, the ninth, I feel I'm finally getting into the swing of vipassana. Most gross sensations have given way to subtle ones, and I've even begun to detach from fantasies, which hadn't revolved solely around Ramon. Thoughts of Zane still arise frequently. Yet today they pass away freely and I revel in the sense of release. But best of all, sitting cross-legged in the main hall not long after lunchtime, I slip into a state I have no words for.

When I return, my attempts to define where I went feel futile. I can't grasp it with my mind. A more complete sense of nothingness, perfect emptiness, I've never known. It's the antithesis of the abyss, the limbo that's claimed me before; unlike a black hole, it's *whole* — pure lightness, the absence of limiting gravity. In the wake of this moment — or minutes? — of non-existence, I float through the next few hours. At last I believe I've discovered the secret to why anyone would meditate. All that bum-numbing, ache-making, dead-boring sitting still does more than help you unwind — apparently it can dissolve your mind, and with no negative side effects. I can't wait to tell Ramon, though it may be hard to convey. If this had occurred on my first course I'd have come back sooner. Then I catch myself. Where's my detachment? I'm supposed to let everything pass away.

Conversation explodes as we stream from the hall on the tenth day. A tall, beautiful brunette turns to me and says, 'Hi, I'm Mona, but I don't expect you to remember. I just had to see if my voice still works.'

'Your voice works great,' I say, testing mine. I have to raise it to hear myself as others rise in a flood tide.

By the time we sit down to eat, Ramon's attracted an audience. 'I nearly ran away on day three and four and five,' he's saying. 'And the snoring in the dorm!' He does a piggish impersonation. 'But the hardest part was finding the willpower not to stretch or do yoga. And *then* — I lost track of the days but it must have been the sixth or seventh — I smelt smoke when I went to the gents one night. I nearly broke down and begged for a drag but then I'd have blown Noble Silence.'

A buxom woman hovers close by him, hanging on his every word as he raves, but Ramon keeps eyeing the tall youth beside me, no doubt taken with his loose grace. I'm intrigued that he hasn't spoken yet, as if he's content to observe instead.

After our last, loving-kindness meditation, the exodus begins. Ramon and I linger, with others we've met today, in the marquee.

'I know a waterfall we could walk to and back from in an afternoon,' says Vin, the violinist from the train. Mona the tall brunette's wandered over, making him look even shorter. 'It's best to re-enter the outside world as gently as possible.' He smiles up at her. 'And a bushwalk's a good way to absorb the shock.'

'Let's us walk then,' the buxom woman says. 'You will come, Ramon?'

'I don't know.' Ramon turns to the tall youth. 'What do you think, Marty?'

'A walk sounds cool.' Marty throws me a look I can't read. His small, shapely skull and deep tan remind me of an African tribesman and his wide, silver-blue eyes evoke alien worlds. No wonder Ramon's entranced. Alongside even his dancer's physique, Marty's an athletic demigod.

'I'm hanging out to stretch my legs,' I say.

We don't have to walk far to lose ourselves, if not our way, in the bush. A well-defined track winds past a lookout. Mona — whose remote smile reminds me of da Vinci's icon — appears to have fallen into step, by shortening hers, with Vin. Baba, the busty woman, bounds along beside Ramon. He's already a head taller than her, yet she's talking hers off, while he keeps turning his to see what Marty and I are up to. We're immersed in talk of past lives and shamanism. Marty asks if I've ever met a shaman, so I tell him tales of Zane, in between identifying bird calls. As we reach the waterfall Ramon throws off his shoes and socks.

'I feel so at one with nature,' he warbles, wading into a shallow pool. 'This is paradise. Smell the mountain air! I'm cured of smoking. Viva vipassana! Yippee!'

If he's trying to get Marty's attention he needn't bother. Marty's doing what looks like chi gung on a flat patch of rock. Baba kicks off her sandals, hoicks up her skirt and splashes in after Ramon.

I walk over to the falls. They look just like a painting I did to represent the watery element. Clouds of fine spray fly heavenwards and float down in a mist as I scramble up onto a ledge beside the roaring wall of water. I resonate my voice and the sound soars out across the mountains, bouncing off their ancient faces, intoxicating me with its power. I keep on calling, longer and louder each time.

'Skye!' screams Ramon from below.

I see shock on his face just as the cascade, somehow swollen in volume, knocks me off my platform. Thighs and buttocks scraping rock amid the surging torrent, I hurtle, half stumbling, half sliding, to the bottom.

214

My heart resounds in my head like the falls on the stone. No bones broken, I guess, as I catch my breath and step out of the pool. I'm soaked and shaking all over. Apart from Ramon and Marty, no-one noticed my tumble. They're still spellbound by the sounds of their own voices. Ramon rushes over as I plonk myself down in the sun.

'You'd better watch out, Skye,' he chides. 'The falls just taught you a lesson. You shouldn't have called up the water spirits.' He regards me the same way he did on the train, with a mixture of anger and fear. Then his eyes relent. 'You need to be more careful,' he says in his most paternal voice.

Marty, who's been listening, eyes me curiously.

By the time all six of us board a Sydney-bound train, the sun's setting.

'I'd invite you all home,' Ramon says, 'but my housemates might be stoned or pissed and I couldn't bear to be near a blaring TV while I'm feeling so sensitive.'

'We can all go back to my place,' I say. 'My flatmates will still be away so whoever wants to can stay the night.'

Unanimous approval greets my offer. We opt to give dinner a miss — as we've done, ten nights running, anyway — rather than brave an inner-city café, and walk from the station to Stella's.

'Oh my God! Look at these!' shrieks Ramon when I let us in and hit the light switch. 'They aren't meant to be death masks, are they?'

Mona sits on the piano stool and begins to caress the keys as if she's hearing the notes for the first time, while Marty does a circuit of the crystals, as entranced by their facets as if he's on acid. I put the kettle on to make tea. The same moment Baba bustles off to the bathroom, Ramon steals into the kitchen.

'My God, Skye,' he hisses under his breath, 'this Baba dame's driving me batty. She won't leave me alone for a moment. Baba Yaga's her real identity — a *vicked* Russian *vitch*! You have to make sure that we sleep in different parts of the house. Tell the women they must all sleep upstairs and the men can stay down here.'

As I fill the teapot, feeling amused by his fix if not by his childish notions of witches, Vin tunes up his violin. Then Baba returns, snaps her fingers and reaches for one of the masks — Aphrodite, goddess of pleasure. Daring Ramon with her eyes, she seizes it and puts it on. Ramon can't resist a challenge, apparently. I must remember that. He lifts down raven-feathered Hades and hides his own face. I suppose I should tell them to replace the masks on Stella's behalf, but I feel like I'm stoned.

At that, Mona rises from the piano and reaches for the only red mask. Though she has no way of knowing, she's chosen Pan. She hands the mask to Vin, who hesitates.

'Go on,' she says. 'Try it on.' And, once he has, she selects Diana. The Madonna-like harmony of the blue mask bears some resemblance to Mona's face.

Then she sits at the piano again and starts to sing a wordless refrain. As Vin begins a violin accompaniment, Baba starts to sway. With the mask of the goddess hiding her face, her curves can speak unimpeded. Not to be outdone, Ramon breaks into a fierce rhythm, clicking his fingers like castanets and keening, framed by the arched kitchen doorway. Baba approaches and circles him, hips shaking. I feel like I'm watching a mongoose and a cobra. Vin cranks his violin and Mona wails like a dark, unhinged diva. Marty takes another mask from the wall.

'This one's yours,' he tells me.

'Persephone?' But I accept it. 'Which one's you?'

He puts on the Hermes mask that Ash wore last, then flows into a chi gung sequence. Though I haven't worn Stella's new mask before, its energy feels familiar. I let its edgy mood and the gypsy strains compel my feet. Movement has never stirred such bliss in me — the fulfilment of excess stillness? Across my whirling vision flashes Baba bent on seducing Ramon, who looks like he could cheerfully kill her. The guise of the god of magic becomes Marty, whose sinuous moving meditation continues even as the music winds down. The others have hung the masks back up willy-nilly. As I try to return them to where Stella put them, laughter floats down the stairs. Ramon's brushing his teeth at the kitchen sink, so Baba must be in the bathroom.

216

'Can I sleep with you, Skye?' Marty's removed his mask. 'Just *sleep*, okay? No funny business.'

'That sounds good.' Relieved, I head upstairs to change my sheets. Sure enough, Vin and Mona have found Stella's waterbed. When the cat's away? I stick my head in and say, 'Sweet dreams — just don't leave any signs of your stay.'

They blow me a kiss and fall upon one another. I close Stella's door. Then I remember that Ramon and Baba will need some sheets. Downstairs, Baba's sipping cold tea. She's already set up the sofa bed. Ramon's vanished into the bathroom so I fetch her some sheets and pillowslips.

Marty's sprawled out on my thin futon when I return. 'Ramon's invited me to stay at his house as long as I like, in his spare room,' he says.

'Really?' I say. '*I* was supposed to move into it in the next few days.'

'I'd rather stay with you,' Marty says. 'Ramon's friendly but he stares a lot.'

'He fancies you. Don't tell me you haven't noticed?'

'Me?' Marty wrinkles his nose. 'I thought he had a thing for you.'

'No way — he's gay. We're just friends. In fact, at the risk of sounding paranoid, I've noticed he's been avoiding me to an absurd degree since before the retreat began.'

Marty groans. 'That's 'cause he doesn't know how to show his feelings for you.'

Unconvinced, I turn off the light and stretch out beside him, and we talk ad infinitum about the visions he saw when he wore the mask and my all-night out-of-body odyssey with Guy.

'That's a sign,' Marty says. 'The appearance of an eagle points to a shamanic vocation. I read where a woman merged with an eagle and then she began to see spirits. Her initiation lasted seven years. That time frame's traditional.'

'Really?' I whisper, in no rush to see more signs, spirits or elementals.

Marty's snoring.

Ramon's first out of bed in the morning. When I descend to go to the toilet he's teaching Baba Yaga yoga. 'It's important to have lots of room to do these poses in,' he tells her. 'Not just for your earthly body but all around your aura.' She looks confounded yet hopeful, ten feet away from him, teetering on one leg.

Vin and Mona rise last and then we all sit down to breakfast together: muesli with powdered soy milk found in the cupboard and mixed nuts from Baba's backpack.

'Shouldn't we all meditate for an hour?' says Ramon. 'The teacher told us to practise morning and night.'

Baba looks willing, but Mona and Marty roll their eyes.

'It's okay to miss a day now and then,' Vin says. 'Getting too attached to it misses the point.'

After he and Mona hug each of us and write down their numbers, they leave together, with the secret of how they scored the romance the rest of us crave. Baba, I sense, won't want to leave unless Ramon comes too, while Ramon's dying to escape her clutches, yet loath to depart without Marty. I've told Marty he's welcome to stay a few days till he goes home to Adelaide.

Finally Marty breaks the deadlock by saying he's got business to do, and takes off with only his money belt, upon which Ramon makes an excuse to leave, remembering some unpaid bill, and Baba insists on accompanying him to the bus stop.

Alone at last, I start to pack so I can move out as soon as Stella gets back, which means giving notice at the last minute, a slip-up: my rents will overlap. But I couldn't face telling Stella sooner. I know she won't be happy. Which reminds me.

Looking at the masks now, I see what's wrong. I'd reversed Hades and Persephone — so I replace them where they belong.

·TWENTY-TWO·

If You Lie Down With Dogmas,

You Will Get Up With Philosophies

Writing things down helps me to remember them. I began at age three, while my mother was breaking down. Though I didn't yet have words to document that, the fear — hers and mine — wrote itself into my nervous system using the language of reflex.

A phone call woke me late one night. I let my machine take it. I'd told Zoe not to ring after ten. She must have forgotten. Now, instead of invading my dreams, she was actively dragging me out of them. I wrote down the time and her message then took the phone off the hook. But I knew Zoe wouldn't let me off the hook.

Sure enough, she confronted me at the next group session. 'Skye, I need to come clean about how I've been avoiding you.'

'You do? I mean, you have?' I scratched my head. I'd braced myself for the sort of attack that, however childish, might still make sense.

'I've called everyone in the group for support except you.'

'You did call me, around one a.m. But any time after ten is too late.'

'I'm sorry, Skye. I didn't know. The others are okay with it.'

A few of them nodded — nocturnal or brainwashed?

'I've never said it would be okay with me.'

'I hear that. But I felt hurt when you didn't call back.'

'Skye can't hurt *you, Zoe,' said Josh. 'You feel* pain *that she didn't return your call.'*

'I figured you'd find someone else,' I told Zoe. I wanted to say, this is getting absurd. But Josh would say that was my shame talking.

'I wanted to talk about us,' Zoe said.

219

'That's not what I heard.'

'I said so in the message I left.'

'No, you said you had "stuff" going on.'

'Stuff to do with us,' she shot back. 'Like I said.'

'Not to my machine. I can still remember your message.'

'I know what it said.' Her gaze withered me. 'I worded it carefully. I feel like I have to tiptoe around you or you'll go off like a loaded gun. Like my mother,' she added shrewdly.

'You said, "I feel fear at ringing so late but I really need someone to hear my stuff." Those were your exact words,' I said.

'The exact words aren't important,' Josh said. 'It's okay not to remember. Zoe's been trying to tell you that it was you she wanted to talk to.'

Zoe beamed gratitude at him. 'I feel heard.' She fired a smug smile at me.

'I heard you fine. But, like Josh says, it's co-dependent to try to mind-read.'

'You don't have to prove you're right,' said Josh. 'It's okay to get it wrong.'

I felt tempted to pull out my diary. But I'd kept track of group dynamics for my sake, not so I could be invalidated, told to trace 'triggers' back to their source. You're no more than the sum of your parents, Josh had said. No more than the sum of your past. In the others' eyes his faults were just triggers, while he was a coveted father figure.

'What makes you so sure that I'm wrong?' I said.

'I don't care either way,' Josh said. 'Your defensiveness is my concern.'

'I feel as if you're negating my reality.'

'That's not a feeling, Skye. It's an accusation. It sounds to me as if you're feeling strong shame.'

'Now you're trying to interpret my reality,' I said.

'You're raging over your fear,' he said. 'It's okay to feel it.'

So why won't you feel your fear, I thought, of what I symbolise? Zane had always despised what he called my critical side. Naive young girls had done more for his ego — like Zoe, *who'd grown up only to go into orbit around Josh. I looked away.*

'Look at us, Skye,' Josh urged. 'You're safe here.'

'I'm angry that you denied my reality.'

'That's not healthy anger. It's rage. Some feedback might help,' he said in his most forbearing tone. 'Are you open to it?'

'Sure.' I shrugged. 'Why not.'

'I thought they were competing,' said Maddy, scared to take any side but Dad's.

'Talk to Skye,' Josh told her. 'The feedback's not for me.'

'Sorry I didn't follow all that. I was dozing,' Morrie Bund said. He'd begun to take antidepressants 'for insomnia'.

'I switch off when you get defensive,' Take-it-away Man told me. Trust him — or his dick? — to side with Zoe.

For the rest of the session I sat in stunned silence. Why hadn't I told them I'd transcribed Zoe's message word for word in my diary? To avoid sounding like the anal-retentive para-noiac I was. Or worse, like my mother, driven to win at any cost. Yet why should I give a toss how I sounded? The others only listened to Josh.

At the session's end we rose to form a circle, holding hands as always. Standing on Josh's right, I felt a current flow from his hand to mine, and from my right hand to Morrie Bund's left one. Just as in magical rites, we formed a circuit and my heart opened. But a dense ball filled my throat, like the clapper in a bell forbidden to peal.

As the others farewelled Josh and filed out, I fled to the ladies. Though they'd given me the shits, I didn't want to miss the post-mortem, so I caught them up downstairs where they stood talking. I felt invisible in the twilight until Maddy spied me. 'Do you want a hug?' she said.

When I gave her what I thought she wanted — a sign that I'd age-regressed — she said, 'Your heart's thudding so hard it feels like it might burst out of your chest.'

The others had settled on the usual coffee bar. Morrie Bund undressed me with his eyes. Had medication suppressed his shy-ness? 'I'll give you girls a ride there,' he said.

'Yes, take us for a ride,' said Maddy, claiming the front seat like Mum, so I sat in the back, and Dad pulled out into the street.

'Look at that.' He pointed up as he drove.

A pair of runners hung by their laces from the power line.

'What a waste,' said Maddy.

And, out of the deep, blue dusk, it descended again — the sense that everything pointed to me; that they thought I was hung up.

'How on earth would they get up there?' said Morrie Bund.

'Maybe they were thrown,' Maddy said, 'by a runner who didn't want them.'

'It's a common phenomenon.' I tried to sound nonchalant — as if I couldn't identify with being run from and feeling unwanted.

'I've never seen it before,' Morrie Bund said. 'Have you, Maddy?'

Still unwilling to take a stand, she said, 'We get what we focus on.'

What the fuck's that meant to mean, I thought. Then we turned a corner, and there, on the overhead wires, I saw another pair. And another. And another. When we swung onto the main road where nine or ten more pairs hung, I wanted to scream, but the impulse died in my throat. If Maddy was right that we got what we focused on, I'd manifested the shoes. The abyss opened.

Morrie Bund parked across the road from the coffee bar. Two lanes of bumper-to-bumper cars blocked our approach. I hung on the kerb, feeling up in the air, until Maddy steered me through the traffic. The others had taken a table inside.

'I thought you might not make it,' Zoe said as I arrived.

'So did I for a bit.' I pulled up a stool. 'It still feels touch and go.'

'I can really relate,' she said, all nods and smiles.

That she'd know what the fuck I meant seemed unlikely; if no more so than those ranks of runners. I struggled to swallow in silence.

'I'm glad you're in the group,' she said. 'I'd hate to see you run away.'

222

Maybe, I thought, I ought to try her medication. But no, this would pass — it had in the past — or so I needed to believe. 'Why?'

'I feel like I've known you for ever.' She sipped her latte and lowered her lashes. 'Well, ever since I was seventeen.'

'But you never knew Zane had a girlfriend.'

She cracked a wry smile. 'My mother told me.'

Was this disclosure a bid for closeness? She'd missed the boat, though I doubted she'd noticed. Zane had fucked her mother, too, but when? Curiosity seized me. What else from back then might Zoe know? Here we go again, I thought, she's bobbed up in another nightmare, only they're getting worse — I can't escape her by waking.

'The usual?' I heard the waitress ask above the roar in my ears.

Sugar makes me manic, I thought, flashing back twenty years. I smiled and shook my head. But I'd made a choice. It was a lucid dream. If I couldn't yet wake from it, I could at least get up and leave.

'Nothing to do with you,' I told Zoe, 'but I've got to run.'

Everyone rose to hug me farewell, obnoxiously friendly away from Josh.

I walked several blocks in the dark, heart hammering, scanning the overhead wires. Josh, I guessed, would say I was running away from intimacy, but I had to know if I'd hallucinated all those shoes. If they were still there, what could it mean — that some sporting team had competed to immortalise last season's footwear? It would mean that I was sane, if strung out. Then I saw them and started counting. Nine pairs just on the main drag. Relieved, I caught a bus home, taking care to avoid reading billboards and signs.

Over the next few days I wrote up a storm in my diary. According to Josh, wounds dealt by our parents could only be healed if we worked with their symbols — the old theory of like cures like, the homeopathic principle. But that didn't mean someone recovering from snakebite should throw themselves into a snake pit.

At the next group session I'd announce my decision to quit.

'One day you'll realise that you've made a big mistake,' says Stella, 'but you're free to choose not to evolve.'

The doorbell chimes again. 'That'll be for me,' I say.

'Well, answer it,' she says and, as I do, tells the walls, 'It's just such a shame.'

'I found a park right outside,' Damian tells me, and nods to Stella, who stares at the scar on his forehead as if it's a neon sign. 'It lights up at night,' he says.

She blushes — he's drop-dead handsome despite it — then disappears upstairs.

We load my boxes, stacked by the door, and leave for Ramon's and *my* new home. I'd never have been game to ask Damian; but, knowing no other car owners besides my father, I called his Buddhist flatmate. She'd gone trekking in Nepal — and left Damian her car keys.

'So how've you been keeping since our last encounter?' he asks at the first set of red lights.

I feel my face turning red too, and not just because I harassed him that night. More than a year later, he still appeals to me. He will to Ramon too, I expect.

'Keeping out of trouble,' I mumble.

'So you haven't seen Zane?' The lights change and the week-end traffic creeps forwards to the next set.

'Not for months.' Several weeks at least. 'Lucky Ramon's not a control freak.' Once I've moved in, I can start to relax.

Damian eyes me sideways. 'And Ramon would be your current flame?'

'He can be a hothead — but no, we're just best friends.' As I contemplate Damian, pinning my hopes on a known homosexual does seem a shame.

'Don't tell me you're single?' says Damian.

I nod, for once grateful it's true. 'And you? I mean, what've you been up to?'

'I've started seeing someone new.'

I meet his sly sidelong glance with a forced grin. 'That's great.' As if he'd go for me.

'And I've been painting houses,' he goes on, 'since I got my diploma.'

224

'How come? Didn't you get high marks for those geometric abstractions?'

His grin mocks me. 'I'm working full-time as a housepainter to pay off my home loan. Twenty-three — this old terrace, eh? It could use a fresh coat of paint.'

The whole street is chock-a-block with cars so we can't park outside. A young, male fashion victim's pushing the doorbell.

'I'll look for a spot,' Damian says, 'while you check if this is the right address.' His raised eyebrow implies he thinks not.

As he drives off I smile at the guy, whose sallow skin clashes with his pink crest. 'I'm Skye.'

'I'm Dino,' he says, as the door swings open. 'Ramon's hairdresser.'

'I thought it must be you,' cries Ramon. He's only seen Dino. 'Sorry to keep you, I overslept — you know how it is? Come on in!' Then he sees me. 'Oh, hi.' He turns back to Dino. 'Have you met Skye yet?' Dino nods. 'I'll just get the key,' he tells me, 'and then you'll have to fend for yourself. Dino's about to do my hair. Your room's the one at the top of the second flight of stairs.' He steers Dino in.

I follow them through to the kitchen, feeling invisible.

Damian's waiting on the porch when I return with the key. 'What, no welcoming committee?' He winks at me.

'Ramon's a busy boy.' I try not to care as we walk round the block.

The sight of my room takes the sting out of Ramon's lukewarm reception. It's the largest I've had since losing my warehouse space. At last I'll be able to spread out paper and canvas and really paint.

'The rest of the house lacks a lived-in feeling.' Damian off-loads a box of LPs. 'But who wouldn't be happy living in a room this big?'

Ramon fails to appear during our repeat trips up and down stairs, though bursts of manic laughter escape from the bathroom.

'Your best friend sounds like he'll be a riot to live with.' Damian's words echo in my space.

'We share the same ideals,' I say, cut by his sarcasm.

'Could've fooled me.'

'Ramon's on a spiritual path and creative to boot.' How could Damian renounce *real* painting just for the sake of putting down roots?

He nods and sets down the last box. 'Well, I'll leave you to it. If you need help again, you know where to find me.'

I want to respond that he knows where to find me, too, now, but why would he bother? He's found someone new and I've thrown in my lot with Ramon.

'Take care,' Damian says. When he goes to hug me I lunge forwards too eagerly and our foreheads collide.

'You take care too.' I walk him downstairs.

The pleasure of spreading my things around the vast room absorbs me for the remainder of Saturday afternoon. At dusk I descend to the kitchen to brew a pot of tea, and run into Ramon, whose gelled, flame-red hair startles me. It looks like his head's caught fire.

'By the way, Skye, everyone here pitches in with the house-work.' He still hasn't spoken a word of welcome.

'That's what I'm used to,' I say. 'I *am* house-trained, you know.'

'Maybe so — but those dishes have been here all afternoon and so have you.'

'None of them are mine. I haven't left my room.'

'In this house we don't just mind our own business. You need to respect the communal space.'

Before I can start washing up to placate him, a loud ring resounds down the hall.

'I'll get that,' I tell him and run for it.

Marty follows me in. 'Did you suss out if it's cool for me to stay?'

'Ramon already told you it'd be okay.'

'Marty, come in, come in!' Ramon appears, beaming, in the hall. 'Welcome to our humble abode. Can I make you a cup of herb tea?'

'No thanks.' Marty looks awkward. 'Far out — what happened to your hair?'

I return to the kitchen to make the tea I forgot when Ramon interrupted me, and bring it back to find the pair of them sitting in the spacious front room, Marty draped in an armchair, Ramon angled forwards on the couch.

'You'll have to come to yoga on Monday morning if you're still here.' Ramon launches into a litany of the benefits.

Marty listens intently. 'It sounds kind of like chi gung.'

'Maybe you could show us some chi gung moves,' Ramon says. 'You'd be into that too, wouldn't you, Skye?' He stuns me with his first genuinely friendly smile since my arrival.

I nod, relieved to see the old Ramon shining through, and realise I've been perched on the edge of my armchair.

'Maybe,' says Marty. 'But Skye and me were just headed out. Weren't we?'

'Uh, yeah.' I'm too churned up to finish my tea.

'Where to?' Ramon asks hopefully.

Marty shrugs. 'On a tour of the backstreets.'

Ramon looks disappointed. 'There's not much to see.'

'Not if you look with your eyes,' says Marty. 'It's different with *inner* sight.'

'I had a big night last night,' says Ramon. 'I might just stay in and watch TV.'

Marty and I roam the local streets. We'd forgotten about dinner, a bit of a habit since the retreat, but the smells of take-away Lebanese remind us. We continue at a stroll as we munch on falafel rolls. Marty wants to know more about magic.

'If we don't consciously honour the gods — and ritual's one way — they can possess us against our will,' I say.

'Has that ever happened to you, Skye — possession by a god?'

'Sure — but more than one god came for the ride.' I explain paranoia as a symptom of anger turned inwards, and lovesickness as an index of blocked creativity. Willpower, I tell Marty, poured from Zane's solar plexus, manipulating the world around him, while mine felt hollow. 'Like a socket he could plug into.'

'That makes you the power source,' Marty says. 'Unplug him and he'd be as useless as a TV set during a blackout.'

I'm surprised at how, with Marty, life makes sense in ways it didn't before, except through Zane's teachings. It's late when we return to 23.

'What the fuck?' Marty stops at the foot of the stairs to look at what's hanging on the wall — a crude figure made of blue-plastic-coated wire wound tightly round and round on itself.

'I'm sure Ramon said one of his flatmates goes to art school. Maybe it's a first-year sculpture project,' I say.

'One of *your* flatmates — this is your home too.' Marty takes the figure down from its nail.

'The artist must've been feeling a tad wound up,' I say, though I don't find his or her creation artistic in any way. The sight of it has set my nerves on edge.

'It looks like a voodoo doll if you ask me.' Marty starts to unwind the wire.

'Let's go upstairs.' I'm in no mood to run into Ramon and be briefed on my domestic duties.

'Can you see auras?' Marty asks, once we're lying side by side in the dark. Streetlights shine through the bare window so I can see his face faintly.

'Only with my eyes shut.' I close them.

He feels for my hands then touches his fingertips to mine, more lightly than the brush of a moth's wings. As our nerve endings connect, fields of electric hues swirl and pulsate across the insides of my closed eyelids.

'What can you see?' he urges.

'Lots of magenta and blue and silver.'

'What's magenta?'

'My favourite colour. A warm shade of purple.'

'What's it mean?'

'Your crown chakra's wide open.'

'Talk normal.'

'You're a loose cannon, but in a good way. You can inspire others —'

A slamming door derails my train of thought, followed by a harder slam.

'Sounds like Ramon went out after all,' Marty says, 'but he couldn't get no satisfaction.'

As clangs, bangs and clatters rise from the kitchen, Marty withdraws his large, splayed hands and clamps them over his ears.

'Oh no,' I confess. 'I forgot to wash up!' I wonder if it's too late to dash down.

'He wouldn't throw a tantrum over a few dirty dishes,' Marty says calmly.

'I've already been warned. He'll say I'm not pulling my weight.'

'He sounds too worked up to worry about that. You know how he's always jumping to assumptions? I bet he thinks we're up here fucking each other's brains out right now.'

'He's got an excess of red in his aura,' I say. We giggle together.

When Marty falls quiet I sense he's asleep. The racket below has subsided too; yet I lie awake, rattled by Ramon's Jekyll-and-Hyde transformation. The house reveals no evidence of the ideals we've discussed, and if he wants my help to implement them, he'll have to regain my trust. Tomorrow I'll be gone before he surfaces, to meet Teresa. Speaking of trust, I don't know why she took so long to contact me. She must have been back for more than two months. After more than two years, won't it be fun to catch up?

The presence of a dark male figure against the pale, high ceiling shocks me. I'm about to scream, but then the looming shape descends and I realise no physical means of defence can repel an astral attack. When I register the impact as sexual, a psychic reflex takes over. I concentrate all the vital force in my being into my solar plexus — as I've done in magic rituals, group and solo, countless times — and shoot forth a ball of light from my centre. With open eyes I see the shadow hurtle back — through the window, past the balcony, across the street and out of sight.

'Skye,' whispers Marty from beside me, 'what was *that*?'

I try to describe what happened, afraid he won't believe me, yet baffled as to how I could have moved enough to wake him.

'Do you think it was Ramon's astral body?' he asks.

'No — it was dense and black. His is light.'

Marty asks how I know, so I tell him about the ritual that freaked Ramon out.

'Ten days of self-denial might have affected his body of light,' Marty says. 'But it doesn't make sense that he'd resent you for trying to heal him. What if he's mad at me being here because he's got the hots for you?'

'If anything, I'd say he'd be mad at me because he fancies *you*.' That we'd each assume it's the other who's irresistible strikes me as wildly ironic. But I don't say so to Marty; don't want to make him self-conscious. I'm enjoying our closeness too much to cloud it with questions of sexual attraction.

'Or,' Marty says, 'maybe Ramon's *mad*, full stop. See, Skye, I'm not sure it matters who the intruder was. It's just lucky you knew what to do to fight him off.'

·TWENTY-THREE·

Leave and Learn

'I didn't know you were leaving,' Josh said. The admission made a welcome change from his all-knowing role, but his face said more. Though he knew better than any of them that I couldn't hurt anyone, I fancied I saw a hurt look in his eyes. A glimmer of little-boy pain. And this little girl felt a glimmer of glee — so he's not as detached as he pretends to be — followed by a guilt attack.

Long ago, when I repressed unbearable feelings, guilt became my identity. Even now, guilt's distracting voice masks the feelings behind choices. Why didn't I? *it says,* I never should have, *and* If only. *Yet the deeper truth is felt. I didn't because I was scared. I did because I was angry. Regret for what might have been feels less overwhelming to me than grief.*

I felt guilty for leaving Josh. But beneath the guilt seethed anger, as my choice revealed. I left without explanation, knowing I owed nothing and wouldn't look back, except in the sense that I'm looking back now — to find closure. I didn't need them to hear me. Only my child self had ever hoped they would, as she'd hung, up in the air, no more noticed than old shoes slung over a wire. Yet on my day of departure they turned their eyes to me enough. They all looked paranoid, even Josh. I could only guess why. That which I've ignored has been the source of my paranoia: anger, my least acceptable feeling, as mirrored by the others.

I know they shared a world view by maintaining a feedback loop, because I moved in and out of it. One foot in what they termed the real world and one foot in another, my, world. I maintained my own feedback loop through a flow of dreams, symbols and synchronicities. My world didn't exist for them, but I charted it in my diary. Sometimes I have an impulse to burn

231

this diary, even now, in case I get into trouble for what I've writ-
ten. But I no longer have to contend with a prying boyfriend like
Zane. And nothing that I write is likely to make my partner
jealous. He understands me far too well.

While I had a foot in Josh's world I could have only one in
mine. Imagine a pair of shoes dangling either side of a power
line — neither foot could reach the ground, nor would anyone
put themselves in my shoes. No-one in Josh's world stretched his
or her mind to understand me. In my world, understanding flows
from random meetings, planets and trees. It's a rhythmic, starry,
elemental, diving, seething, soaring world; not a waiting room
with walls of jargon, a ceiling on rapture and prescription door-
ways.

A cockroach scuttled across the floor just before we all said
our goodbyes. That Josh noticed, let alone stomped on it, took
me by surprise.

'Bugs are distracting,' he said, sitting back down as swiftly
as he'd risen.

Come on, admit that you feel distracted, I thought, and
explore what's behind that.

A few of them said they felt responsible for my desire to
leave. I made a little speech about needing all the help I could
get. I've never known when to move on, I confessed, sometimes
I've had to be forced out. I couldn't even leave my mother's
womb without forceps clamping my skull. No need to mention
the headaches I'd suffered during group sessions. As if the cos-
mic midwife was trying to guide me out, but the exit of the stuffy
little room wouldn't dilate. On my last day there my head felt
fine, I've noted in my diary.

When Morrie Bund gave me a lift to the coffee bar one last
time, he spoke of seeing cast-off runners hanging from power
lines all over town. 'You've opened my eyes, Skye,' he said, 'but
I can't stop feeling paranoid now. I keep wondering what else I
haven't been noticing.'

I tell Teresa about the phantom attacker as we loll in deck chairs
under a beach umbrella in a backyard overlooking the sea, at her

homecoming party thrown by the friends she lived with before me. A salt breeze blows the smell of charred steak and onion towards us, and one of our hosts refills our glasses with yet more bubbly.

'It doesn't sound like a haunted house' — Teresa takes a long swig — 'but I'd smudge it. Cleanse each room from top to bottom,' she responds to my shrug, 'with sage smoke by burning a bunch of the dried leaves. If some resident ghost wanted you gone it would've attacked Marty too.' She looks restored now, if thinner than when I last saw her, having just spent two months at her parents', laid low by some virulent Indian parasite.

'What if the ghost was hetero?' I say.

'I don't follow.' She fingers her newly long hair.

'Whatever it was that tried to rape me didn't go for Marty.'

'How well do you know this Marty?'

My explanation — that, though we've just met, we both feel as if we've known each other for ages — sets Teresa off on the subject of past lives. She talks about living in a culture where it's taken for granted that so-and-so's son is a reincarnation of such-and-such's dead husband. And she was her husband-to-be's wife in a life in Nepal, centuries ago.

'Is that what *he* told you?' I wonder how she can know so specifically.

'He remembers too,' she says, 'but it came to me in a vision.'

'You mean while you were awake?' I thought that after a two-year break, things might have changed. But no, lying here, watching her friends roll monster spliffs and get spiflicated, I'm still feeling inferior to Teresa. How I fucking well hate it.

'Yes,' she says. 'At the time it came to me I was meditating.'

That reminds me of the vision of Ramon that I took for fantasy. Curious to hear her slant, I relate my waking dream of our wedding.

She nods intently. 'That doesn't sound unlike a past-life memory. Ramon's desire to live with you might mean he yearns to return to the past. Maybe you two were happily married in Spain once upon a time.'

'I don't know.' I watch a joint approach from the corner of my eye. It's three overlapping papers long and as fat as a cigar.

'Why would he incarnate as a Spaniard twice?' I wave the joint away, so the bare-chested bearer offers it to Teresa.

'Look at it like this.' She takes a deep, luxurious drag. 'He might have journeyed across the world from his homeland to find you again.'

'But,' I say, 'he's found two other women to live with too, puerile, brittle, trivial bleach-blonde bimbos. Me and him and the pair of them — how's that going to work?'

'Maybe' — she passes the joint on, having taken one more toke — 'Ramon and you raised a couple of children after you married in Spain.' She exhales a cloud of smoke.

I badly want to believe her version. 'From what Ramon's told me, he left an unhappy home behind in Spain.' I tell her about the domestic violence he grew up with, which reminds me of the kitchen when I came downstairs this morning — pots, pans, knives and spoons strewn across the floor. I put them away as noiselessly as I could before leaving.

'Maybe' — she pauses to drain her champagne — 'he's been possessed by his father's demons.'

'You can't mean' — was she stoned when her Nepalese past life flashed before her eyes? — 'that one of Ramon's father's demons tried to rape me?'

'The possibility hadn't entirely escaped me,' she says. 'But Marty and you aren't lovers, I take it?'

'No. More like brother and sister.' Or Hansel and Gretel trapped in the gingerbread house with the witch, since Ramon's transformed into Baba Yaga.

'It's almost too obvious,' she says. 'No wonder I missed it.'

'What are you getting at?'

'My instinct tells me that your attacker was probably Marty's astral body.'

'Here's to Teresa,' says one of her many friends, and we all raise our glasses.

That night, as Marty and I relax on the TV-room floor, I show him the saffron shawl Teresa brought back for me — 'It's been

234

blessed by one of her gurus,' I say — then I recount highlights of our exchange, omitting her suspicions.

'So your friend's love affair with this swami dude's a big secret?' he says.

'Yeah. Apparently.'

'And he's let her come back to Australia on her own?'

'Only because he has to keep his hostel going.'

'Uh-huh.' Marty studies his fingernails. A crescent moon edges each one. 'I predict they're as likely to wind up hitched as you're likely to marry Ramon.'

'Really?' A firebomb of shame ignites behind my diaphragm. I pray that red won't spread over my face. 'What makes you say that?'

'It's a cliché,' he says. 'Older, wiser guy exploiting a young, gullible girl.'

'No, I mean about me marrying Ramon.' My face has begun to burn.

'Just a throwaway line,' he says. 'Ramon's not the marrying kind.'

'Of course not,' I say. 'Even if he *wasn't* gay.'

'That's just his security blanket,' says Marty, 'like your consecrated shawl. We've both seen him flirt with the others.'

I draw the shawl around me. I've seen one like it before — on Sophia, the woman who blessed me at my first vipassana course. 'Yeah, okay,' I say. 'Speak of the devil.' I know it's Ramon who's just come in by the staccato thud of his boots on the hall floor. His footsteps proceed to the kitchen, then double back.

'Hi.' He stops in the doorway. 'Will you both be around for dinner?'

'I ate too much at a barbecue today,' I lie. Two serves of salad.

'I haven't felt hungry at night since the retreat,' Marty says.

'That's okay.' Ramon looks bereft. 'Do you know if the girls are in?'

'Obviously not,' says Marty, 'unless they've got TVs in their rooms.'

'Well' — Ramon straightens his shoulders — 'I might just get takeaway.'

Marty and I still haven't heard him come back when we turn in hours later. Oblivious to astral visitors, we sleep until the sun bursts in.

By the time we leave for yoga, Ramon hasn't stirred. Nor has he arrived by the time I conclude the class. After coffee Marty wants to go walkabout. I head back, seized by an urge to paint. A gypsy plays violin in my mind's eye while the three Graces dance — Vin, Mona, Baba and me on a post-vipassana high? Then the gypsy turns into Ramon and it's Brittle and Trivial holding my hands. Suddenly I'm afraid to go home.

'Oh, Skye.' Ramon's coming from the kitchen when I steal in. 'It's about time I saw you.' He looks like death warmed up; puffy-eyed, pale, overwrought. 'You've been here for two days now. Perhaps you could make yourself useful.'

'Where's the best place to start?' I say, bent on redeeming myself asap so I can escape and prepare to start painting.

'If you need to be told, you're shockingly out of touch,' he retorts. 'It's obvious at a glance that the garden needs watering.'

Hopeful to the point of elation, I slip out the back door. I don't want to hole up in my room; I want us to be best friends like before. The shrubs growing in the bed by the garden shed look thirsty, tips drooping in the noonday sun. I find the hose, a long, blue serpent, and uncoil a suitable length, reminded of the blue wire doll that Marty began to unwind. Then I turn on the tap and wave the jet up and down the garden bed, a thumb jammed in the end of the hose to diffuse the flow; someone's mislaid the rose. I try to send most of the spray into the earth beneath the shrubs. But my thumb lacks the myriad evenly spaced tiny holes designed to finetune control. Some droplets spatter onto the foliage. Nothing else in the yard looks desperate, but I water the rest for good measure. When I'm satisfied that I've bought myself some time out, I go upstairs.

Though I want to make the most of my space by working big, I decide to sketch a few small studies first. By the second one, the gypsy violinist's gone and the Graces resemble Mel, Teresa and me. Any day now, Mel, too, is due back from overseas. So

236

much has happened since I last saw her. I've gotten back with Zane, broken up with him, and enrolled in a drama course that starts in three weeks. Zane asked scornfully why I thought I needed more drama.

Boots pounding on the stairs startle me. They rap a rhythm across the landing, stop at my door, and a fist takes over. 'Skye! Open up!' Ramon rants as he hammers. 'Come and see what you've done!'

Heart thumping, I close my sketchbook and open the door.

'You need to be more careful.' His face is bright red, if not compared to his hair, and his black eyes glitter with fault-finding intent. 'Come downstairs.'

He leads the way and I fall in behind, wilting in the sun of his righteousness, a lead ball of guilt filling my throat. I shouldn't have visualised him to make myself come while masturbating; should never have told him about that ritual, I berate myself, or even done it.

'You didn't shut the storage-shed window,' he berates me as I follow him out. 'Look at that!' Inside the shed he swipes at a tarp slung over some boxes. 'When you hosed those bushes the water splashed in.'

'Sorry,' I say. 'I didn't know the water spirits had played up again.'

'I'm not joking, Skye, and neither should you. This isn't good enough. Now mop it up!' He stomps back to the house, leaving me quaking.

Is he going crazy? What the hell could have made him so mad? But he can't be insane as long as he's venting his pain. I recall how I held all mine in, just like now, and when Marty returns I tell him everything.

'Don't let him get to you. A few drops of water's just an excuse.' Marty shrugs. 'Maybe he's copped some blow to his sexual ego,' he says with a smile.

'You're probably right.' But Ramon's ego's not the only one that feels fragile.

Neither Ramon nor Marty comes to yoga the next morning. Just as well. I'm not at my best. Coffee would only exacerbate the jittery state of my nerves, so after the class I go home for breakfast. Brittle — or is it Trivial? — drifts in to empty an ashtray and brew yet more coffee as I search high and low for the muesli. She's so thin I suspect she's anorexic or bulimic; a glorified clothes hanger, yet she and Ramon get on like a house on fire. I fill a bowl with muesli, wonder what the fuck she eats if at all, then tip roughly half back into the jar where I found it.

The sound of footfalls on the stairs kills what little's left of my appetite, as Brittle trips off to the TV room with her coffee. 'Hello, darl,' Ramon says when they pass in the hall; no wonder I keep forgetting her name. Uninspired by my dry muesli, I borrow a slurp of the milk that whitened darl's coffee, resolving to buy more later today. But Ramon sweeps into the kitchen before I can replace the milk in the fridge door.

'Skye,' he roars, 'I want you out of this house!'

'I'll go and buy a fresh carton,' I say. 'As soon as I've had breakfast.' Not what I'd intended; that'll make me late for work. But I need to placate him, at least until I can think straight. I'm shaken to my core. He doesn't look like himself anymore, and it's not just his hair, that's only a symbol. His eyes look shifty, his jaw's set and he's holding his arms and shoulders stiffly.

'You're not contributing energy to the household.' His tone sounds militaristic.

'I haven't had time to unpack yet,' I shrill, 'let alone settle in, Ramon. I've been here less than three fucking days.'

'And you've done nothing but damage in those days,' he snaps back at me.

'Spilling a few drops of water? C'mon! Give me a break.'

'You've been taking a break ever since you moved in. You haven't contributed anything!'

'Unlike the Barbie twins painting their nails and smoking in front of the telly.'

'I never knew you were so judgemental, Skye.'

A lurch in the pit of my belly tells me I've underrated his bond with the blondes, and I panic. 'I just thought we'd planned to try to live our ideals,' I say.

238

'You have to start somewhere.' He sounds almost reasonable. Then his face contorts. 'And you're doing sweet fuck-all!'

'Let's talk about what we expect of each other,' I say, even as the truth penetrates — *my* expectations carry no weight. The realisation makes me feel like I'm walking on the moon and Ramon's the sole reference point for gravity.

'The time for talking is past,' he says. 'Only actions matter now.'

'So tell me what you want done,' I say. 'Fuck playing guessing games.'

'I needed you to put energy into our household,' he says, and for a moment I think I see recognition flicker in his eyes — as if the veil's lifted, permitting a glimpse of the Skye he used to like.

'I thought that was why you wanted me to live here,' I say, more gently, 'to raise the vibration by working with *subtle* energy. And I've begun to. The other night I managed to drive out an astral intruder, and the next thing this place needs is a good smudging.'

Ramon's nose quivers like a horse's that's caught a whiff of a carrot. 'What's *smudging* involve?' he says, rapt.

'You smoke out the negative vibes to purify the entire space.'

His eyes grow round until I'm gazing, relieved, into the old Ramon's face. 'It sounds like a good idea,' he says. *'Purification?'* But then the veil falls again. 'You're full of cosmic ideas, aren't you, Skye. Too bad it's all just talk.'

'Ramon,' I plead, 'you've tried meditation. Don't underrate the power of thought.'

From the way his brows converge in a thick, black line below his flaming crest, he seems to be running with my provocation, until he pins me with an unblinking stare and jabs a stained finger in the air. 'If you're not out of here first thing in the morning,' he screeches, 'I'll throw all your stuff onto the street!'

·TWENTY-FOUR·

After a Storm Comes Karma

After all these years you could call me an initiate — if not in the way I once envisaged. While I'd always been a magnet for certain types of misfits, my own descent into hell has deepened my sympathy. Those who suffer from psychic anguish (and the stigma of clinical labels like 'schizophrenic', 'delusional' or 'bipolar') have often singled me out; on the street, at parties — many go undiagnosed — or in the fantasy world of the new-age network.

Forget their frantic antics; I know them by their eyes. They see differently — not better or worse, but they look beyond surfaces, gravitating to me because they feel seen. At bus stops, everyone ignores wild-eyed ranters and ravers. And everyone's accosted, except me. It's not as if the misfits ignore me. I'm just not someone they need to convince. I don't remind them of misguided doctors, parents or other authority figures. And if they know I'm different, how crazy can they be?

I never accosted strangers, nor drew attention to myself — not if I could help it. Loss of sanity can't make an introvert extroverted. Nor does it involve some fundamental change. It's more like falling overboard — or being pushed, in some cases — and finding oneself terrifyingly separate. Adrift in the night sea of the unconscious. Voices or visions only heighten the separation — unlike religious epiphanies, which make one feel closer to God and others.

Did I break down or wake up? Go mad or come to terms with my demons? Was I avoiding or facing reality? Was Zane a trickster or a teacher? Such bipolar labels aren't mutually exclusive. Taken in isolation, though, they strike me as delusive. These days, it's reductionists with simplistic answers who sound schizoid to me.

Tonight, my fourth in this madhouse, I'd hoped to finish un-
packing. Yet now no choice remains to me but to reverse the
process. With Led Zeppelin on my turntable to drown out the
sounds of psychosis — Ramon doing a war dance in his room —
I start folding clothes. Then the rock beat gets into my feet so I
dance, and sing along to lyrics about a long, lonely, lonely,
lonely, lonely, lonely time. I should have known better. Rat-tat-
tat. Wham-bam-bam. Phoomp-boomp-boomp. Here we go.

'Skye, turn that record down now — unless you want to pick
up the pieces from the street outside your window!'

'Don't make me sick with your hypocritical shit, you psycho
fuckwit,' I say — Ramon can't hear — then I grudgingly adjust
the volume to low. 'I thought you'd like it!' I holler through the
closed door.

He catches that bit. 'Not when I need to rehearse,' he hollers
back.

Is that what he calls the frenzy of stamping vibrating my
walls and floorboards? As he rampages back to his room, I crank
up the music and hurl myself down on the futon. My dreams for
the future have been entwined with Ramon's for months. Centuries, if Teresa can be believed. He's been my best friend, my
biggest fan, my fantasy, my flamenco teacher and the hottest
dancer I've ever known. But lately his glance makes my blood
run cold. If only he'd spell out what I've done wrong, besides
not renovate the whole fucking house, I'd bend over backwards
to make amends.

As a child I used to drown my pillow in tears just like I am
now, after my mother yelled about whatever the hell I'd done.
She often reached a hysterical pitch to rival Ramon's. My father,
on the other hand, would yell about what I *hadn't* done. Dishes
not dried, a mother not minded. *You mind your mother*, he'd
warn. Though I minded her no end, I dared not answer back. I'd
hold my breath instead, flattened against my single bed, and
pray that he'd forget me temporarily. If only I hadn't still felt
forgotten after the storm blew over.

Isn't Ramon forgetting something? He's skipped yoga since I
moved in, so who'll take over when I'm gone? We both
promised Mel we'd look after her class. It's my duty to confront

him. I blow my nose, smooth back my hair, inch open my door, steal downstairs, and stand on the landing until his heels stop clicking. Then I knock.

The door swings inwards and he peers out, his upper lip beaded with sweat.

'Sorry to bother you.' Scared is more like it. 'But' — I clear my throat — 'I can't make it to yoga tomorrow so hopefully you can, otherwise one of us should leave a note.'

He nods agreement. 'I'll lead the class. I need to do yoga again. And Mel's due home any day. Things should return to *normal* then.'

A spasm of jealousy grips me. Once Mel's back, I'll cease to exist for him. He didn't need me until she left. The floor starts to drop away. But no, I think, digging in my heels, the bond I shared with Ramon was real. I have to make a last-ditch bid to save it.

'Ramon — can you level with me about what I've done wrong?' I choke out. 'I know it can't *all* just be to do with the house.'

'Hell, no,' he says, and I sigh with relief. 'You act like the *world* owes you a living.'

Even as I reel from his words, I sense he's avoiding the issue. 'Okay,' I say. 'That's your opinion. But what have I actually *done* to you?'

'It's what you *haven't* done.' As he looks away for an eternity, I stare at the holes in his singlet. 'You disappoint me, Skye.' He sounds old for his years, paternal, sad.

'Can't you give me a second chance?' I could kick myself straightaway; he's not my goddamn dad. But before I can tell him how disappointed *I* am, he rounds on me.

'No, you won't get another chance to fuck with my soul. And if you want to manipulate others you'll have to do it somewhere else.'

'What do you mean by that?' I yell. 'Give me one example.'

'Get lost,' he yells back. 'Just get out of my face.' And he slams his door in mine.

I'm lost already. It's like I'm descending as I stumble upstairs, feeling weak and unsteady. I crawl under my doona,

shuddering. *Manipulate?* That's what we used to say about
Zane. The pressure in my chest erupts. Tears start to roll. I've
lost Ramon and the pitiful, bitter awareness undoes me, rips me
open from throat to gut, and all the strings hang out. All the
psychic cords with which I unwittingly tried to bind him are
useless now he's torn them loose at his end. I feel as if I'm unravelling.

The last man I loved turned into a monster when he lived
with me. Others blamed Zane. But this time the change happened faster. Is it *my* fault it's happening again? Stella said I'd
made a big mistake. But what difference does magic make? If it
can't heal the rift between Ramon and me, how can it heal a
whole planet? Maybe the storm will blow over, I think. But how
long will it take? Maybe one day Ramon will realise he's made a
big mistake. But by this time tomorrow I'll be out of his sight,
and maybe he won't be out of his mind, and the yoga household
will be like a dream — or a nightmare — that fades upon
waking.

After we've stacked my boxes on the porch beside Marty's
pack, he and I talk while we wait for my parents. He'll soon see
his in Adelaide. We've traded family addresses and numbers so
that we won't lose touch. Friends like Marty don't come along
often.

'Ramon can't seriously believe that you're manipulating me,'
he says. 'He must just be jealous because no-one's trying to
manipulate him.'

'I did that healing ritual,' I remind Marty.

'You meant well. Your only mistake was to tell him.'

'But he hates me with a vengeance, so I can't pretend it's
helped him.'

'Vin reckoned vipassana speeds up our karma,' Marty says.
'If you and Ramon had unfinished business, maybe it's time to
let go. Hey — is that your folks?'

'Yeah.' I stand up and wave as they climb out of the car
parked across the street, but they just blink and squint at house
numbers; my mother in a pantsuit, my father in a sports shirt,

shorts and long socks. She spots me first and steers him by his elbow. Then he recognises me, and smiles, until he sees Marty.

'Can we drop Marty at a train station?' I ask.

My father grunts assent and we sling my gear in the boot.

'Where are you off to, Marky?' asks my mother.

He hefts his pack onto the back seat beside me, then folds his long limbs in. 'Any town far enough out of the city to hitch from.'

'Isn't that risky, Marky?'

'Nah,' he assures her. 'Someone always stops eventually.'

'Whose house will you stay at *now*?' she says after we've left Marty at Central.

'It's a *ware*house, not a house, and I won't be staying.' To escape the third degree, I did consider enlisting Damian. But I feel too much shame, let alone desperation, at having to move yet again.

'She didn't stay long at the last address,' my father mutters under his breath.

Once he's parked in the narrow lane behind Jake's studio, the three of us carry as much as we can round the block and up to the second floor. I find the key above the door where Jake said he'd leave it, and we enter the disaster area that passes for his workspace. My mother takes one look and complains of feeling faint, so my father tells her to wait there while we fetch the rest.

'You know you're always welcome to come home if you're stuck,' he says, safe from eye contact ahead of me on the stairs.

'Thanks. I thought you were glad to get rid of me.'

'That's not true. We never —' The roar of a passing semi cuts him off as we reach street level.

'I don't mean my mother. I could've sworn that *you* were relieved when I left.'

'No, love, but you must've known you made your mother very upset.' We round the first corner, then the second, walking in step. He's still looking away.

'She upset me, too, but that never seemed to bother you,' I say.

'You could take care of yourself. But your mother, she's always been nervous.'

'What, ever since I was three?' She might as well have blamed me for her breakdown. *Handful*, indeed. 'What do *you* think pushed her over the edge?'

His stride lengthens so I have to rush to keep up. 'That's going a *long* way back.'

'You've forgotten?'

'Your mother feared for you.' He sounds so pained that I feel guilty asking, yet it's too late to pull my head in now I've started.

'Why was that?'

'She wanted to protect you from what she went through.'

'How do you mean?'

'You'd have to ask her.' He groans. 'But it might be for the best if you don't.'

Trust him to clam up for her sake. I hope *I* meet a man that devoted one day. '*You* didn't worry about me, did you — or not in the same way?'

'You've got your head screwed on right, despite all your funny ideas.'

So, during those years I felt unseen, my father had more faith in me than I did. 'What would you say, Dad, if I told you that I'd been out of my tree?'

Not till we reach the car does he turn his faded brown eyes to me. 'I'd say you always fall on your feet, love.'

We plod back to the studio in silence with the last of my load to find my mother chewing a hangnail and facing one of Jake's canvases, a loose, expressionistic mess that nonetheless represents three figures, the middle one horned. Though I know Jake meant them to be Theseus, the Minotaur and Ariadne, I just see him, his wife and me.

'No disrespect to your friend,' my mother says, 'but he can't believe that anyone would *buy* these, can he?'

'He leaves that to his dealer,' I say. 'They sell for tens of thousands.'

My mother steps up to the canvas then backs off, her watery eyes narrowed. 'I know I'm no expert,' she says, 'but with all your talent, Skye, I think you could do better.'

'Yes, much better,' my father agrees.

They decline my offer of black instant coffee, seeing no-where clean to sit, and my mother slides a small bundle from her string bag. 'I thought maybe you could use this.'

I flinch at the threat of extra baggage, but what I unwrap takes my breath away, a beautiful patchwork cushion cover. 'Did *you* make it?' But I know the answer.

'I thought it might come in handy. You said that you sit on the floor to meditate.'

'Thank you so much.' I hug and kiss her then my father.

Once they've gone, after making me promise to visit, I sit down on a box and admire her gift. I never used to like what she made, because of what I sensed went into it: stifled emotions, her need for control and a million and one neuroses. But today I see only her artistry, which I've inherited, and her devotion.

Five years had flown by the time I saw Ramon again. I'd taken my live-in boyfriend to a showcase of fringe dance, and Ramon waved from across the crowded foyer. My long, blonde hair hadn't deceived him. He left the companions I recognised vaguely and wove his way over. As he drew close, I could see he'd lost weight, and he'd been wiry before.

'Hello, Skye.' He grasped my hand and we embraced, then I introduced Damian.

'I *must* get back into yoga,' he gushed. 'Have you kept up vipassana?'

'No, but I try to remember to breathe.' I'd fleetingly forgot-ten, wondering if he'd have been as pleased to see me without my handsome companion. 'And you?'

He shook his head. Though he had his black hair back, he didn't look like his old self. His face had lost its youthful roundness — still, mine had too, we were both pushing thirty.

'Don't laugh,' he said, 'but I actually went back to do another retreat.' A mischievous spark flared in his eyes. 'I lasted less than two days.'

'At least you tried.' I longed to hear more over coffee, but fell quiet, fearing rejection.

'You look absolutely amazing, Skye.'

He must have been impressed because he'd never seen me in a dress, let alone a sexy one. I wanted to return the compliment, but it wouldn't be true. He'd matured in five years, deepened, and yet he seemed more rueful. Soon after our falling-out I'd gone to a psychic who'd read his birth date. I see you two collaborating in future, she'd said. With such compatible numbers, you'd be the best of friends.

I've missed you so much, I wanted to say, seen your jaunty walk on countless strangers. I'm sorry for doing that ritual without consulting you first, and if it's any consolation, *I'm* the one who's cursed.

'It's good to see you,' I said instead, not wanting our contact to end.

'It's good to see you, too,' he said and the shine in his eyes convinced me he meant it, 'but I must get back to my friends or they'll miss me.' Smokers, I noticed over his shoulder as we hugged goodbye. Then he beamed at Damian and swept off to rejoin them.

A year or so after that chance meeting, I ran into Mona from vipassana. And, as our talk turned to mutual friends, she mentioned Ramon's recent death, from pneumonia.

No, I thought, as my throat constricted, not with the rift between us unhealed. Now I'd never hear his riotous laugh or see him dance flamenco again. Then came shame — that I'd been so insane as to want him to be more than a friend.

'Damn cigarettes.' I shook my head.

'He had AIDS,' Mona said. 'He'd known for a while.'

'Is it possible he knew a year ago?'

Mona nodded.

And yet he'd said nothing. My eyes stung.

'He went peacefully,' she said. 'He was living alone, but he had friends. Near the end, he lived the lifestyle of a celibate monk.'

'That's what he said he wanted,' I said. '*Celibacy* — not to cark it at thirty.'

'According to his passport,' Mona said, 'he was almost thirty-two.'

So the psychic reading I'd drawn solace from would never come true. Like Zane, Ramon had lied about his age. Some psychic, I thought bitterly.

Even after so long, at times I think I see Ramon, in a stranger's straight stance or the flash of dark eyes, most often on Oxford Street. And Zane still haunts my dreams at intervals. He rarely speaks, just stares as if he's trying to psych me out. Rumours reach me now and then of his inappropriate conduct with patients, but no-one I know who knew Zane has seen him for years.

My wish list eventually manifested a light, airy home with a long-term lease, space to paint in and a view of the sea that avails me the occasional whale sighting. Teresa, who's a mother now, visits when she's in town. The rivalry between us has waned; maybe since she, too, has found her soul mate.

Or maybe, as I'd like to believe, because we're more enlightened?

www.ingramcontent.com/pod-product-compliance
Lightning Source LLC
Chambersburg PA
CBHW020651030726

47498CB00002B/469